DOVE

A James Acton Thriller

Also by J. Robert Kennedy

James Acton Thrillers

The Protocol	Wrath of the Gods
Brass Monkey	The Templar's Revenge
Broken Dove	The Nazi's Engineer
The Templar's Relic	Atlantis Lost
Flags of Sin	The Cylon Curse
The Arab Fall	The Viking Deception
The Circle of Eight	Keepers of the Lost Ark
The Venice Code	The Tomb of Genghis Khan
Pompeii's Ghosts	The Manila Deception
Amazon Burning	The Fourth Bible
The Riddle	Embassy of the Empire
Blood Relics	Armageddon
Sins of the Titanic	No Good Deed
Saint Peter's Soldiers	The Last Soviet
The Thirteenth Legion	Lake of Bones
Raging Sun	Fatal Reunion
Wages of Sin	The Resurrection Tablet

Special Agent Dylan Kane Thrillers

Rogue Operator	The Agenda
Containment Failure	Retribution
Cold Warriors	State Sanctioned
Death to America	Extraordinary Rendition
Black Widow	Red Eagle

The Messenger

Kriminalinspektor Wolfgang Vogel Mysteries

The Colonel's Wife	Sins of the Child

BROKEN

DOVE

A James Acton Thriller

J. ROBERT KENNEDY

Copyright ©2012, 2017 J. Robert Kennedy

ISBN: 9781990418396

For Brent, the "brother" it took me years to realize I always had. We are all very proud of your dedicated service to your country.

BROKEN

DOVE

A James Acton Thriller

"Even while living in the world, the heart of Mary was so filled with motherly tenderness and compassion for men that no-one ever suffered so much for their own pains, as Mary suffered for the pains of her children."

Saint Jerome, circa AD 380

"I hope that real love and truth are stronger in the end than any evil or misfortune in the world."

Charles Dickens

PREFACE

Before the ninth century, all papal processions from the Patriarchium, the Pope's residence, to St. Peter's Basilica, would travel a route known as the Via Sacra, the most direct route between the two points. After the death of Pope John VIII, a pope later stricken from the records, the Via Sacra, or "Sacred Road," was renamed by the locals, "the shunned street," and since then, no papal processions have taken this road.

After the death of Pope John VIII, for over six hundred years, during the papal consecration ceremony, the newly elected pope would sit on the *sella stercoraria*, a seat with a hole in the middle like a toilet. The newly elected pope's genitals were then examined, and after confirmed male, the examiner would announce, "Mas nobis nominus est," or, "Our nominee is a man." Once this announcement was made, the new pope would receive the keys of St. Peter.

In AD 1276, Pope John XX, after ordering an exhaustive search of the records, renamed himself Pope John XXI, in recognition of two Pope John VIIIs.

To this day, the Roman Catholic Church denies the original Pope John VIII existed.

Outside Tyrus, Judea
AD 342

With one hand, Berenice gripped the book hidden beneath her robes tight to her chest, the other grasping the seat of the cart in which she sat. Flanked on either side by two of her sisters, she awaited word from the advance scouts sent ahead almost half an hour ago. It felt as if she had been holding her breath the entire time. Her ears pounded, her palms sweat profusely, her flushed cheeks were like fire upon her face.

The snort of a horse ahead had her perking up, her companions sitting with her, and the guards surrounding them on horseback, all stirring. Pounding hooves echoed through the pass they were waiting for their scouts to declare safe before they entered.

This cannot be good.

She closed her eyes and prayed to the Blessed Virgin as the thunderous sound neared.

"Prepare for attack!" yelled one of the guards. "Protect the Word at all costs!"

Berenice opened her eyes. There was no retreat. Roman soldiers were behind them, half a day's ride at best. If they couldn't go forward, these treacherous mountains would become their tomb, and the Word would be lost. The decision to move it had been hers, and she had made a mistake. The hope had been to not only escape the never-ending searches by the Romans, but also to deliver it to the Coptic monks of Abba Antonious, still sympathetic to their cause, where in a single week, they could make dozens of copies of what she now held, the last copy known to exist. A book so terrible, so blasphemous, so apocryphal, the Emperor had ordered it and all others like it destroyed after the Council of Nicaea had concluded any teachings not fitting their narrow beliefs must not exist. Emperor Constantine's edict had resulted in the destruction of thousands of precious

2

works, some indeed blasphemous, others innocent, but burned from ignorance, hate, or opportunism.

Including the few dozen copies of this collection of pages she now held.

And today, if those pursuing them had their way, the last copy would be lost.

"It's Sister Joanna!"

Berenice exhaled her held breath. Joanna raced to a stop in front of the wagon, breathing as hard as her sweat-caked horse. Both appeared ready to collapse. "We can't go that way!" she gasped. "The end of the pass is sealed by a contubernium of soldiers." She sucked in some more air, too exhausted to continue.

Sister Sapphira, sitting beside Berenice, spoke. "We have double that behind us. If we can't go forward, and we can't go back, what do we do?" The panic in her voice was evident to them all.

And they all shared in it.

"We fight!" One of the guards on horseback shook her fist in the air as those around her cheered, her steed rearing on its hind legs.

"And we die," said Berenice, calmly. The group fell silent. She looked from face to face with a smile as she remembered how she had met each over the years. She patted the book under her robe. "This is worth more than our lives, is it not?"

Every head around her nodded in agreement.

"Then what happens to us is irrelevant. This book must survive and be delivered to the monks. If we fail in that mission, all is lost. The Word is lost, and that is something I fear will damage the teachings of our Lord, and the Blessed Virgin, for eternity." The smile disappeared from her face. "One of us must survive."

"Let it be you, Sister Berenice," said Joanna. More nods of agreement were followed by a few calls of her name. "You are the best of us, the most learned of us.

3

Should the book be lost, as long as you survive, at least the Word can still be passed on."

Berenice smiled at Joanna. "I thank you for your faith in me."

"Then it shall be so!" announced Joanna, raising her sword in the air. "Long live Berenice! Long live the Word!"

The guard echoed the call, thrusting their swords in the air.

Berenice blushed, the shame of their praise at once filling her heart with love, and wounding it with her unworthiness. She raised a hand to quiet them. "There was a farm not far back, where the farmer seemed a good Christian, and sympathetic to us."

"The one who gave us fresh milk this morning." Joanna nodded. "Yes, you must return there, hide until the troops pursuing us have passed, then make your own way when it is safe. We"—she circled her sword indicating the others—"will proceed forward and engage the troops blocking our way. Should we succeed in vanquishing them, we will return for you. Should we fail, we will have died in the name of our Blessed Virgin, and shall dine tonight in Heaven, at her side!" Her sword thrust in the air, the morning sun glinting off the blade as she closed her eyes, staring up at the heavens, her compatriots doing the same.

Berenice lowered her head in silent prayer.

Should any of us survive the day, it shall be a miracle granted by the Holy Mother herself.

Natanz Nuclear Facility
20 miles NNW of Natanz, Iran
Present Day

Command Sergeant Major Burt "Big Dog" Dawson froze.

Something difficult, considering he was hanging at the end of sixty feet of rope, held from above by a pulley system and a hulk of a man named Atlas. He gently placed his gloved hands against the sides of the ductwork he was hanging in and waited. Below him—five feet below him—stood two guards, chatting in Farsi, who were not supposed to be there. Intel had said this level was always free from guards, as what took place here was too sensitive even for them.

The Natanz facility, identified over a decade ago, was now one of the primary uranium enrichment plants of the Iranian nuclear effort, with over 7000 centrifuges in the one-million-square-foot facility. This level led to the two main centrifuge facilities, each over a quarter-million square feet in size, and two of the most secure rooms in Iran, with boots on the ground security provided from above.

Not here.

At least according to Langley.

Yet for some reason, today of all days, they were here, and he didn't speak Farsi to know what the hell they were talking about.

But someone at Control did.

"One of them is asking the other how long they think he will be. I think they're talking about a third person."

Dawson said nothing. He couldn't. One sound and they would look up, and if they did, the mission could be blown. He took deep, steady breaths, but his muscles screamed for relief. A drop of sweat rolled down his forehead. The tiny, translucent dot raced along the bridge of his nose, then sat there. He slowly moved his left hand to wipe it away, but his balance shifted and he stopped. Raising his head, he stuck out his lower lip and breathed in, sucking the bead toward his mouth.

It dropped.

Not into his mouth.

He stared down and watched it fall through the grate and onto the shoulder of the guard directly below him. No reaction. At least not from him. His partner, however, pointed at his shoulder. Dawson reached for his sidearm, removing it from its holster, and as the two men looked up, placed one bullet between each of their eyes. They crumpled to the ground.

"Two hostiles eliminated. Our cover might be blown. Zero-Two, status of security override?"

"Security override in place and functioning." Master Sergeant Mike "Red" Belme's voice came across the comm crystal clear and confident. Dawson never doubted his second-in-command and best friend. They were known to the public as the Delta Force, their official designation 1st Special Forces Operational Detachment–Delta, the best-trained group of special operations soldiers the US military had to offer, and his team, Bravo Team, was the best of the best, in his utterly biased mind. He was their team leader. As with all Delta teams, the command structure was very flat, with everyone ranked at some level of sergeant. He happened to be the highest-ranked in his unit, and by default, was in command. Yet he had earned that position, leading his team of operators on missions throughout the world, successfully, and unseen.

And today better be another one of those.

He grabbed the power screwdriver off his utility belt, slid the head through the grate, then pushed forward on the slide, adjusting the angle of the head. It snapped several times as it bent to a 180-degree angle, a small mirror showing him the position of the head. He adjusted it, then pressed the button, providing power. The screw unwound, then the magnetic charge held on to it when it was freed. He pulled back on the slide with his thumb, pulled the head with the dangling screw through the grill, and pocketed it. Repeating this three more times, he pulled the grate up and into the duct with him, placing it against the side, resting on the lip. Snapping the screwdriver back on his belt, he pressed a button on his harness to lower the final few feet, then unhooked, dropping to a knee, his weapon drawn as he confirmed the area remained clear.

Both ends of the long corridor were empty, the two gunshots, muffled with a suppressor, not drawing any attention. He peered through a small window on the door nearest him and found the room vacant. He tried the knob. Locked. A quick glance showed it to be a standard tumbler type. He pulled his pick gun off his belt, stuck it in the keyhole, and squeezed a few times, sensing the tumblers fall into position. The door unlocked. He pushed it open then pulled both bodies inside.

The door clicked shut behind him as a voice in the hall called out. He checked the floor and breathed a sigh of relief. No blood trail, his shots at enough of a downward angle, there were no exit wounds. He pulled the bodies out of sight from the door's window, then positioned himself on the side of the frame, knife at the ready. The light pouring in from the hallway dimmed as someone put their head to the glass. Dawson shifted his foot so his boot would block the door if whoever was on the other side gave it a casual push.

Then he remembered the missing grate.

Don't. Look. Up.

He heard footsteps walking away from the door, along with what he guessed was cursing. A few moments later, a click echoed through the emptiness. He opened the door to his hiding place and peered quickly up and down the hallway. It was clear. "Control, Zero-One, proceeding with mission, over." He jogged to the end of the hallway where a door with an electronic keypad stood, then activated his comm. "Zero-One in position."

Updates came in from other members of his team.

"Zero-Five and Zero-Eight in position."

"Zero-Six in position."

He punched in the code from memory, provided by someone not too thrilled with the idea of a jihadist state having nuclear weapons, and the door clicked open. He drew his gun and a breath.

"Proceed on my mark. Three...Two...One...Execute!"

He shoved the door aside and stepped into a brightly lit room the size of five football fields, the ceiling extending over one hundred feet above him. Stretching in long rows before him were thousands of centrifuges that, according to his briefing, were used to enrich uranium. Two technicians to his left stopped and gaped at him. He put two bullets in each of their chests. They dropped, and he began a clockwise round of the massive room. Another technician, sitting at his desk engrossed in a display, never knew what hit him. Dawson rounded the first corner, eliminating three more scientists with clipboards in a heated debate over something, when the alarm went off.

Shit!

"Control, Zero-One, we're compromised. The alarm has sounded, say again, the alarm has sounded, over."

"Zero-One, Control Actual, assessment?"

"Stand by, Control." Dawson recognized Colonel Thomas Clancy's voice. He was always happy knowing Clancy was in charge of an op. He trusted him. In the past, there were occasions when he had no idea who Control was, and on some of those occasions, he and his men had been left hung out to dry, or compromised in some way, left to their own devices to save themselves.

But not today.

Scientists and technicians were poking their heads out from among the centrifuges as the alarm wailed overhead. Dawson picked each off as he ran, and began pulling magnetic explosives off his vest, tossing them toward the centrifuges as he raced by. As he threw each one, he could hear a satisfying clank as they attached to the metal.

Two more down.

Running toward him, he could see Sergeant Trip "Mickey" McDonald, his distinctive ears hidden away, doing the same, having entered from the other end.

"Control, almost finished clearing the room, explosives being set. Estimate exit in two minutes, over."

"Copy that, proceed at your discretion."

Dawson and Mickey met up and turned inward, clearing several rows of centrifuges, then broke off again, heading back toward their entrance points. Dawson continued to toss explosives and only encountered one more tech on his way out. He closed the door behind him then sprinted down the hallway toward the missing grate in the ceiling. "Zero-Seven, drop the rope."

As he skidded to a halt, the rope, drawn up earlier by Sergeant Leon "Atlas" James, dropped in front of him. He hooked on then pressed the control to begin pulling him up. As his head cleared the ceiling, he heard something, then the pounding of footsteps and yelling. Hands grabbed his feet, pulling him back down, and he spotted a military uniform with markings indicating a Colonel. Dawson, weapon still drawn, took a bead and fired. The man crumpled to the ground, freeing Dawson's legs, and he ascended, the machine pulling him up, assisted by the massively muscular Atlas yanking on the rope at the other end.

Within moments, he was at Atlas' position. He propped himself up on an intersecting duct and disconnected from the rope as Atlas folded up the equipment. Dawson rapidly crawled down the duct, Atlas bringing up the rear. "Zero-One to Zero-Five and Six, status?"

"Zero-Five and Zero-Eight, clear."

"Zero-Six, clearing now."

Dawson stared ahead and could see feet dangling from the next junction disappear. Moments later, he was there and shoved to his feet then raised his arms. Two sets of hands grabbed him and hauled him up, Atlas pushing on his boots from below. He rolled onto the concrete slab housing one of the more remote exhaust ports for the facility and cleared it as they hauled Atlas out. Sergeants Vince "Stucco" Stewart and Danny "Casey" Martin replaced the cover as Dawson gained his bearings, then they began a fast sprint across the desert sand, away from the alarms and lights.

"Control, we're clear, over."

"Copy that. Execute, over."

"Roger that. Executing, over."

Dawson signaled Red who flipped a cover protecting the detonator switch, then pushed his thumb down on the exposed button. The entire area rumbled, the ground shaking as the explosives below detonated. Dawson glanced back and saw nothing at first, then, as the explosion spread, the roaring flames forced their way through the ductwork his team had just been in, and out the exhaust ports, lighting up the entire desert behind them as they sprinted for cover.

"Overseer to Zero-One, you've got a vehicle in pursuit. Stand by."

Dawson checked over his shoulder and saw the bouncing headlights as he and his team mounted a crest and disappeared down the other side. He skidded to a halt at Sergeant Carl "Niner" Sung's position as he fulfilled his Overseer duties, squeezing off another round. Dawson looked back over the hill and saw steam hissing from the engine block of the vehicle.

He slapped Niner and his spotter, Sergeant Gerry "Jimmy Olsen" Hudson, on their backs. "Okay, let's go."

Both rose and followed the rest of the team, cresting another hill, revealing their salvation in front of them, an ultra-top secret Gen-3 Ghost Hawk chopper, or "Jedi Ride" as they liked to call it, its remarkably silent engines powered up and ready to go. As Dawson took up the rear, the rest of the team piled aboard then hauled him inside.

"Go! Go! Go!" he shouted, and their pilot, Sergeant Zach "Wings" Hauser, pulled up on the stick, lifting the chopper from the ground. Within seconds, they were racing across the barren landscape toward Iraqi soil.

Niner, his nickname provided by himself after a racial slur about his Asian heritage resulted in a bar fight, looked at Atlas and gave a thumbs-up. "Man, that was more fun than that time we planted the fake drone!"

The entire team chuckled.

"You'd've thought they'd at least get suspicious when it supposedly crashed and had no damage," said Atlas.

Niner laughed. "Yeah, and the few hundred dollars of Radio Shack parts didn't even raise an eyebrow."

Sergeant Will "Spock" Lightman's eyebrow shot up, and Dawson smiled as the camaraderie enjoyed after a successful mission played out. "Control, Zero-One, we're on our way out." He muted the comm and yelled to Wings. "ETA?"

"Fifteen minutes!"

"Control, ETA fifteen minutes, over."

"Zero-One, Control Actual. Copy that. As soon as you're clear, I have a Priority One mission for you and your team, over."

Dawson shared the expressions of confusion on the exhausted faces surrounding him.

"Control, Zero-One, confirm that last transmission, over?"

"Zero-One, Actual, we received an SOS from an old friend, over."

An old friend? Who the hell could that be?

The Vatican
Three Days Ago

Father Granger held the flashlight far in front, its beam slicing through the pitch-black confronting him. As he slowly made his way, the light bounced off the contents of the dusty shelves revealing dozens of priceless pieces of history with each step. And he had examined every single one. His heart pounded as he waved his free hand ahead to catch any cobwebs, confident he would find few if any here, this particular section searched just yesterday. Today, he continued his methodical hunt in the adjacent section. An hour each day, before the rise of the staff. In secret. No one could know he was in the Vault. No one could know the Vault existed.

If they knew what I was doing, where I was!

The scandal could destroy the Church, though he would never let that happen, no matter how important his purpose. He would die before he would let anything happen to the Church or his beloved Father. It was at the Pope's request that he was here, searching for something about which the world knew little. And of those few who knew the truth, most had no knowledge of this mission.

The *Archivum Secretum Vaticanum*, the Vatican Secret Archives, was massive, with enough history to make all of the museums in the world envious. The Secret Archives were in themselves huge, and if you didn't know what you were looking for, you weren't getting it. The entire collection was available and indexed, however anyone wanting to view something had to request it specifically—there was no browsing in the archives.

But where he searched now was something completely different. No catalogs or indices showed the location of artifacts, no tour guides answered questions. Where he was now, merely a handful knew even existed, and in almost two millennia, little more than five hundred were made aware, and of those, three, maybe four-score, had actually laid eyes upon it.

And that was why, when he rounded the last stack he had previously searched, he was shocked to not only see fresh footprints in the dust, but a hand swinging through the flashlight beam, followed by the excruciating pain of something hitting the side of his head.

He dropped to his knees, the flashlight rolling away from him, revealing the boots of his attacker, and nothing more. He raised his hands to cover his head when a second blow landed, breaking the fingers interlaced over his scalp. He cried out, the desperate plea's lonely echo falling only on his own ears, and that of his assailant, whose merciless assault continued with blow after blow.

And with pain racking his body and the assault showing no signs of letting up, he put himself in the hands of God and prayed.

Apostolic Palace, The Vatican

"What do we do?" whispered Eugenio.

"I don't know!" hissed Giorgio. "This has never happened before!"

Eugenio stared at the intricately carved door in front of them, then down at the fresh, hot towels as they rapidly cooled. He frowned, then made a decision he wasn't sure was his to make. "We can't wait any longer." He reached forward and knocked three times as he had seen Father Granger do every morning, then opened the door, the others gasping as he did so.

"It's not permitted!"

Eugenio glanced over at Giorgio as he stepped through the doors. "And what would you have us do? Wait for *him* to come and get *us*?"

This halted Giorgio's protests. Eugenio looked at the others whose heads bobbed in agreement. They had no choice. A duty was to be performed, as it had been for years, every day, without fail, regardless of where he might be on God's blessed creation. He stepped into the chambers then stopped, unsure of what to do. Somebody leaned into his shoulder then whispered in his ear.

"What is it?" asked Nicola.

"I'm not sure what to do. Father Granger does this. I've never done it before."

"We're in here because of you. *You* better do it." Nicola gently pushed on Eugenio's back with his elbow, his own hands occupied by a steaming bowl of water for the morning ablutions.

Eugenio nodded.

You opened the door. This is now your duty.

He took a breath and stepped deeper into the chambers, his eyes on the two-tone checkered floor. With as much confidence as he could muster, he walked toward the small, humble bed. "Good morning, Your Holiness."

"Good morning."

15

Eugenio froze and Nicola ran into him from behind. The water lapped against the side of the bowl and Eugenio suppressed a curse as it dampened his robes. He looked at His Holiness, something he had failed to do moments before. He was propped up in bed, a slight smile drawn across his face.

"You're late."

There was no reproach. No malice. No criticism. Just a statement of fact.

Eugenio stepped forward. "I'm terribly sorry, Your Holiness. But—" He wasn't sure what to say, and stood frozen like a child debating on whether to tattle.

"What is it, my son?"

The voice was gentle, calming.

What did you expect?

He had never heard him raise his voice. Eugenio was sure he did on occasion—enough maddening things happened in the world every day that he must get angry at something. After all, he might be the head of the largest church on Earth, but he was also a man. Eugenio looked at the man, and not the Pope.

"Father Granger—" Again, he paused, then inhaled deeply. "Well, Your Holiness, he's not here."

The expression changed to one of concern, the Pope's eyes narrowing and his head tilting slightly. "What do you mean, 'he's not here?'"

"We waited, Your Holiness, but he never arrived, so we"—somebody grunted—"I mean *I* decided we should enter, rather than wait any longer."

"Has anyone looked for him?"

"Vincenzo went to his chambers and knocked, but there was no answer."

The Pontiff turned to Vincenzo. "Did you enter?"

Vincenzo shook his head fiercely, as if the very thought of it were a mortal sin.

The Holy Father smiled at him. "Do not worry, my son, I am sure it is nothing. But"—he reached for the

16

edge of the duvet covering him—"I think we should find him."

Giorgio raced forward, grabbed the corner of the duvet, and pulled it aside as His Holiness swung his legs out and over the edge of the bed. He turned to Vincenzo. "Please visit the Father's chambers again, and enter if necessary, with my blessing. Should the Father merely be sleeping in, wake him. Nothing more, I am sure, will need to be said. After all, we all sleep in on occasion, and when woken, immediately recognize our error."

Vincenzo bowed and rushed off, half walking, half jogging, in an attempt to maintain dignity and decorum within the chambers of their most venerated leader. Eugenio watched him go then turned back to His Holiness, who clapped.

"Well, how about we begin?"

Outside Father Granger's Quarters
Apostolic Palace, The Vatican

Vincenzo hammered on Father Granger's door, now desperate. The last thing he wanted to do was walk in on the Father. He pressed his ear against the door and still heard nothing. Or was there something? He pressed harder. The door creaked, protesting against his weight, and…

An alarm clock!

He stepped back and fished the key from his robe. If the Father's alarm clock were still going, he might be hurt, or worse. Vincenzo's trembling fingers found the keyhole. Shoving the key in, he turned it and the click of the metal lock radiated through the ancient wood door. He turned the handle and pushed the door open. The moment a crack was revealed between the door and its frame, the unmistakable sound of an alarm clock, its electronic beeping sound desperate for escape and attention from someone, surged into the hall.

He pushed the door fully open and stepped inside, not sure what he'd find. This was a room in which he had never been. It was large compared to his, but still humble considering the position the Father held. He had to remind himself, however, that in the era during which these rooms were built, this would have been considered huge. Today's decadent society expected large rooms for the lowliest person, and enormous for anyone with any sort of status or position.

God help us.

He stepped forward and spotted the bed to the left, against the wall. Strewn across the bed were a bundle of sheets and pillows, along with a large down-filled duvet. He couldn't see the Father, nor could he hear any breathing. He stepped to the right side where the alarm clock was blaring, and reached out to turn it off. As he stepped forward, something touched his leg. He looked down and yelped, scurrying back.

Sticking out from under the duvet was a bloody hand.

Father Granger's Quarters
Apostolic Palace, The Vatican

Inspector General Mario Giasson stood in the doorway, his trained eye surveying the now emptied room of the Father. As the head of the *Corpo della Gendarmeria dello Stato della Città del Vaticano*, or the Corps of Gendarmerie of Vatican City State, he was essentially equivalent to what many would call a chief of police, as well as the head of the FBI and Homeland Security. And murder was his business, though none had ever happened on his watch.

When he had received word of the death, and the apparent nature of it, he and several of his Swiss Guard had sprinted to the room. And to his dismay, had found it filled with priests and laymen, touching the body, praying, and, most annoyingly, destroying his crime scene. Without setting a foot inside, he had ordered everyone out, including several bishops not accustomed to such treatment.

He didn't care.

If a murder had indeed been committed here, it would be the first in decades. And it had to be solved as quickly, and quietly, as possible. The very idea of one of the most important commandments being broken on this hallowed ground was too much to fathom. The scandal could damage the Church at the very time it could least afford it.

He stepped inside.

It was a small room, though slightly bigger than the room His Holiness occupied, Pope Pius X having refused to move from his own humble chamber when elected pope, thus leaving the actual papal chambers abandoned since 1903, no other pope having dared to suggest he merited bigger quarters. It was a shame, the original papal chambers remarkable, now relegated to a museum curiosity.

However, papal chamber choices were hardly of importance at this point in time. He stepped around the bed and saw the bloody arm of the victim sticking out. The duvet had been turned down, the entire body exposed, apparently by one of the staff. The victim was facing away from him. He leaned over the body and confirmed what he already knew. It *was* Father Granger. His face was barely recognizable, but his distinctive long hair, lean body, and the ring indicating his position, left little doubt.

But why is he in his robes?

A quick glance was all he needed to know the murder hadn't been committed here. There was no blood spatter. Merely the body, and some stained sheets.

And he was fully dressed.

Had he been waylaid on the way to waking His Holiness?

Impossible.

The chambers were not that far apart, and the grounds too well guarded for there to be an intruder.

Then how do you explain this?

Clearly, there had to be an intruder. For if there weren't, then one of their own had committed this ghastly act. He pointed at one of his men. "Photograph everything before anybody else comes in the room." The man began snapping photographs as Giasson stepped back into the hallway. He looked at Vincenzo, whom he recognized as one of the Papal valets. "You discovered the body?"

Vincenzo's eyes were red, his cheeks stained from tears now gone. "Yes, sir, not half an hour ago."

"And why were you here?"

"His Holiness sent me to find him, as he did not appear for the morning ablutions."

Giasson frowned.

He would never miss that.

"Has His Holiness been informed?"

"No, sir, he's at morning prayers."

There are more important things in life than death.

"Very well, I will inform him." He turned to Gerard Boileau, his second-in-command. "This is not the murder scene. Search the entire grounds."

"What are we looking for?"

"Blood. Signs of a struggle. Anything out of the ordinary." He paused for a moment, his finger poised in the air, then marched back into the room. He pressed the *Alarm* button on the clock. *5:15 a.m.* That seemed reasonable. He looked again, noticing another button labeled *Alarm 2*. He pressed it. *4 a.m.* The display on the clock indicated both alarms were active.

Why would he be getting up so early?

He returned to the hallway. "Check the camera footage. See if you can track him."

"There are no cameras in this section."

Giasson shook his head as he walked away. "I told them we needed coverage everywhere." His voice trailed off. "Check the footage."

"Starting from last night?"

"No, four a.m."

Papal Office Antechamber
Apostolic Palace, The Vatican

Inspector General Giasson stepped into the outer office and acknowledged Father Morris, sitting behind a desk older than most countries. One of the things that never ceased to fascinate him was the history contained within the massive Vatican walls. Thousands of years, preserved from wars, famine, looting, the fall of mighty empires. It was all here, preserved lovingly in the archives using state of the art techniques, or in offices such as this, a utilitarian desk, used in a utilitarian fashion, as it was meant to be. It would never know abuse, it would never know carelessness, it would always be maintained with the utmost of care. And it would never be hidden away, like so many of the treasures of this vast complex.

"I assume you're here about Father Granger."

"He knows?"

Morris bowed slightly.

"Is he receiving visitors?"

"He will see *you*."

It was stated as if he were the exception, and his interpretation was probably correct. Father Granger was not only His Holiness' private secretary, but his friend. They worked side by side, every day, for years, their relationship predating His Holiness' appointment. It was inevitable that a bond would form between the two, especially considering the nature of their work. This was not an office building housing corporations where everyone was in a constant struggle to move up an imaginary ladder to get a foothold over their officemate and survive the recession intact. This was the Kingdom of Heaven's embassy on Earth. This was a place of love, of peace, of mutual rejoicing in the Lord's sacrifice for our benefit.

But today, it was a city like any other city. A city with a murder to solve.

Father Morris rose from his desk, knocked on the large oak doors, then pushed them both open, walking in as he did so, the effect as if he were presenting the room to Giasson.

"Inspector General Giasson to see you, Your Holiness." He bowed slightly to Giasson as he moved aside, allowing the security chief to step toward the Pontiff's desk. The doors closed almost silently behind him.

"Mario, my son, so good to see you." The Pontiff struggled to push from his chair when Giasson waved him off.

"Your Holiness, please do not trouble yourself on my account."

The Pontiff smiled slightly and sank back into his chair. "Thank you, my son. These bones grow weary. Lately, I feel years older than I think I should."

"It is a difficult life God has asked of you."

The Pontiff indicated for him to sit. "That it is, and days like today make it even more so when the evil that men do seep through our protective barriers, both physical and spiritual, and strike down one of our own." He paused, as if deep in thought, his eyes gazing unfocused at the cross on the far wall. Giasson didn't say anything, sensing he wasn't finished. His attention returned to Giasson. "Today, we all mourn the loss of our friend and colleague. And today shall be a day of prayer, not work, for those of us who can afford to do so. You, however, cannot afford to rest. I am not so sheltered from the world surrounding me not to know that time is of the utmost importance." He leaned forward, lowering his voice as if he didn't want anyone else to hear. "You may not know this, but before this calling consumed all of my time, my idea of a good time would be to 'kick back' as the kids might say, and watch a gripping episode of Frost or Morse on the telly. Midsomer Murders, Poirot, Marple. I loved them all. They were my guilty pleasures of

a sort, acquired over the many years I spent in England."
He leaned back, the slight signs of remembrance at a life
forgotten slowly wiped from his face as the reality of the
moment returned. "I assume you have questions for me?"

"Yes, Your Holiness, a few."

"Proceed."

Giasson pulled out his notebook and pen, flipping to a
blank page. "First, do you know of any reason why Father
Granger would be waking at four in the morning?"

The Pontiff's eyebrows rose slowly. "That is awfully
early, isn't it?"

Giasson agreed. "I checked his alarm clock, and the
alarm, at least for this morning, was set for four a.m."

"Perhaps his ablutions are far more involved than this
old man's?" A wry grin spread across the Pontiff's face as
he leaned back, folding his arms, his head pressed against
what appeared to be leather far more sumptuous than
anything in Giasson's office. "He was a very prim and
proper man, for one of the cloth. He took great pride in
his appearance, to the point where he even had to confess
it several times, vanity being one of his greatest sins." He
sighed then returned his eyes to Giasson. "He is to be at
my door at six a.m. every morning to wake me. Why all
the pomp and circumstance surrounding my morning
routine, I'll never know, however who am I to question
over a millennium of tradition? It would seem at some
point in our history, men of my apparent stature were
above bathing themselves."

Giasson smiled, though awkwardly. "So, he may just
be an early riser?"

The Pope spread his fingers, bending his hands at the
wrist, exposing his palms, and shook his head slightly. "I
must admit I find it hard to believe he could take two
hours for such things, but this is his private time." His
voice trailed off, as if not wanting to intrude any further
on what he had just referred to.

"Had he ever been late or missed—"

"Never," interrupted His Holiness. "In all my years, he was never a moment late. It was really quite remarkable. In fact, I don't believe I've ever known him to be ill, or to have even taken a day's vacation."

"Routine question, of which I'm sure I already know the answer, but"—he paused, searching for the right words—"did he have any enemies that you know of, anyone who might do him harm?"

A slight smile creased the Pontiff's face, revealing his understanding of the necessity of the question. "No, none that I'm aware of. And"—he raised his finger—"before you ask, I was in my chambers, sleeping, and I do not have an alibi, except for the two Swiss Guards on either side of my door at all hours."

Giasson flushed. "I never would have asked you, of all people, that question."

"Which is why I saved you the trouble."

Giasson nodded. "One other thing, Your Holiness. It appears he was not murdered in his chambers, but elsewhere, then carried to his bed."

"Really?"

Giasson regarded the Pontiff closely. If he didn't know better, he would guess he seemed caught off guard. "Yes. Can you think of any reason he might be out of his chambers late at night or very early in the morning?"

The Pope stared at the cross on the far wall, his voice a whisper. "No, no I cannot."

Giasson rose. "Thank you, Your Holiness. That's all I have for now."

The Pontiff continued to stare at the cross, saying nothing. Giasson took that as his dismissal and made for the doorway, surprised to find it swing open as he approached. Father Morris bowed slightly as he passed, but Giasson barely noticed, lost in his own thoughts.

Why do I get the feeling I was just lied to by the Pope?

26

Triarii Headquarters
Fleet Street, London, England

The Proconsul of the Triarii, Derrick Kennedy, leaned back in the sumptuous leather of his office chair. He gazed at the history the room contained and smiled. His mind wandered back to the day they were forced to evacuate, the physical scars to the building repaired, but not the mental ones—those would take longer.

So many friends lost.

It had been a brutal attack, yet they had survived. Not all the souls, but the history. And their charges. The Oracles of Jupiter and Apollo had been saved, their history had been saved, and they were back.

And with a tantalizing new opportunity.

He sipped his 1968 Macallan scotch, the harsh bite quickly replaced by a crisp, fresh, numbing effect as it slid down his throat and rushed through his veins. This was his reward for the end of a long day. Though things had settled down since the attack, since the enactment of the Protocol, it was still busy. Running a 2000-year-old secret organization descended from the Roman Empire was mentally exhausting. With the large number of deaths at their headquarters, they had been forced to start bringing in members from around the world to staff the positions left vacant.

The Triarii had become a corporation of sorts. It was inevitable. Just like any army had its administration, so did the Triarii. Here at their Fleet Street headquarters, they ran a worldwide organization with thousands of members, mostly made up of people whose families had been members for hundreds, if not thousands, of years. And with the meticulous records kept by the Triarii, they could trace back each and every one of them, to the beginning when Emperor Nero had sent them north, to protect the Empire from the skull.

With a dozen skulls now found, tracked, and protected around the world, they needed manpower. And that meant administration. Their records went back two thousand years. And that meant preservation. Like any archive, they had their own initiatives underway, computerizing the records, scanning in the ancient scrolls, and securely backing up everything electronically. With the attack last year, this project had taken on a new urgency.

And that vexed him. Some had thought him a fool to return to this building, insisting that a new location be found. He had overruled them. The enemy was no more, those who knew of the location trusted to not tell of it, and in a generation, it would be forgotten. And with the scandal that had rocked the world after the events of that night, everyone was eager to keep details to a minimum.

And it didn't hurt that several high-placed government officials were members of the Triarii, including the head of the commission charged with investigating the incident.

They were everywhere. Pervading every level of society.

And it took an army of clerks and administrators to keep it all going.

He sighed and eyed his empty glass.

Another?

His phone beeped for his attention. He leaned forward and pressed the intercom button. "Yes?"

"Sir, urgent call for you, Line One."

"Who is it?"

"Herr Roessel."

Now that's unexpected.

He pressed the button for Line One, picking up the receiver. This was not a call he wanted on speaker. "Good evening, Your Holiness."

Corpo della Gendarmeria Office
Palazzo del Governatorato, Vatican City

Detective Inspector Martin Chaney sat in the outer office of the Vatican Chief of Security, Inspector General Mario Giasson. He could see him through the glass, and Giasson didn't look happy. Sweat beaded on his shaved head and ran down the back of his neck, slowly dampening the crisp white dress shirt he wore. The phone he had cradled on his shoulder while his hands slammed the keyboard in front of him continually slipped, frustrating him even more. He was speaking in Italian, leaving Chaney in the dark as to what he was yelling about.

I hope it's not me.

There had been surprise in the Security Office when he had arrived to present his credentials as a courtesy. He hadn't been summoned there by them. He had been summoned by their boss. And, apparently, their boss hadn't deemed it necessary to inform them. In fact, even *he* had no idea why he was here. He had received a phone call last night from the Proconsul telling him that a leave of absence had been arranged at Scotland Yard, and he was to fly to the Vatican to meet with the Pope. Less than twenty-four hours later, he was here, not as a police officer, but as a member of the Triarii.

And for what purpose, he had no idea.

What possible business could the Triarii have with the Roman Catholic Church?

It wasn't his position to question, especially the Proconsul. He had seen him several times at the headquarters, though had never spoken to him.

I'm a mere plebe compared to him.

And last night, when the coded message arrived, and the voice of the very man himself rumbled through the earpiece, he had trembled, intimidated by his mere position. The power the man exercised was awesome in scope. He could, and indeed had, influenced elections, *told* elected governments what to do, freed those in jail, and had put some behind bars.

His power was as absolute as you could get in what the populace thought was a free society.

We're just fortunate he's one of the good guys.

Had the Triarii killed? Yes, especially in the past. Hundreds, if not thousands, had been sent to their deaths in the two millennia since leaving Rome. But in the twenty-first century? None. Except during the events surrounding Archaeology Professor James Acton over a year ago.

Though that was all in self-defense.

I wonder what he's *doing.*

Acton had saved his life, yet they had never really connected. Hugh Reading, his former boss at Scotland Yard, had kept in touch and become good friends with Acton and his now partner, Laura Palmer. All three of them had recently been mixed up in the business with the death of the previous pope, but he had no idea where they were now. He made a mental note to call Reading and see how he was doing.

The phone slammed down in Giasson's office. Chaney looked up and Giasson waved him in. He rose from his chair and entered.

"Close the door, please."

Uh oh.

He closed the door and sat at a chair indicated by Giasson, who had Chaney's credentials sitting before him. And a frown.

"What is Scotland Yard doing here, Detective Inspector Chaney?"

Chaney smiled in an attempt to defuse the situation. "It's not, I assure you. I'm here on personal business."

Giasson leaned back. "Personal business? At the Vatican? What possible business could a London police officer have at the Holy See?"

Chaney shifted in his chair, slightly uncomfortable. "Unfortunately, I cannot say. It is"—he paused, searching for the right word—"*private* business."

A vein pulsed faster on top of Giasson's bald head.

Wrong word?

"My question stands, though slightly modified. What type of *private* business could you possibly have here?"

Chaney raised his hands in front of him, palms outward. "I'm sorry, but I can't say. As I said, it's private."

Giasson's frown creased his face even deeper. "And who is this *private* business with?"

"The Pope."

Giasson's thick eyebrows shot up. "His Holiness?"

Chaney nodded.

Giasson chuckled. "You know, millions have *private* business with His Holiness. But"—he raised a finger, pausing dramatically—"*he* doesn't have business with *them*."

Chaney displayed his palms again, raising his shoulders, his head sinking slightly into his neck. "I assure you, I do."

The phone on the desk rang, interrupting the awkward moment they were sharing. Giasson grabbed it. "Allo?" Chaney peered through the glass surrounding the office at the dozens of staff at their desks. Too many heads whipped back to their computers, their curious stares caught. "Monsieur Reading, how are you, mon ami!"

Chaney's head spun around.

Reading?

Could there be more than one? Of course there could, but that would be one hell of a coincidence. Had Giasson called Interpol to have him checked out? That, he could see. Yet how did he know Reading?

The bombing!

"We must get together the next time you are in our beautiful city and have some tea."

31

That's definitely my Reading.

His former partner's legendary penchant for tea at all costs had apparently spanned the Continent.

"Listen, my friend, I have someone here I need you to vouch for. Do you know a Detective Inspector Chaney of Scotland Yard?"

Chaney couldn't hear the other side of the conversation, however he did notice Giasson drop a few shades of red as the vein on his temple settled down. His frown disappeared, though not replaced with much, if any, of a smile.

"And he can be trusted?"

Again, Chaney was left to wonder what was being said at the other end of the line.

Giasson held out the phone. "He wants to talk to you."

Chaney slid forward and took the phone. "Hello?"

"Martin! How are you?"

"Hugh, I'm fine. You're about the last person I expected to hear from."

"Well, our friend Monsieur Giasson and I had some dealings recently with the attack, as I'm sure you heard. Going through something like that, dealing with the aftermath—well, you know how it is."

"Yes, I understand." Chaney had never been a soldier, though he had dealt with his fair share of horrors in his career, and the ones you went through it with were friends for life. Not necessarily friends you called every week, or even headed to the pub with on a Friday. But if you needed something, they were there. If you bumped into them, even years later, it was like picking up right where you left off, as if they were family, because they knew who you were, what had created you, what had created both of you, the bond forged under fire stronger than any other. He looked at Giasson. "Can I assume you've vouched for me?"

"You? Never! I said he should immediately escort you off the grounds, as you could only be up to no good!" Reading roared in laughter and Chaney joined in.

I miss him.

His new senior partner was friendly, and they got along fine, and in time he was confident they would form the same bond he and Reading had enjoyed after years of working side-by-side, however their relationship was still fresh, and that camaraderie had yet to gel.

Give it time.

Chaney looked at Giasson but spoke to Reading. "Can I assume we're okay?"

Giasson nodded with a slight smile as Reading confirmed it. "Yes, you're fine. I told him I trusted you with my life. When you get back to London, call me, and we'll do tea."

"Absolutely. Goodbye, Hugh."

"Goodbye, my friend. Now put that Swiss blowhard back on the line."

Chaney handed the phone to Giasson, who took it and spun around in his chair, his back facing Chaney. He lowered his voice, but Chaney had little difficulty hearing him.

"So, he is who he says he is?" A pause. "And he can be trusted?" Another pause. "That is all I needed to hear, mon ami. When you are next in Rome, we will have tea. Au revoir." He spun his chair and dropped the phone into its cradle.

"Monsieur Reading seems to think very highly of you."

Chaney smiled. "And I of him. We were partners for many years."

"Hmm. So, you claim to have an appointment with His Holiness." He raised a finger, cutting off Chaney before he could set him straight. "Let us check." He picked up the phone and dialed an extension. A brief conversation in Italian ensued, Giasson's eyebrows

33

shooting up at one point. He hung up then looked at Chaney. "I'm sorry I doubted you. You are requested to join His Holiness in his office as soon as is convenient for you."

Chaney could tell just from the bewildered expression on Giasson's face that this was unusual. Even he was surprised when he wasn't given a specific time to meet the Pope, but was instead to simply present himself as early as possible.

"I think it's best if I go immediately."

"I concur."

"If you could point me in the—"

Giasson wagged his finger. "No, I shall accompany you personally."

Chaney followed Giasson through the complex, thankful he had a personal guide, as it was far vaster and more confusing than he could have imagined. Minutes later, they were in an outer office, and an elderly priest sitting at the desk rose, bowing slightly at Giasson.

"Mr. Chaney?"

Chaney was about to extend his hand when he noticed the priest's were neatly tucked in the opposing arms' sleeves. "Yes, umm, Father?"

The man smiled slightly. "Follow me." He stepped away from his desk and pushed open two large doors, the woodwork something he would expect at Buckingham Palace, and not in a house of God.

God's palace on Earth?

He stepped forward, as did Giasson. The priest shook his head. "Only Mr. Chaney."

Giasson halted in mid-step. Chaney shrugged. "Sorry." Following the priest in, he found himself in a large office, though not ostentatiously so, brimming with history. His eyes traveled the shelves lined with books older than him, artifacts from throughout the ages, walls adorned with priceless works of arts, and behind a stunning handcrafted desk, the holy man himself.

Chaney, though not Catholic, gulped.

"Mr. Chaney of Scotland Yard," announced the priest who promptly left, closing the doors behind him.

The Pope rounded his desk, his hand extended. Chaney had seen the ring kissed on many occasions, but wasn't sure what he was supposed to do. He erred on the side of caution and reached out, taking the hand. He bent over to kiss the ring when the Pontiff's other hand touched Chaney's shoulder, stopping him in mid-stoop.

"That is not necessary, my son."

Chaney, upright again, instead shook the proffered hand. "I'm sorry, sir, I wasn't sure."

The man grasped Chaney's hand in both of his, looking deep into his eyes, slowly nodding, then suddenly grabbed Chaney's left hand and flipped it over, exposing his wrist. With his opposing thumb, the Pontiff pushed the strap of Chaney's watchband up, revealing his Triarii tattoo, two small, thin lines, with a third, slightly curved and thicker, underneath. The man quickly let go and stepped back, smiling. As he did, he flipped his own wrist over.

Chaney gasped as he saw a tattoo matching his own. "You're Triarii!" He instinctively revealed his own tattoo again, staring at it to compare, not trusting that his eyes were not deceiving him.

"Yes, my son." The Pontiff indicated a set of chairs near a window, the afternoon's light pouring through stained glass accents, reminding Chaney of church when he was a child. He followed, on autopilot, and dropped into one of the leather chairs. The Pontiff sat across from him, his elbows resting on the chair's high arms, his fingers interlaced under a slightly jutting chin. "Would you like the full story?"

Chaney nodded.

"Very well, I will tell you as much as I can." He drew a deep breath, as if this would indeed be long, then began. "You of course know the Triarii protect the twelve crystal skulls, discovered over the past two millennia." He stopped, raising his eyebrows. "You are familiar with the history?"

"Of course, I was taught it as a boy by my father."

"Good, good." The Pontiff's head bobbed. "Then I will skip to recent events. I was a Cardinal, a prince of the Church, for almost two decades." He paused. "Has it been that long?" His eyes stared at the ceiling, or more likely, toward God. He returned his gaze to Chaney and smiled. "I apologize, my son, this old man sometimes drifts."

"It's okay, sir."

"Thank you, my son, now, where were we? Oh yes, I was a cardinal, which, in case you aren't aware, is a very high rank, and is usually the pool from which the next pope is chosen. When the events of several months ago occurred, I was automatically a candidate to replace the poor soul, and had, over the years, been positioning myself to be a serious contender."

Chaney cleared his throat.

"Yes?"

"Well, sir, I hate to ask, but—" He stopped, not sure of how to ask the Pope, of all people, the question on his mind.

"You wonder if I even believe in God, in the Roman Catholic Church. You wonder if I, by occupying this very post, defile it."

Chaney's cheeks flushed. "Yes."

"I'm glad you asked. And please"—he leaned forward and touched Chaney's knee—"don't hesitate to ask me anything. If we are to get through this, we must be as trusting of each other as we can."

"Yes, sir."

The Pontiff returned to his position of contemplation. "Do I believe in God? Absolutely. Do I believe in our Lord, our savior, Jesus Christ? Absolutely. Do I believe in the teachings of the Holy Bible and the way in which this church has interpreted it? Absolutely. I am, in every way, a staunch Roman Catholic. I am Triarii by birth, and honor its history and mandate, and will honor the vow I made when I formally joined the Triarii to fulfill the duties my ancestors have for thousands of years, but that in no way affects my ability to believe in God, to have religion. The two are not in opposition to each other." He stopped and pointed a finger gently at Chaney. "Do *you* believe in God?"

Chaney shifted in his chair. "Yes, I suppose I do. Nothing formal. I mean, I don't go to church, but I guess I believe."

"And does it interfere with your duties as Triarii?"

"No, I suppose not."

"Of course it doesn't. The Triarii have always allowed all faiths to be members, as even the Triarii have no idea what the source of the skulls is." He leaned forward. "Now, as I was saying, I had been positioning myself for years, at the request of the Proconsul, as we became aware of something after the war that demanded investigation."

"The war? World War Two?"

"Yes. As I'm sure you're aware, Hitler was a zealot when it came to historical relics. He had teams spread across the globe chasing down everything and everyone in an attempt to find things that may help him in his efforts to conquer the world."

"I thought that was just in the Indiana Jones movies."

A smile spread across the old man's face. "Ahhh, Indiana Jones. How we were concerned when that movie was announced!"

"The last one? I saw it. Once I realized the premise, I knew we had nothing to worry about."

"I think every member of the Triarii around the world saw that movie opening weekend."

Chaney chuckled. "Probably boosted its numbers."

"No doubt, no doubt," agreed the Pontiff, his head bobbing with laughter. "But you brought up Indiana Jones. Though fiction, the premise of the first movie was based on fact. Hitler had his Nazis spread out across the globe, seeking everything, including crystal skulls."

"Yes, one in Warsaw was lost, was it not?"

"Yes, and eventually recovered by the Soviets before we could get to it. Luckily, it was later retrieved, as you are well aware." He leaned forward, lowering his voice. "The confusion after the war allowed us to put several operatives into their defunct archaeological branch and investigate what they had found out about the skulls. In fact, my father led the team, which is why I know what I know."

Chaney leaned forward as well, the distance separating the two men mere inches. "And what is it you know?"

"That they found evidence of a thirteenth skull."

Chaney jerked back in his chair, his jaw dropping. "Are you serious?"

"Would I joke about something like that?"

Chaney shook his head.

Of course he wouldn't.

His mind raced with the ramifications. The fabled thirteenth skull. Some had thought it existed, that it must exist, superstition winning over science. But if it did exist, not only was it a fascinating discovery, it was a dangerous one. If there was a rogue skull out there, unprotected, the consequences could be catastrophic.

The Pontiff leaned back, his voice still low. "I see you understand the implications."

"Of course. What's being done about it?"

"The records gave the location."

"And where is it?"

The Pontiff pointed his finger at the floor. "Here."

"It's here?" exclaimed Chaney.

The Pontiff's finger flew to his mouth, urging him to lower his voice. Chaney flushed. "I'm sorry." He leaned

38

forward and lowered his voice to a whisper. "Have you found it?"

The Pontiff shook his head, all traces of joy leaving his face. "No, and I'm afraid this is why you are here."

"You want me to find the skull?"

"No, I want you to find out who killed Father Granger, one of our own, who was searching for the skull."

"There's been a murder? At the Vatican?" Again Chaney was admonished to keep his voice down. "I'm sorry, sir, I just—" He stopped. He wasn't sure what to think. He had to process this new information.

And calm his racing heart.

A murder at the Vatican. The fabled thirteenth skull here. Triarii running the Roman Catholic Church. It was all too much. He closed his eyes and leaned forward, dropping his head between his knees and clasping his hands behind his neck.

I wish Reading were here.

A hand gently squeezed his shoulder.

"Are you okay, my son?"

Chaney nodded, then unclasped his hands and slowly sat back up. "This is fantastic. Simply too fantastic."

The old man returned to his seat. "It is indeed. I can understand your confusion, your shock. It's almost too much to take in all at once."

Chaney took a breath then tweaked on something just said, his eyebrows shooting up. "Father Granger was Triarii as well?"

"Yes." The Pontiff leaned back. "In this position, I get to choose my own aides, so I naturally chose one of our own. He is fully qualified to execute the duties of the position, is as devout a Catholic as any man I know, and is also loyal to our cause. As well, he was a dear friend who had worked by my side for years."

"And he was murdered?"

A frown creased the Pontiff's face. "Yes. Yesterday morning, his body was discovered in his chambers. He was beaten to death."

"Did anybody hear anything?"

"No, they think he was killed elsewhere and his body moved to his room."

"Has the murder scene been found?"

"No, and it won't be."

Chaney's eyes narrowed. "Why not?"

"Because I know where he was killed, and it is a place known only to me, and until yesterday, Father Granger."

"Where?"

The Pontiff took in a breath then slowly exhaled. "What I'm about to tell you is the most well-guarded secret the Church has. It can be repeated to no one. It is a secret you must take to your grave."

Chaney's heart thudded.

What possible secret could a church have?

"I understand."

"You have heard of the Vatican Secret Archives?"

"Everyone has. They're not exactly secret."

The Pontiff chuckled. "No, and 'secrecy' is not the definition of 'Secret' in this case. It is actually 'Private,' meaning they are owned by me. The archives are public, scholars are allowed to view the items, the inventory is public. No, I'm not talking about the Secret Archives." He leaned forward. "What isn't known, what can't be known, is that there is another archive."

Chaney said nothing, instead leaning closer as the Pontiff's voice dropped further still.

"Beneath these very walls, under the foundations of this church, is an archive created and maintained by my predecessors." He struggled to his feet then stepped over to a table, his hand extended toward a wooden box. Chaney joined him as the elderly man placed a hand on it. "Each pope, upon their election, is presented with this chest, with a lock that only the papal ring can open. It is presented with instructions that it must be opened in private, and on the first day of his reign. Inside is a letter, written on stone, with no name on it, but there is a fish carved at the bottom."

"A fish?"

"The fisherman. St. Peter himself."

"Wasn't he—?"

"The first pope, the first head of the Church of Christ, the man who laid the foundation of what would become this very church, the Roman Catholic Church, the greatest church to have ever existed, with more followers than any other, and through the centuries, more power than it ever should have wielded."

"What did it say?"

The Pontiff shook his head. "No one knows, the words were either worn away with time, or purposefully destroyed, perhaps by one of my predecessors too upset by what he had discovered inside the chest. But I can tell you this. Other documents inside refer to it, and from what I gather, it ordered all future popes to protect the Church. Not only from blasphemy, but from truths that could damage, or worse, destroy. And over the years, over nearly two millennia, items were collected that my predecessors felt may hurt the Church, shake people's beliefs, and they have been hidden away, eventually in secret chambers built under Saint Peter's Basilica itself."

Chaney wasn't sure what to think. There was no doubt the old man took this extremely seriously.

A super-secret archive hiding things that could hurt the Church?

"What kind of things are hidden?"

"An inventory is kept in the Unus Veritas Chest of everything that has been hidden over the years, but the parchments are old, and some have crumbled to dust. Only the past seven or eight hundred years are known, and now, thanks to His Holiness, John Paul the Second, the inventory was archived on computer disk to preserve it. Unfortunately, the first thousand years or more of the archive is mostly unknown."

"Can't you just go down there and look?"

The man appeared mortified. "These are forbidden items. Things that could shake mankind's very belief in Christ, in God, in the Church."

"What could possibly do that, especially in today's day and age?"

"My son, I have merely *read* the inventory and am terrified."

"But what—?"

The Pontiff raised his hand, cutting him off. "There are some things man is not meant to see. Some things man is not meant to know." He dropped his hand, sighing. "At least until man is ready. But when that will be…" His voice trailed off.

"Well, we do know one thing that's in there."

The Pontiff raised his drooping head. "Yes?"

"Something worth killing for."

The old man agreed, then took a piece of paper from a nearby folder. "This is a copy of the map handed down to each of us, showing how to get to the Vault."

Chaney looked at what was clearly a scan of a very old document, the fresh new paper begging to be held gently, the color printout leaving a distinctly genuine impression. "Where are we on this?" The old man pointed with a shaking finger. "And the Vault?"

"You must follow this path." He traced a route from the chambers that would take him down several hallways and to a seemingly dead end. The Pontiff tapped a room to the left with his finger. "In this room, you will find a large wardrobe. Open it, step inside, then close the doors. Inside there are a series of clothes hooks. Push the second from the left up, and a secret door will open. This will lead you into the Vault."

"Seems simple enough."

"Yes, but keep this in mind. There is no electricity. You will need to bring your own light. And, beyond that door, there is no further way I can help you."

"What do you mean?"

"I have never been there. I have no idea what you should expect on the other side of that door."

"You've never been there? Aren't you curious?"

"Of course I'm curious, but it's forbidden. If an artifact is found that should be hidden away, only then can you enter. I have not yet had occasion to do so." He paused and looked at Chaney. "And I hope never to have to."

Chaney retraced the route with his finger. "Are there any cameras around here? Me disappearing into a room for some time is bound to raise questions."

The Pontiff shook his head. "No, this area has no cameras for this very purpose. These are all the private chambers of myself, my staff, and some guest rooms. Our privacy has been given as the reason for no cameras, however the true reason is the Vault."

Chaney pushed the map across the table. "You keep this. I know where to go and I don't want to be found with it on me."

"Very well. What will you do now?"

Chaney leaned back. "Well, I'll need a base of operations. Just a room that I can use as an excuse not to be seen. You mentioned guest rooms?"

The Pontiff smiled. "I've already arranged a room for you, only twenty meters from the Vault entrance. I've had some supplies you may need placed there."

"Perfect. I suggest someone show me to my room, then I'll go exploring."

The Pontiff rose, as did Chaney. "I will have Father Morris show you." He took Chaney by the arm. "And be careful, my son. One is already dead, and that is one too many."

Guest Chambers
Apostolic Palace, The Vatican

Chaney listened and, hearing nothing, slowly turned the knob and pulled the antique door open, the apparently well-maintained hinges silently doing their job. He poked his head out and, seeing no one, stepped into the hallway, closed the door, then strode with purpose to the end of the hall. A quick glance to the right confirmed the coast was still clear, and a sharp turn to the left had him swallowing his heart.

"Lost?"

Chaney shook his head at the priest standing in front of him. "Ah, no, Father, simply playing tourist."

The young man smiled. "You must be easily entertained if the residential wing holds any fascination." He stepped around Chaney and continued on his way, Bible clasped in his hands. He motioned down another corridor. "That way will lead you to far more interesting things."

"Thank you. I'll go there next."

"As you wish." The man turned a corner, out of sight.

Chaney stood in place, calming his thumping heart.

Keep it together!

He inhaled deeply then slowly exhaled. He walked briskly to the end of the hall. With a look to confirm all was clear, he opened the door in front of him and entered. Closing the door, he made a swift survey of the room, relieved though not surprised to find himself alone. He stepped toward the wardrobe, the large wood structure filling half the wall of the small chamber. He ran his hand along the simple, functional design. The skilled craftsmanship was evident, the wood lovingly measured, cut, and fitted, but the design was utilitarian, as if not to attract attention.

Probably so no one would get the idea of wanting it in their room.

He pulled on the handle and the heavy door swung silently open. It was empty inside save for a few metal hangers pushed to one end of the rail. The hooks the Pontiff had spoken of were empty, six of them spread across the back from one side to the other. From his pocket, he pulled a flashlight left in his room. He snapped it on and stepped inside, pulling the door shut behind him. Though the wardrobe might have been large, it was still a piece of furniture, and claustrophobia gripped him. He reached and pushed up the hook, second from the left. It took some effort, and for a moment he wondered if he had remembered correctly, though with a little more muscle it moved, and a clicking sound echoed through his small waystation. With the hook pushed all the way up, he waited, but nothing else followed.

Did I do something wrong?

He let go of the hook and it remained in place.

Should I pull it back down?

He thought about it, but figured that would merely lock whatever mechanism he had just heard. He pushed on the rear panel. It swung open and away from him, sending him stumbling forward a step before he regained his balance. He played his flashlight into the newly discovered opening and sucked in a breath.

Stone walls, clearly ancient, revealed themselves to the beam of his flashlight. A quick look at the floor had him step down slightly into the corridor now before him. He pressed forward, the click of his shoes echoing off the walls that stretched out ahead.

With more confidence, he continued forward no more than twenty feet when he found a pulley system of clearly ancient design, the chains dull with age, the wood still sound, though covered in dust and cobwebs. He peered over the edge where a platform, attached to the pulley, was free to descend. He shone his flashlight yet could see nothing below. He examined the platform and whistled.

You could move a car on that.

He stared down the hallway he had just traveled.

But how the hell would you get it here?

He shone his flashlight to the other side of the platform and found a wide corridor stretching farther than the beam could reach.

There must be another entrance.

He listened, making sure he was still alone. He heard nothing.

I wonder if he knows there's more than one way in here.

He made a mental note to ask, then shone his flashlight ahead. A few more feet of walking and he was met with a set of stone stairs, spiraling down toward what he assumed would be the Vault below.

Beginning his descent, he found his heart beating faster with each step, his footfalls echoing off the walls, giving him the distinct impression he was being followed. He stopped. The clicks of shoes continued for a few moments, then stopped. He took a few more steps, the echo once again resuming. And stopped. Again, the delay.

You're going barmy! It's just your mind playing tricks on you!

He continued his descent, this time quicker, struggling to block out the footsteps echoing through the confined space. After descending several hundred steps—he had lost count in his momentary panic—he came about the final turn and into a large, gaping space.

And froze.

He wasn't prepared for how massive the Vault would be. He shone his flashlight about him, his arm stretched as far as it could to gain those extra inches, and still he could see no end in sight. At this level, there were shelves, tables, and other items simply sitting on the floor, but he could see no ceiling and no walls other than the one behind him where the exit to the stairs he had just descended stood, along with the other end of the pulley system he had observed earlier.

He looked at the floor and gasped. Kneeling down, he ran his fingers over the stone, still rough from centuries of feet never there to polish its surface through repeated abuse. He rubbed the dust between his fingers, the thick layer of centuries of neglect surprisingly dry to the touch. In fact, he found the entire place to be fairly dry. Not too dry, simply not damp as he had expected.

Humidity controlled?

It would make sense, but how? He shook his head.

Not your concern.

He shone his flashlight about the floor and smiled.

This might be easier than I thought.

There were clear footprints in the dust, leading into the darkness. It seemed as though several trips had been made, the impressions appearing to be the same size. The Pontiff had mentioned that the Father had been searching, so repeated trips made sense. And the fact there was no evidence of other footprints suggested no one else had descended the stairs, or platform, behind him.

So where did they come from?

An unease swept through him, goosebumps raising the hair on his arms. A quick spin, the beam of light cutting through his surroundings, his eyes squinting in anticipation of seeing something, only set his heart racing more than it already was. He stopped.

No, your best bet is to use your ears, not your eyes.

He took a deep, slow breath, then closed his eyes and listened for any hint of company. And found none. Satisfied for the moment, he followed the footprints around a shelf and found it to be the first of many stretching into the distance. A single set of footprints led down each shelf and back up the adjacent. Confident this was merely the Father searching, he continued forward along the path in the dust for several shelves and stopped.

Hello!

A new set of prints, the feet distinctly larger than the Father's, with a tread pattern indicating a boot of some type rather than a dress shoe as the Father had been wearing, met the last of the Father's steps. He knelt down, shining his flashlight over the floor, searching for any clue as to what happened, though he was pretty sure he already knew.

Blood!

There was no mistaking it. Several small pools of blood and spatters stretching for at least a ten-foot radius. This was where the Father had been beaten to death. And it appeared to be a vicious beating. Chaney found himself making the sign of the cross, something he couldn't recall doing in his entire life. But it seemed appropriate. He stood and surveyed the area.

What's this!

Leading away from the jumble of feet where the assault had taken place were two long, solid lines, stretching between the shelves. He followed them to the end of the line of shelves, then back toward where he had come from, only on the opposite end. They led directly to the pulley system he had found earlier.

They must have used this to get his body back to his room.

Retracing his original path, he moved up and down the shelves, searching for anything out of the ordinary. The beam of his flashlight revealed secrets that scared even the Church, but they were meaningless to him. Nothing more than scrolls, books, talismans, crystal balls, and other items that appeared to be benign and untouched for centuries, if not longer.

Bloody hell!

He froze, his flashlight aimed at a large jar, several feet high, sitting on the bottom shelf.

What the blazes is that?

He leaned forward and shuddered, the light revealing a small body inside the jar. And a face definitely not human.

This looks like it should be in Area 51.

He stepped back, taking one final look, then moved on.

Must be some sort of mutation.

He satisfied himself with that explanation and continued until he reached the scene of the crime. Nothing had been touched as far as he could tell, the thick layer of dust preserved in every case.

So why was he killed here *of all places?*

It didn't appear to be something he had discovered. The shelves were undisturbed, and he was clearly walking to the next set.

Something he was about to discover?

This sent a rush of excitement through Chaney.

The thirteenth skull! Could it be here?

He stepped clear of the bloody scene and rounded the unsearched shelf, the beam of his flashlight cutting through the dark revealing more of the same assorted artifacts.

A shoe scraped the stone floor behind him. He spun, his flashlight cutting an arc through the darkness, revealing an arm swinging down at him, something gripped in its hand glinting. He moved to block the blow, but it was too late. Something jabbed his shoulder, the sharp pain replaced with a warm, tingling sensation as whatever had stuck him began its work. Weakness swept through him and he fell to his knees, his eyes drooping. He shone the flashlight up at the figure now leaning over him, lowering him to the floor, yet saw nothing but black robes and a hooded face. With the last of his strength, he reached up to pull the mask off and reveal his attacker, but he fell short, instead yanking at the robe, and for a moment, the light flitted across his attacker's chest, revealing something white underneath, and part of a symbol he recognized from somewhere, an upside-down cross with two keys.

His hand let go and the flashlight rolled from his grasp as he finally succumbed to the blackness.

Interpol, United Kingdom Liaison Office
New Scotland Yard, London, England

Interpol Agent Hugh Reading slammed his phone down for the umpteenth time. He hadn't reached Chaney all day, and now he was officially worried. Chaney had never failed to return a phone call promptly, even when on an investigation. An hour or two was fine, but eight hours wasn't. Reading didn't know exactly why Chaney was at the Vatican, though he was certain it was Triarii business, what with his former partner and the new pope both from that ancient organization.

What the hell could the Triarii want with the Vatican?

They had never shown any malevolence toward the Church that he could tell, although his knowledge of the organization was extremely limited. Acton had told him everything he and Laura knew, and it had matched up with what Chaney had said. The Church must have something the Triarii wanted, and the only thing he could think of was another crystal skull.

Here we go again!

He didn't care if he ever saw another one of those monstrosities again, but when the news report broke about rumors of a murder at the Vatican, why Chaney had been brought in became obvious. The Pope clearly wanted somebody he could absolutely trust to investigate.

I can just imagine what Mario thought of that.

He grinned as he pictured the bald man's vein throbbing over his temple. Then frowned at the thought of why he had gotten to know the man in the first place.

The horror. The evil upon which some men acted.

He shook his head, ridding himself of the images from that day, but failed. He would never be able to. Not completely. The carnage had been something for which he could never have prepared. It had kept him up at night for weeks, and only recently had he managed to get a full night's sleep on occasion, many nights still tortured by nightmares leaving him soaked in sweat. Those nights were slowly getting fewer, and he'd get over it eventually, though it would take time.

And now his friend was back in the thick of it, and not answering his phone.

He checked his watch. There was no way Chaney would have ignored his call this late. He grabbed his phone and dialed. It rang once then was picked up.

"Giasson."

"Hi, Mario, this is Hugh Reading. How are you?"

Giasson cleared his throat. "I was wondering when I was going to hear from you."

Reading's heart rate increased slightly. "Why?"

"Oh, I figured you'd be checking up on your old partner."

Reading chuckled. "You know me too well." He lowered his voice slightly. "Listen, I've been trying to reach him all day, but he hasn't answered, and hasn't returned any of my messages."

"Really? And he's in the habit of returning your calls promptly?"

"Absolutely. We've known each other for over ten years. Even after leaving the Yard, we've kept in touch, and he's never not returned my call, usually within minutes, sometimes an hour or two. Never this long." He paused and took a quick breath. "I'm worried."

"I will check into it personally and get back to you as soon as I have something."

"Thank you, mon ami."

The line went dead and Reading reclined in his chair, resting his head against the high back.

Martin, you tosser, what have you gotten yourself into?

Guest Quarters
Apostolic Palace, The Vatican

Giasson stood in front of the quarters assigned to Detective Inspector Chaney and knocked again, his first attempt having gone unanswered. He had, however, knocked quietly so as not to disturb any other guests, the stone and wood construction of these quarters causing every sound to echo loudly.

Or maybe it's just your imagination?

He checked his watch. It was after midnight. He put his ear to the door and heard nothing. He tried the handle and the door opened, the lock on the inside obviously unused. This wasn't unusual, as it was rare for a visiting man of the cloth to lock his room while in the Vatican, likely the safest place there was in the world. But a police guest? He would have expected the door to be locked every moment he was in the room.

And this could mean only one of two things.

Either he wasn't in the room, or he had met the same fate as the Father. He pushed the door open and poked his head into the small, dark room. "Detective Chaney?" It was a faint call. He still wanted to try and avoid a ruckus at this hour, if possible. He stepped deeper inside, reaching for the light switch. He flipped it up. The lone bulb in the ceiling flooded the room with a gentle, warm glow, revealing the sparse furnishings, closed drapes, and an unslept-in bed.

This can't be good.

A quick search of the room confirmed it was empty. If it weren't for yesterday's incident, he might not have been as concerned. But even so, this wasn't a hotel. Guests of the Vatican didn't simply go out for a night on the town. While here, they behaved themselves and went to bed at a decent hour.

Something is definitely wrong.

He closed the door and jogged back to Security. Rushing through the doors, the sparse night shift all looked up, not accustomed to seeing their boss running and now out of breath. Giasson sucked in a few lungsful of air, hunched over, making a mental note to hit the gym more often. He stood and turned to one of his underlings, Paolo D'Onofrio. "Paulo, check the logs. I need to know if Detective Inspector Chaney has left the grounds." He swept his arm at the room at large. "Check all security footage since our guest arrived. I need to see where he went. Start with entrances to the residential quarters. We need to see if he left there." He stopped for a moment.

Should I?

He pointed to the woman sitting at the reception desk. "Call the front gate, have them seal it. Nobody leaves without my permission."

He headed into his office and closed the door. Grabbing the phone as he rounded his desk, he dropped into his chair and dialed Reading's number. He answered immediately.

"Reading."

"Allo, mon ami. This is Mario."

"Any news?"

"None good, I'm afraid. It appears his bed has not been slept in. You know him better than I. Would he be out late, perhaps on the town as you might say?"

"Not Martin. Not when there's a job to be done." Giasson heard Reading inhale deeply. "Something's wrong. I can feel it."

"I too."

"What are you doing about it?"

"As of this moment, I have locked down the Vatican and am treating Mr. Chaney as a missing person. We're reviewing security logs and camera footage. Once I confirm what I already suspect, that he never left the grounds, I will begin a search."

"Do you know why he was there?"

Giasson shook his head slightly, recalling his frustration at being left out of the loop. "No, I'm not privy to that information."

"Then ask."

Giasson grunted. "Mon ami, one does not wake His Holiness up in the middle of the night and ask him why he invited a guest."

"One does when there's already been a murder. It seems quite obvious to me that Martin was brought in to investigate for some reason. And if he stumbled onto something quicker than your own investigation, he must have had some sort of inside information, supplied by the Pope. You need to find out what he told him. That could lead you to him."

Reading was right.

But to wake His Holiness!

He glanced at the clock on the wall.

Well after midnight.

"Of course you are right. I will see to it and call you back when I hear anything more."

"Do that. I'll be there in the morning."

Giasson smiled. "I would be shocked if you weren't, mon ami. I will see you then."

He hung up the phone as D'Onofrio knocked on the door. Giasson waved for him to come in and the young man opened the door, poking his head inside.

"Sir, I checked the security logs and we have no record of Detective Chaney leaving the grounds. I also checked with all three shifts of guards, and none remember him leaving, though he could have ignored procedure and just mixed in with the tourists rather than signing out."

Giasson pursed his lips as he debated what to do. "Okay, pull his face from when he arrived, then get facial recognition working on the crowds exiting after he left his meeting with His Holiness."

"Yes, sir."

D'Onofrio closed the door and returned to his desk as Giasson picked up his phone again, dialing the extension for the Pontiff's office. What many people didn't realize was that this was a country like any other, and the office was always manned. Though the smallest in the world, it too never entirely slept. Someone was always on staff in case of emergencies around the globe involving the Church, or mankind in general.

The extension was immediately picked up.

"Papal Offices, Father Silvano Benedetti speaking."

"Good evening, Father. This is Mario Giasson. We have a problem here."

"Yes? Is there a threat to His Holiness?"

Giasson noted the concern, understandable after recent events.

"No, however one of his guests, Detective Inspector Chaney from Scotland Yard, is missing."

"Are you certain? He is not simply elsewhere?"

Giasson knew what was about to happen, and a little "white" lie could prevent it, but he was the security chief at the holiest of places—lying wasn't an option, for he was a deeply religious man. "No, we are not certain, but so far, all indications are that he is."

"And what do you need from us?"

"I would like to speak to His Holiness."

"At this hour? About a man you aren't even sure is missing?"

"Yes."

"I don't know about that."

Giasson took a slow breath, struggling to remain calm. *God, give me strength.*

"You are aware of the murder yesterday?"

"Of course."

"And now we have another person missing."

"*Presumed* missing."

"A personal guest of His Holiness, here at his invitation, specifically in relation to the murder..." His tone left each point dangling as he gave every opportunity for the Father to grasp what he was implying.

There was silence.

He was about to open his mouth to bluntly connect the two events when Benedetti sighed. "You have all the subtlety of a hammer, Monsieur. And you are right. His Holiness would never want to be left sleeping if one of his guests were possibly in trouble. There is one problem however."

"And what is that?"

"His Holiness left strict instructions that neither he nor Mr. Chaney were to be disturbed for any reason tonight."

Okay. Wasn't expecting that.

"I assume that is unusual?"

"Very. In fact, in all my years as night watchman, I have never heard such an instruction given."

Maybe he isn't missing after all?

Giasson drew a breath, not sure if he should ask this question. "How certain are we that His Holiness is in his room?"

"Of course he's in his room! Where else would he be?"

He was right to ask the question, as it was a reasonable one.

On any other night.

With a murder, and now a guest showing no evidence he had stayed in his room for more than a few minutes, and His Holiness giving an order he had never given in the past, it was a question that deserved only one answer.

"Are you willing to take that risk?"

Benedetti immediately grasped the implication. "You don't think—"

"I don't know what to think. But can we take the risk?"

Evidently, Benedetti, to his credit, didn't think so. "I will wake his personal valet immediately."

"Good. Tell him I will meet him at His Holiness' chambers."

He hung up the phone and rose from his desk, swiftly crossing the floor and leaving his office. Leaning on the desk of the nightshift's most senior staff member, he lowered his voice. "Alfredo, I need you to pull the procedures for Broken Dove."

Alfredo Ianuzzi's eyebrows shot up and his eyes widened in surprise. "Did you say Broken Dove?" he asked in a harsh whisper.

Giasson looked around, making certain no one had overheard. Satisfied, he leaned in even closer. "Yes. Pull the plans, just in case. Don't let anyone know, but start reviewing them right now."

Ianuzzi made the sign of the cross and Giasson walked from the offices then broke into a jog toward His Holiness' quarters.

God save us all if something has happened to him.

Outside the Papal Chambers
Apostolic Palace, The Vatican

Giasson waited outside the door, his heart still pounding from his sprint over here.

Where the hell is he?

He checked his watch. It hadn't been ten minutes since his request for His Holiness to be woken.

And where the hell are the guards?

Two should be stationed outside the door at all times, yet they weren't to be found. He put his ear to the door, listening for anything. Heavy breathing, snoring, some sign he was in there. Nothing. Though that actually *did* mean nothing. Many people were quiet sleepers, including himself. Not his mother-in-law, though.

Mamma mia, could she wake the neighborhood.

She wasn't a fan of his, and the feeling was mutual. When she visited, it was a nonstop verbal tirade about how he neglected his family by working such long hours, and if he loved his wife as much as he loved his job, her daughter would be that much happier.

Funny how she's always happier after you leave, Mamma!

He was Swiss. French-Swiss, though still Swiss, which meant his parents had made certain he spoke Italian and German as well. He knew when he married an Italian girl, he was marrying her entire family, whether he liked it or not. Yet he loved Marie-Claude. Her father was French, hence her French name, but his father-in-law had been absorbed into the Italian side like Giasson feared might happen to him. Her mother insisted on calling her Maria, though he always went with the French.

They had met almost twenty years ago when he was a young man. He had graduated from the University of Lausanne with a Bachelor of Theology degree. His dream had always been to work at the Vatican. Not as a priest— he wasn't strong enough for that. He liked women. A lot. And there would be no denying that side of him. Though to serve the Lord in any other capacity was open. He had applied for, and won, a position in the Pontifical Swiss Guard, and served for several years as a Hauptman, or Captain, then was promoted to Major. When a job came open in Security, he applied, and again won.

And he had never looked back. It was celebrating his new job with some of his former guardsmen that had him run into Marie-Claude. Literally. He had stumbled from the bar they were celebrating in and bowled her over. He picked her up, apologizing profusely, then pursued her down the street, his mid-twenties testosterone-fueled ego determined to get the name of the lovely vision he had just encountered.

She had refused, climbed in her car parked down the street, and left.

His buddies didn't let him live that down for the rest of the night.

It was six months later that he saw her again, or rather her car. It was a distinctive orange Citroën, and he had remembered the plates, an ability he had always had, turning numbers and letters into patterns he could recall later. So, he set up surveillance at a local café with a clear view of the car, and waited. And waited. It had been hours before she finally appeared, several shopping bags and what appeared to be a freshly coifed head of hair the explanation.

He smiled as he remembered her reaction when he approached her.

"Do you remember me?"

She had looked at him, puzzled at first, then her mouth opened slightly. With a frown. "You're the drunk who knocked me over, and wouldn't take no for an answer. What do *you* want?"

He had blushed, and his face must have revealed his disappointment at her reaction. He had stood there, tongue-tied for several moments, then mumbled an apology and began to walk away when she cleared her throat. He had spun around, new hope written all over his face, and she had smiled awkwardly.

"Can you help me open my trunk. My hands are full."

Six months later they were married.

Tears filled his eyes as he pictured her walking down the aisle, more beautiful than he had ever imagined possible, her tanned skin contrasting sharply with the white of her gown, the veil doing little to hide the beaming smile behind it.

Footfalls echoed through the hallway and he pulled a handkerchief from his pocket, dabbing his eyes dry. Father Jenner, the temporary replacement to the now-dead Father Granger, rushed up. "Monsieur Giasson. Are you sure you want to do this?"

"Do we have any choice?"

The man frowned, clearly not pleased by having his question answered with another. "Very well. I pray we are about to make fools of ourselves."

"Informing His Holiness that one of his personal guests is missing I think will be greeted with concern, and gratefulness at us bringing him this information promptly. I, too, pray that Mr. Chaney is found shortly, and all of this proves to be of no use." He detected a slight wavering of the Father's resolve. "However," he said, raising his voice slightly, "at this point in time, Mr. Chaney *is* missing, and His Holiness, I am certain, would want to know, and may even be able to help us."

Father Jenner stared at him for a moment. "Very well." He knocked lightly on the door. "Your Holiness, it is I, Father Jenner. I have important information."

They both listened, but heard nothing. Father Jenner knocked harder, repeating his appeal. Again nothing.

"Open the door," ordered Giasson.

Father Jenner paused, regarded Giasson, then opened the unlocked door, a practice all popes had followed since Giasson had been here, despite his pleas—after all, this was the Vatican. What possible harm could come to His

Holiness here, in his own bedchambers? His thoughts flashed to Father Granger, and his badly beaten body.

Perhaps it is time to revisit the unlocked door policy.

They both stepped tentatively into the room. "Your Holiness!" Father Jenner's whisper was harsh yet received no response. Giasson listened but heard no sounds of sleep in the small room. He reached around Father Jenner and flipped the light switch.

They both gasped.

The bed was empty.

It had been slept in, or at least occupied, for some time, the sheets and covers messed from use. Giasson rushed over and placed his hand on the sheets, feeling for any warmth from residual body heat, but found none. He checked the bathroom and found it empty. A whirlwind search of the rest of the room left him standing in the middle, staring at the shocked Father, who hadn't left the entrance the entire time.

"He's gone!"

Giasson reached for his phone and dialed Ianuzzi's extension.

"Ianuzzi here."

"Broken Dove."

Corpo della Gendarmeria Office
Palazzo del Governatorato, Vatican City

Ianuzzi couldn't believe the two words he had just heard.
Broken Dove. His heart slammed as he flashed back to
recent events and the death of the last pope. "Are you
sure?"

"He's not in his chambers. His bed has been slept in,
but he isn't here *now*!"

"Should I begin—"

"Yes."

"You realize—"

"Yes."

"Okay, you'll have backup in a few minutes."

He hung up the phone and stood, clearing his throat.
"Attention, please!" The room stopped, the entire night
shift turning to face him. "We have a Broken Dove
situation." Gasps filled the room, and at least one person
cried out. Ianuzzi fought to keep control of his emotions
as he stared down at the procedure manual in front of
him, tears welling in his eyes.

*We can't lose a second pope, not this soon, not in this way
again.*

"I need the following things done immediately." He
began reading, pointing to a different member of the staff
as he read each point. "One, lockdown the city. Two,
recall all staff. Three, send a contingent of the guard to
His Holiness' quarters. Four, notify the Polizia
Municipale." He paused, looking to where his finger was
pointing. "Discretely." The man nodded, turning to his
phone. "Five, wake all of His Holiness' personal staff and
determine when he was last seen. Six, review the threat
file. Seven, contact all of His Holiness' visitors for the
past week and interview them to determine if anything
unusual occurred. Eight, review the latest Papal
correspondence for anything unusual. Nine, begin a
systematic search, radiating outward from His Holiness'

last known location. Ten, pray for his safe deliverance from whatever evil may have befallen His Holiness." He turned to who he was pointing at and frowned. "I guess we'll all do that one."

He dropped into his chair, staring at the page he had just read. His hands gripped the arms, his knuckles white, his forehead beaded with sweat. What many didn't realize was that a job at the Vatican wasn't just a job. It was a calling. And he, like everyone in the room, was deeply religious, and to say they loved their pope would be an understatement. That he would lay down his life to save a man he barely knew should never be doubted. It wasn't the man. It was what he represented. The Lord's voice on Earth. A direct conduit to all that was holy, all that was pure.

And it was missing.

He breathed deeply then released his grip, stretching the fingers out for a moment. He surveyed the bustle of activity about him as everyone did their jobs like the professionals they were. Emotions streaked their faces, but they continued to work, despite a part of their core having been cleaved from them.

Francesco Greco, sitting next to Iannuzzi, hung up his phone and spun in his chair. "Sir, all gates are sealed. All entry and exit logs are being brought here. Also, no one has reported anything out of the ordinary, and they are all contacting their earlier shifts to confirm."

"Very good. Review the logs when they come in for anything unusual, and match them against the security footage. I want to know if anyone entered or left without signing the log, and if the names match the faces."

"Yes, sir." Greco turned back to his desk and hammered away at his keyboard.

The officer managing the front desk waved her hand, her pale face suggesting she might be too shaken to make the walk over. "Polizia Municipale have been notified." She looked down at a notepad, apparently not wanting to miss anything. "They are sending a contingent of unmarked cars to help in the search, along with dogs. They also will be reviewing all footage, tickets, and reports from outside the walls to see if anything unusual was reported or can be spotted, and a point man, sorry, woman, Yvonne Peori, will be here any minute."

"Excellent. Tell the front gate to let them in when they arrive, and to notify us so we can coordinate the effort from here."

She grabbed her phone and dialed.

"Sir, look at this."

Iannuzzi glanced up at the young Swiss Guardsman who held out a sheet of paper, his face covered in sweat from the run he had apparently just undertaken.

"What is it?"

"It was found taped to the northern wall."

Iannuzzi flattened the page on his desk and stared at it. "What does it mean?"

"I have no idea. I've never seen that symbol before."

Iannuzzi examined the page, running his hand over what appeared to be ancient parchment, but felt new, not hard and dry as he would expect something truly old to feel. A large red X covered the page from corner to corner, as if applied with a heavy brush. Yet it was the symbol that puzzled him the most. Two straight lines, with a third, heavier line, curved slightly upward, underneath them.

What could it mean? And is it connected to His Holiness?

Via della Conciliazione, Vatican City

Reading flashed his badge for the umpteenth time, making his way through the cordon of security blocking all of the entrances to the holy city. He had asked a few of the officers what was going on, and all had shrugged or waved him on without answering. He had the distinct impression that no one knew. Crowds of the faithful, along with curious onlookers and pissed off tourists, had already gathered by the time he arrived. And so had the media.

This is turning into a circus.

He finally made it to the security station at the main gate and flashed his badge. "Agent Reading, Interpol. Monsieur Giasson is expecting me."

The man scanned a list then picked up a phone, requesting an escort. "Please wait over there for your escort to arrive." He pointed to a cordoned-off area, devoid of people except for two of the Pontifical Swiss Guard in their clown outfits.

If the bobbies had to wear those, we'd never get anyone to join the force.

He acknowledged the guards and they ignored him, standing at attention, their eyes staring straight ahead.

Disciplined.

He always got a kick out of the tourists attempting to annoy the Queen's Guards at their posts as if they were mascots at Disney World.

Don't you nutters know these are highly trained soldiers?

He smiled at the memory of a video that had made the rounds of one tourist nearly soiling her drawers when the soldier had abruptly moved for the changing of the guard.

Reading glanced through the fence and into St. Peter's Square. The sight wiped the smile off his face. There were dozens of officers, Swiss Guard, K-9 units, and priests, sweeping the area, obviously searching for something or someone.

Would they risk this much publicity for Chaney?

He hoped so. If Chaney were indeed missing, he would hope they would spare no effort and risk any negative press to find him.

But that means Chaney is missing.

His thoughts turned to his longtime partner and friend. And the dead Father. He looked up at the heavens and said a silent prayer as a young man in a suit ran across the cobblestone of St. Peter's Square and came to a stop on the other side of the fence.

"Let Agent Reading in, please," he said to the guards manning the gate. One opened the iron gate and Reading stepped through, shaking the man's hand. "I'm Francesco Greco, sir, I don't know if you remember me from when you were last here—"

"Of course I do." He glanced quickly at the balcony then at the surrounding area. There was no evidence of what had happened here just a few short months ago. "What's going on?"

"I think it's best Monsieur Giasson tells you that, sir."

He briskly walked back across the square, and Reading had to jog to keep up with the clearly agitated man. "Is Detective Inspector Chaney okay?"

"I really cannot answer any questions. Not here. Not now." He glanced over his shoulder at the main gate. "Too many cameras, too many tricks."

Reading was curious now. What could possibly have this young man, so full of confidence the last time he had met him, so nervous now, to the point he didn't want to risk someone behind a high-powered camera reading his lips? As they crossed into the main administration building, it hit him like a ton of bricks.

This has nothing to do with Chaney.

He grabbed Greco by the shoulder, spinning him around. "Hey, what's going on?"

"Hugh!"

They both turned as Giasson walked up to them, arms extended. Reading hid his grimace as Giasson leaned in, planting a kiss on both cheeks. It was a habit he had never become accustomed to, and refused to return, instead shaking Giasson's hand on the rebound and slapping his shoulder.

"Good to see you, mon ami." Giasson lowered his voice. "Come with me, and I'll bring you up to date on everything that has happened." He dismissed Greco with a nod and took Reading by the arm, leading him deeper into the complex.

"What the bloody hell is going on? Is Chaney all right?"

Giasson raised his finger, silencing him. "Wait just a minute, mon ami."

It was more than a minute before they reached Giasson's office. He pointed at a seat and closed the door. Reading sat, now ready to explode, the sheer volume of people running around, searching, moving things, sweeping things, too much for this old cop to handle without knowing the purpose.

Giasson dropped in his chair and leaned back, sighing. "Mon ami, you would not believe what is going on."

"Try me."

Giasson smiled, as if he knew exactly how Reading felt. He leaned forward, lowering his voice. "When we could not find your friend last night, we initiated a search, and around half past midnight, I decided to wake His Holiness to make him aware of the situation, and to gain any insight into why DI Chaney was here, as it may provide a clue as to where he went." Giasson paused, staring up at the ceiling, then down at his desk, as if searching for words he himself could believe.

"What is it? What did he say?"

Giasson raised his head and looked directly at Reading. "Nothing."

Reading wasn't expecting that. "What do you mean?"

"He wasn't there."

"You mean—" Reading stopped, unable to say the words.

"His Holiness is missing."

Reading's jaw dropped. "You don't think—"

"I pray not, but with the Father having been murdered just the day before, I can't help but think the worst."

"Any leads? Any clues? Anything?" Reading's mouth was spouting whatever he could think of, his anxiousness removing the brain-mouth filter. He drew a slow breath. "Tell me where you're at in the investigation."

Giasson frowned. "Almost nowhere. We're searching the entire grounds, top to bottom, even in sections long closed off. Basements, attics, sewers, everything. As well, we're reviewing any security footage we have. The Roma Police are doing the same, checking cameras, tickets issued, interviewing their officers to see if they saw anything unusual. So far, nothing."

Reading shook his head. "Unbelievable," he muttered.

"All we know is that his staff confirmed His Holiness went to bed at his regular hour. His bed was slept in, but his room was empty at approximately one a.m. when we entered. No one has reported seeing him leave his room, and we have no cameras in the residential quarters. All we know for certain at this point, is that he didn't leave the quarters through any of the known entrances, and he ordered his customary guard dismissed until the morning."

"Dismissing the guard. Is that unusual?"

"Unheard of."

Reading leaned forward, his interest piqued further. "*Known* entrances?"

"This city is old, built in a different time, a paranoid time. There are secret passageways and hidden doors throughout. We know of many of them, but there could be others we are simply not aware of."

"So, you don't even know if he just wandered off, or if he was taken."

Giasson shook his head. "No, not for certain, however I lean toward the latter."

"Why?"

Giasson lifted a folder off his desk and handed it to Reading. "This was found taped to the outer wall last night."

Reading took the folder and flipped it open. He gasped. Inside was a single sheet of paper with the symbol of the Triarii, crossed out in red.

Somebody knows the Pope is Triarii!

Corpo della Gendarmeria Office
Palazzo del Governatorato, Vatican City

Father Morris appeared pale, the old man approaching the age of his charge, the Pope. He had been the executive assistant for three popes, and Reading was sure he had no desire to fulfill the same job for a fourth. He sensed no fear from the man, no guilt, simply worry. They both looked up as Giasson reentered the office, handing the trembling man a glass of water before closing the door behind him. Reading sat casually in his chair and Giasson took up a similar posture on a couch lining a portion of the back wall, both attempting to keep the man at ease.

"Is there anything out of the ordinary you can tell us about His Holiness' meeting with Detective Inspector Chaney?" asked Giasson

Father Morris lowered the glass from his lips. "The entire meeting was quite out of the ordinary."

"In what way?"

"First, I never arranged it. Usually, if His Holiness wants to meet someone, he asks me to contact them and arrange a meeting. In this case, I had no involvement, and was merely told to expect him the next day, and that when he arrived, to have him sent in immediately." He took another sip. "He also had me clear his morning schedule."

"And that's unusual?" asked Reading. "Clearing the schedule, I mean?"

Father Morris' head bobbed. "Absolutely. His Holiness never canceled a meeting. In fact, I cannot recall any of the popes I've had the honor to serve canceling a meeting unless there was an illness or emergency of some sort. In this case, there was no indication of any such thing."

"Anything else?"

Father Morris glanced away and shifted in his chair. He raised the glass then lowered it without drinking. He looked from one man to the other. "Do you really think His Holiness is in danger?"

"Absolutely."

Father Morris sighed. "Very well. What I'm about to tell you cannot leave this room. Ever. You must swear to God himself that what I am about to tell you will never leave your lips."

Reading and Giasson exchanged glances. Reading wasn't a religious man, and personally believed that God would forgive him for breaking the promise he was about to make if it meant saving His mouthpiece on Earth. "I swear." Giasson echoed this, and Father Morris leaned forward, lowering his voice.

"The first evening of every pope's reign is marked by a special, private event. It is secret, known only to a handful of people, one of which is me. No one, however, knows the nature of the event, as only the new pope is present."

Reading's curiosity was piqued. "What can you tell us?"

"After all of the day's activities are completed, a chest is brought from the Secret Archives and placed in His Holiness' office. It is fitted with a lock that only the Papal ring can open. The new pope is instructed that it is his duty to open this chest, inspect its contents, and then to let us know when he is finished."

"What's inside?" asked Giasson. Reading could tell from the excitement in his voice he had never heard of the chest, or this ritual.

"No one knows. However, I do know this. Of the three pope's that I have seen the chest presented to, not one has gone to his chambers that night. All have remained in their offices through the night, and the next day, were changed men."

"Why are you telling us this? What does it have to do with the meeting?"

"Because, for the first time I am aware, he requested the chest be brought from storage, and placed in his office. And"—the man paused, as if for effect—"immediately after DI Chaney's meeting ended, he requested the chest be returned to storage."

"Could he have shown Chaney what was inside?"

Father Morris shrugged. "I have no idea."

Reading didn't need convincing. "It's too big a coincidence for him not to have." He turned to Giasson. "We need to see what's inside that chest."

Both Father Morris and Giasson gasped.

"It's forbidden!" exclaimed Father Morris.

Reading returned his gaze to the elderly priest. "If no one knows of this chest, then how is it forbidden to look at it? Is it written somewhere?"

Father Morris said nothing.

"I didn't think so." He turned to Giasson. "We need to know what was so important that Chaney and now the Pope have disappeared. The key is in that chest."

"But it's locked. Only the Papal Ring can open it."

"Don't worry, I know someone who's an expert at opening ancient locks."

Acton Residence
Stowe, Vermont

Archaeology Professor James Acton lay on his side, facing the sleeping form of the woman he loved, Professor Laura Palmer. He smiled at the rose-covered pajamas she had insisted on wearing while visiting his parents, her normal nighttime attire usually a little more provocative. It was his dad's birthday this weekend, and it was rare he was there in person, life usually forcing him to resort to a phone call and a mailed gift. But when Laura had found out about it, she had thought it the perfect opportunity to see them again, so had surprised him with two first-class airline tickets from their dig in Egypt to his parents' home in Vermont.

Being rich has its advantages.

Laura's brother had died several years ago, leaving her the many millions he had made selling his Internet company before the bubble had burst. She had remained a professor, even lived in the same apartment as before, and used the money to fund her digs, and indulge herself by flying first class, staying at five-star hotels, and generally enjoying life with no barriers. And since he had become involved with her, she had been spoiling him in little ways. He had protested at first, as he could honestly claim he had no idea she was rich when he first fell in love with her, but she had insisted that it made her happy, and she had so much money, why not spend it on each other? He had acquiesced, and yes, life was better. He still had the same beat-up Jeep in his garage, the same mortgage-saddled modest home that he barely saw, but it was the barriers he hadn't even realized were there, and their removal, that truly made the difference.

Money buys freedom.

They flew whenever they needed, always as comfortable as possible. If one of their digs needed some equipment, it was purchased without a second thought. If there were a student who couldn't afford to come because of family circumstances, they would pay for that student, quietly so the student wouldn't be embarrassed, anonymously if possible. Acton usually said the university had an anonymous benefactor, and to keep it quiet. The joy on their faces was worth every penny. Freedom to do what you wanted, when you wanted. It was a wonderful feeling. Especially when doing it with the woman you loved.

He shuffled closer to her, the double bed making it a short trip. Spooning her, he buried his face in her long, auburn hair, inhaling her scent. He kissed her neck and she moaned softly. He kissed her again, and something stirred below. She slowly awoke and turned to face him, smiling, her eyes still closed. He kissed her lips and she responded, reaching out for him as he kissed his way down her neck. He reached to unbutton her pajamas when she suddenly awoke fully and grabbed his hand.

"James! Not here!" she said in a harsh whisper, her eyes fully open.

"Why not?"

"Your parents! They could hear us."

He continued to unbutton her top. "I'll be quiet."

She swatted his hand away. "Behave."

"But, honey, we have company."

She glanced down at his boxers and burst out laughing. It wasn't the reaction he was used to, but even he chuckled. They were both cut short by a knock on the door. "You two awake in there? Breakfast is in ten minutes."

"Yes, Mom."

He looked at Laura holding her breath, struggling to stifle her laugh. Failing, air burst from her lips causing them to vibrate momentarily. He joined her, hugging her tightly, then whispered in her ear. "I love you."

She pushed him onto his back and straddled him. "Okay, maybe a quickie." She dropped down on top of his chest and whispered. "But *be* quiet!"

He grinned and was about to accomplish something in this bedroom he had never managed in his entire teenage life—score—when his cellphone vibrated on the nightstand.

"Leave it." Her whisper was hoarse, as she too was now aroused, her lips kissing his neck and chest. The phone went to voicemail, then vibrated a moment later indicating a message. He tore open her top, revealing her naked chest, and was about to provide his own form of support when the phone rang again. Laura sat up, clearly as frustrated as him. "You better get it."

He grabbed the phone, the call display showing him a number he didn't recognize. He pressed *Talk*. "Acton."

"Jim, old boy, it's Hugh."

Acton's eyebrows shot up. "Hugh? Do you have any idea what time it is?" He lowered his voice. "And that you just interrupted a dream thirty years in the making?" Laura swatted him, then ground her hips playfully. He threw his head against his pillow, frustrated.

"Sorry, but I need your help, urgently."

Laura's lap antics continued to distract him. "Wh-what is it?" He reached up with one hand to participate.

"Chaney is missing, and so is his *friend* in the Vatican."

Acton's hand stopped in midair. "What?"

Laura grabbed his hand and placed it on her chest. He pulled it away and raised a single finger. She stopped, concern on her face. "What's wrong?" she whispered.

"Listen, I can't really tell you much on this line. It's not secure. But I need you here, now."

"In Rome?"

"Yes, I'm here now, and there's something we need you to help us with that's urgent." Reading's voice lowered. "Listen, one person is already dead, two more are missing, and I think you can help. How soon can you get here?"

"I'll have to check the flight schedule, but Laura and I will be there as soon as we can."

"Okay, let me know the details, and I'll have you met."

"Okay, see you soon."

Acton ended the call and looked at Laura as she rolled back to the other side of the bed.

"What's going on?"

"That was Hugh. Somebody's dead at the Vatican, and now Chaney and the Pope are missing."

"What!" Laura's hand flew to her mouth. "Missing?"

He nodded. "We need to get to Rome right away."

Laura flipped her legs out of the bed and grabbed her phone. "I'll call our travel agent."

"I'll go let Mom and Dad know." He hopped out of bed and headed for the door when Laura cleared her throat. "What?"

She pointed at his waist. He looked down and found Jimmy, Jr. still peeking out. He grinned. "Better put some pants on."

Outside Tyrus, Judea
AD 342

Berenice bit her knuckle, stifling any cries of terror she might accidentally let loose. She gripped the Word tightly against her chest as only feet away footsteps pounded, shaking the ground under which she now hid. The kindly farmer, so helpful earlier, stood above, terrified. From her vantage point in a dugout root cellar, she could see his hands clenching and unclenching through a small gap in the heavy rugs covering her hiding place. His steps were tiny as he shuffled from one spot to another while avoiding being tossed aside by the soldiers like the furniture now scattered about the floor, revealing how insignificant he now felt in his own home.

"We know they passed here. Your denial of having seen them makes you guilty. You could not have missed them if you were tending your fields as you claim."

The soldier was right. There was no way the poor farmer could have missed them. They were ten on horseback with a carriage, and all women, most in armor. A sight that would stop even the most pious of men. And it had stopped him. The moment they rounded the bend, he had looked up. They had drawn to a halt, asked him about the road ahead, and if he had seen any soldiers. He had told them of the narrow pass, and that he had seen no soldiers for days. He had offered them fresh milk from his goat, a goat he seemed particularly proud of, a goat that seemed his only possession of value.

"Perhaps I know a way of loosening your tongue!" The soldier snapped his fingers. "Get me the goat."

"Yes, Decanus!" Another soldier left the small house, and a moment later, the poor creature bleated in terror as she was tugged against her will into her master's home.

Berenice watched in horror as the soldier grabbed the creature by the tuft of fur atop her head and yanked back.

The short sword drawing from its sheath caused her to start, and the poor farmer to cry out.

"Please don't, not my goat, please! She's all I have!"

The soldier pressed the blade to the beast's neck. "Where are they?"

The farmer dropped his head onto his chest. "They were here."

"When?"

"This morning."

"Where did they go?"

"Into the pass."

"And you haven't seen them since?"

The farmer hesitated, looking directly where she was hiding.

The goat cried out as the soldier pulled his sword slightly, slicing the exposed neck a fraction. The creature bleated in fear more than anything else. The farmer fell to his knees, his hands clasped, shaking them in a desperate plea to reach the heart of the soldier.

"Please, please don't hurt her!" He stole another glance at Berenice, huddled in her hiding place among the root vegetables that were its regular occupants.

"It is you, by your silence, by your lies, that hurt this foul creature." He yanked her head back again. "Now, I will ask you once again. Have you seen them since?"

The farmer collapsed, prostrate on the floor, sobbing. "Oh, God, forgive me for what I'm about to do," he whispered through the floor, into her tiny hiding space. Berenice looked at him and nodded, giving him a smile of understanding, then made the sign of the cross.

"I forgive you," she whispered, gripping the Word tightly.

He pointed at the tiny root cellar. "Under there."

She closed her eyes and prayed as overhead the carpets pulled aside.

"Get out."

78

She opened her eyes, blinking at the interrogator staring down at her, hands on his hips. She slowly rose, then, with the help of a shaking and apologetic farmer, climbed from her hiding place. She stood before the soldier, gripping the Word to her breast, and stared at him, fear filling her heart, but her outward countenance stolid. She would not let this man see her cower.

"Father, come in here."

An old man entered the abode, his priestly robes simple, humble, unlike many in the Church who adorned themselves in gold and lace. He held his hands out to Berenice, indicating she should give him the book. There was no point in resisting.

She handed it to him.

He took it, gently, respectfully, reverently, and opened the hard cover protecting the precious words inside.

"Well, is that it?" asked the impatient soldier.

The old man trembled. "Yes, yes it is."

"Very well."

The goat bleated a horrible scream as the soldier sliced her throat through, blood spilling on the floor. The farmer cried out and fell to his knees, grabbing the poor creature as she gasped for air. Berenice stared in horror then anger at the soldier. "You didn't need to do that! I gave you the book!"

The soldier regarded her, then without emotion, without a muscle on his face moving, jabbed his sword forward, burying it in her belly, then, pulling it out, wiped both sides on the fallen farmer's shoulders as she slumped to the ground. "Let's go, I want to make it back to camp before nightfall."

The priest took a knee in front of Berenice. "We will leave when *I* say."

"Now, Father."

"Not until I have read this poor girl her Last Rites."

A growl of frustration erupted from the soldier before he stepped outside. The priest placed a hand on her

79

shoulder. "Would you like absolution for your sins, my daughter?"

She shook her head. "Listen to me. Please, please don't destroy the book. It is the last copy."

"I'm sorry, child, but I must."

She reached a bloody hand up and squeezed his. "Then promise me one thing. Read it before you destroy it. And if you can still destroy something so beautiful afterward, then do so. But please, do not simply toss it on a fire without looking at it. You must promise me." She coughed, and the taste of blood filled her mouth. She grew weaker as her time grew short. "Promise me."

The old man sighed. "I promise you, I shall read it first."

"And should you not destroy it?"

"I will have it placed in the Church's archives in Rome."

Berenice smiled. "Thank you, Father, I am ready."

The old man proceeded with the final confession and the Last Rites, and she soon lay at peace, a smile of contentment on her face as she was certain she had succeeded in having the book ultimately preserved.

No person could read those words then destroy them, no matter how much hate filled their hearts.

The priest rose. "Is there anything I can do for you before I leave, my child?"

"Parchment. Ink."

He left for a moment then returned with several long scrolls and a supply of ink and quill pens. She took them and smiled. "Thank you."

He patted her shoulder then left, the book gripped in one hand.

She stared up to the heavens and prayed for strength, then began to write a note to her sisters about where the Word might be, then everything she could remember written down in those most blessed of pages.

And as she wrote, she weakened, her eyes drooping, her hand continually slipping, but she pushed on for as long as she could, until finally, her hand fell to her side and she gasped her last few breaths. The farmer, who had watched in silence, sitting on the floor, his dead goat's head resting in his lap, crawled over to her. Her head lolled to the side, her eyes barely focused on him. In a final surge of effort, she stared him in the eyes. "Should any of my sisters return, give them what I have written."

Then she heard the wings of angels and sensed the gentle caress of the Blessed Virgin on her cheek as she rose toward the light.

Acton Residence
Stowe, Vermont
Present Day

"So why *do* you call him James? I think you're the only one who does unless I'm scolding him."

"Which almost never happens," interjected Acton as he held his plate up for the pancakes his mother, Dorothy, was rationing out.

"Oooh you, when you were a teenager, it was nothing but!" She made her point with the air-jab of a lifter.

"Now that's true. It was always, 'James Edward Acton, how many times do I have to tell you to clean your room,' or 'James Edward Acton, what's the point of having an alarm clock if you never actually turn it on,'" said Acton, impersonating his mother's voice.

Acton's father, Ellsworth, laughed. "That's your mother, all right."

She served the last of the pancakes. "That kid was constantly driving me crazy!"

Ellsworth grabbed her by the waist. "And you'd have those days back in a heartbeat if you could."

She flushed, tears filling her eyes slightly. "You know I would." Her voice cracked. "Oh, now look what you've done." She hip-checked him, breaking his hold, and took her seat. She dropped her head for a moment in silent prayer, a ritual Acton knew well, their family never saying 'Grace.'

"So, Laura, why *do* you call him James?" she repeated.

Laura cut into her pancakes and stabbed the portion with her fork. She looked at Acton. "The night we met, he actually asked me to call him Jim, but I had been following his work for years, and in my mind, I had always thought of him as James. I guess I never noticed, he didn't say anything, and when we first kissed, he was James, and I never wanted that memory to be spoiled by later changing what I called him." She leaned forward and placed her hand on his cheek. "Besides, I don't think he minds."

He turned his head and kissed her palm. "Not at all."

His parents exchanged glances, his mother all smiles. "Look, dear, our boy's in love."

"Awww, ma!" Acton cried in mock embarrassment, giving Laura a quick wink. She removed her hand but he grabbed it and held it for a moment. "And yes, I'm in love." Her eyes glistened as he kissed her fingers.

"I love you too," she whispered. She put down her pancake-filled fork and dabbed her eyes with her napkin. Across the table, the matriarch of the family did as well.

"Now look what you've done."

Acton glanced at his father, who nodded toward his mother.

"Sorry, ladies. I get my romantic side from my father."

That elicited a grunt from the senior Acton. "These pancakes are gettin' cold."

They all ate in silence for a few moments, Dorothy breaking it. "So, why is it you need to go to Italy?"

"Hugh needs our help, something with a case he's working on." Acton sighed and put his fork down. "Listen, I don't want you to worry, but just in case something happens"—his mother's hand flew to her mouth with a gasp—"no, Mom, not that kind of something, I mean if you see something on the news, or see us on the news—" He stopped. "Full truth?"

"Always," said his father.

"Fine. You heard about the murder at the Vatican?"

They both nodded.

"Well, Hugh's former partner, Detective Inspector Chaney—"

"The one who was in that Roman thing?"

"Triarii, dear," whispered his mother.

"Yes, him. He was at the Vatican, and is now missing."

83

"Oh, how terrible. Do they think he's—" She stopped, apparently not wanting to say it.

"We don't know. But that's not all." Acton looked at Laura, who nodded. "The Pope's missing as well."

Dorothy gasped and made the sign of the cross despite not being Catholic.

"I don't remember seeing that on the news."

Acton turned to his dad. "I don't think it's public yet."

"They're not going to be able to keep a lid on something like that for long."

"Agreed. That's why we need to get there as quickly as possible."

Laura glanced up from her cellphone. "And speaking of, just heard from Mary—"

"Her travel agent," explained Acton.

"—and she's chartered us a private jet. We leave in two hours."

"Private jet!" His dad looked at him. "Must be nice."

Acton smiled and patted Laura's leg. "She treats me well."

"Nothing you wouldn't do for me if our positions were reversed, I'm sure," she replied.

"You know it, babe." He grabbed his utensils. "Now, let's power this down. We don't have much time, and I don't want to miss a chance at Ma's pancakes." He took a bite, as did Laura and his dad. His mother simply sat there, staring at him. "What?"

"How do you keep getting mixed up in these things?"

He shrugged. "Lucky I guess?"

"Lucky!"

He took another bite and swallowed. "Sure. In London I met Laura, best thing to ever happen to me."

His mother smiled at Laura. "I'll give you that one, but you both almost got killed."

"*Almost* being the key word."

"Don't you dare make me attend your funeral, young man."

84

Acton gave her a look. "Young man? I haven't been called that in years."

"I'm still your mother. I brought you into this world—"

"—and you can take me out, I know. So, if I get myself killed, you're gonna kill me again?"

She shook her fork at him. "Just watch me."

He laughed and reached over, squeezing his mom's arm. "Don't worry, Mom, I'll be careful. Besides, it's the Vatican. What's the worst that can happen?"

"Oh, I don't know. What happened the last time you were there?"

He didn't reply to the rhetorical question, the memories of that day flooding back. He put his fork down, no longer hungry.

How do I get myself into these things?

Ciampino Airport Approach
Rome, Italy

Acton stood and stretched. Hard. He didn't mind flying, having flown in every manner of airplane with every standard of safety from Western to none, though flying in a private Gulfstream was the most comfortable by far. He slipped his shoes on, his habit of taking them off at the beginning of the flight still applicable even when flying with more leg and arm room than most would know what to do with. Laura mirrored the stretches, both of them having been unsuccessful at sleeping until the final hour of the flight.

Isn't that the way it always is?

This time, however, he had a private stewardess—flight attendant—to wake him ten minutes before landing so he could enjoy the view. He never tired of looking down over an area from the air, especially a city, where you could make out the details of not only daily life, but the layout of the town. To see what the urban planners were thinking hundreds, even thousands of years ago was fascinating. London was a mess of streets, New York was a near-perfect grid of blocks. But Rome. Rome was a mix of the ancient with the modern.

He pointed at the Coliseum. "Look."

Laura peered out the window. "Perhaps we'll have some time to tour the city. I've been here before, of course, but never with another archaeologist. I wonder if we can pull some strings and get access to some of the non-tourist parts."

"That'd be cool." He sat and tightened his lap belt. "I have a funny feeling we're going to have our hands full, though." He pulled his cellphone off his belt. "I've got a signal but there are no new messages."

"So, they're still missing."

"Appears that way."

She lowered her voice and leaned in. "They're both Triarii. Do you think that might have something to do with it?"

"The thought had crossed my mind. But then why was the Father murdered?"

"He might have been Triarii too for all we know."

Acton pursed his lips. "Hadn't thought of that." He leaned back. "So, someone knows who and what they are, decides they don't like them hanging around, running their church, so kills them?"

Her hand darted to her mouth. "Oh God, I hope not."

"Well, if they were murdered, then I would think we'd know by now. After all, they had no problem having the Father's body discovered, so why not Chaney and the Pope?" He shook his head. "I hope Hugh can tell us more when we get there."

They both sat back in their chairs as the plane touched down. Minutes later, they had taxied to the charter terminal and were descending the steps, a limousine with Vatican flags waiting at the bottom. The driver tipped her hat and opened the door. "Mr. Acton, Miss Palmer. I trust you had a good flight?"

"Yes, thank you," replied Laura as she climbed into the limo, Acton following. The door closed behind them and interior accent lighting kicked in, revealing they weren't alone.

Laura gasped.

Across from them, facing the rear, sat a woman Acton didn't recognize, pointing a gun at both of them.

"Welcome to Rome, professors."

Acton instinctively slid closer to Laura, putting his shoulder over hers, partially blocking her body from the woman. "Who the hell are you?"

"Tsk. Such language. Do you not realize where you are? Why you are here?"

"Don't act so pious with me. You're the one with the gun."

She flicked the weapon, as if dismissing it. "Purely to illustrate a point."

"And that point is?"

She leaned forward. "That *I* am in control. Not you."

The driver's door opened then slammed shut. The car moved and Laura gripped his arm. "Where are you taking us?" she asked.

"To the Vatican of course."

What the hell is going on here?

"Then why the gun?"

"Because I am not *with* the Vatican."

Laura's hand squeezed tighter. "Then who are you *with*?"

"The Order of the Blessed Virgin."

Acton exchanged a quick glance with Laura, who shook her head slightly.

"What the he—" He stopped himself, and sneered slightly. "What is that?"

"We worship the Blessed Mary."

Acton's eyes narrowed. "Then what do you want with us?"

"We want you to retrieve something that was stolen from us long ago."

"What?"

"The Gospel of Mary."

"There is no Gospel of Mary."

The smile grew. "So you've been told."

"What does that mean?" asked Laura. "There are four Gospels. Matthew, Mark, Luke, and John."

"No, there are several more, however they didn't fit in with the likings of the Nicaea Council."

Acton knew what she was talking about. Roman Emperor Constantine had convened the First Council of Nicaea in Bithynia in AD 325. The month-long meeting defined the nature of Jesus, leading to the Nicene Creed, and ultimately the Bible as it is known today, with many texts describing the life and teachings of Jesus abandoned for various reasons, mostly due to them conflicting with the newly agreed-upon truth. After the definition and dissemination of the Bible, all other texts were destroyed as blasphemous. Over the coming thousand years, the Church slowly tightened its iron grip over Europe, and none questioned the contents of the Holy Book, most not capable of reading it, and none outside of the Church allowed to possess a copy, aside from royalty.

Until Luther and others translated it, and printed it.

Once the masses understood the words, the Church's grip loosened. When people realized they had been lied to, that the words had been distorted and the Catholic Church had become nothing but a business designed to fleece the population of their money in exchange for passage into Heaven for them or their loved ones, the separation of Church and State had begun. It took hundreds of years, but it was done. And both the State, and the Church, were better for it.

Now we need a separation of State and Business.

"So, you're saying the Gospel of Mary, Mary the mother of Jesus, exists."

"It does."

"Where?"

"In the very place you will be going tonight."

"I don't understand."

"After Nicaea, all copies of the Gospel of Mary were destroyed but one. The founders of our order had the original, written some say by the hand of Mary herself, and her son, the only Gospel to be written while our Lord was alive, and by someone who knew him perhaps better than anyone could."

"So—"

"So, it is the only honest Gospel. The only true Gospel."

"How do you know? Have you read it?"

Her chin dropped into her chest. "No. None have." She raised her head. "Our order was almost wiped out in a clash with the Church's troops. The few copies we had managed to transcribe were lost in that battle, but the original saved. But only two weeks later, we were betrayed by a farmer who had taken our leader in. All in exchange for a goat."

"A goat?" exclaimed Laura. Acton looked at her, and had the distinct impression she had forgotten their situation.

Their captor shook her head, as if still in disbelief over an event almost two thousand years ago. "Yes. A goat." She sighed. "Roman soldiers from the local garrison were in pursuit of the few remaining members of our order when they came upon this humble man's farm and threatened his goat. He pleaded with them, it being his only goat, then betrayed our Sister Berenice who he had agreed to hide. They killed her, and the goat, and took the original text to Rome, where it has never been seen since."

"Have you asked?"

"Of course. With the opening of the Secret Archives, we immediately petitioned, but the Church repeatedly denied its existence."

"So, you don't even know if it really exists."

The woman glared at him. "It exists. Of that, have no doubt."

He shrugged. "I guess we'll have to take your word for it." He pointed at the gun. "Now what does that have to do with us?"

"Everything, if you want to see your friends again."

He leaned forward. "You have them?"

"Yes."

"Why?" asked Laura. "Is this because they're Triarii?"

"Try what?"

He exchanged a quick glance with Laura. "If it's not because they're Triarii, then what did they ever do to deserve kidnapping?" he asked slowly.

"As the head of the Church, His Holiness is participating in and perpetuating the fraud that is the Roman Catholic Church."

"And Chaney?"

"A pawn, caught in the middle. Of no value to us, but of value to his friends, who will be motivated to do our bidding to save his life."

Acton scowled. "And what do you want from us?"

"To retrieve the book, of course."

"And just how are we supposed to do that?"

"Well, you're being brought in, aren't you? Two archaeologists? Did you think you were being brought in because of your legendary policing skills?" The woman laughed, flicking the weapon. "The arrogance of you Americans—"

"She's British."

"Even worse!" She leaned forward. "Your country rules the world, so you think you all as individuals are so superior to the rest of us. But in reality, you are all pawns in the grandest corporate takeover in history."

"What the hell are you talking about?"

"America is owned."

"Are you one of those Occupy nutters?" asked Laura.

The woman chuckled. "No, but the original protestors were right, which is why they were quickly taken over by the unions and others so their message could be distorted."

Acton sighed. "Okay, I'll bite. How were the original protestors right?"

"America. Is. Owned." With each word she stabbed the air with her weapon before leaning back. "Think about it. The average American doesn't donate to a political party or candidate. They can't afford to. Those that do, contribute a little bit, maybe a few hundred, even a few thousand dollars. That can't run a campaign. It costs a billion dollars to run for president today. That doesn't count all the Senate and House seats. Or governors, state senators, judges, sheriffs, district attorneys, etcetera, etcetera. Every few years, your entire country is bought, over and over, by big business. Only they can afford to donate the millions, even tens of millions, needed to win. And now with your Super PACs." She tossed her head back and laughed. "Even your own Supreme Court is owned! What kind of moron can seriously think that a corporation has the same rights as a human being? Until Texas puts a corporation to death, I think we can safely say they aren't human."

"So, there's a huge amount of money involved. It's always been that way. It's that way in every country."

"Well, that's where you're wrong. Many countries limit people's donations, and in many cases, no companies or unions can contribute, only citizens." She scratched her head with the barrel of her gun. "Think about this. If you donate a thousand dollars to your Senator's campaign, and she"—she pointed at Laura—"a part of the uber-rich elite, donates ten million, whose phone call do you think he's going to take? I think we all know the answer to that." She jabbed the air with her gun, emphasizing each point. "And, when she says she wants him to vote a certain way on an upcoming bill, she merely threatens to not donate to his campaign at reelection time. And since your election cycles are so short, your politicians are in constant campaign mode. They can't risk losing the big donors, so they do their bidding." She sat back and threw her hands in the air. "So, your government is owned. From the top elected official, right down to the bottom. And it's only getting worse."

The woman made some good points. But he wasn't here to listen to conspiracy theories or debate campaign finance reform. Of course big money should be taken out of it. Any sane person understood that. Though just try getting that kind of reform through Congress. It would never happen.

Because they're owned.

He shook his head. He had to focus on the problem at hand. "Thanks for the civics lesson. Now, once again I ask, how are we supposed to get the book?"

"As I said, you are archaeologists, not police detectives. There is only one reason you are being brought in, and that is to examine something of archaeological interest. You must use this opportunity to find the gospel and return it to us."

"And what will you do with it then?"

"Release it for the world to see. To see what has been hidden from them for thousands of years." She leaned forward, scratching her ankle with the barrel of the gun. "And destroy the foundation of the Roman Catholic Church."

"How could a fifth gospel, regardless of who wrote it, destroy the Church?" asked Laura.

The woman smiled. "You don't know what's in it."

Acton grunted. "Neither do you, apparently."

A nod. "True, we don't know the exact words, but we know the general content, the spirit. Immediately after the gospel was seized, our dying leader wrote down everything she could remember, to preserve some of what had been lost."

There was a knock on the window separating them from the driver.

"We're almost there." She fished a cellphone from her pocket and handed it to Acton. "Speed Dial One when you've found it. And keep that with you at all times in case we need to reach you." She leaned forward, the gun dancing in her hand, bouncing between pointing at Acton then Laura. "If you want to see your friend and His Holiness again, do as you're told, find the book, and return it. It's as simple as that. If not, they die."

The car came to a stop and the driver's door opened. A moment later their door opened, revealing streetlights mixed with police cherries flashing outside. They climbed out and the driver had the gall to tip her hat at them smartly, as if nothing were wrong.

"We will be in touch, Professors," said the woman who remained hidden from sight inside. The driver closed the door, returned to her post, and their captors slowly drove away.

The car out of sight, Laura threw her arms around Acton and squeezed tight. "Thank God that's over."

"Let's get inside." He eyed all the police and camera crews who were now turning their attention to the two strangers who had just arrived in a limousine displaying Vatican markings.

"Professor Acton, can we have a word with you?" A young female reporter raced toward them, arm outstretched, microphone in hand, her camera crew struggling to keep up. Acton grabbed Laura by the arm, steering them away, but it was too late. Just the mention of his name sent the gathered press into a frenzy, his name and Laura's, perhaps pushed out of the press since the events in London, still apparently recognizable to the media. Within seconds, they were surrounded, dozens of microphones within inches of their mouths, bright lights in their faces, harsh camera flashes blinding them. They both raised their arms, shielding themselves, and in the jostling and confusion, he lost his bearings.

He picked a direction.

With one arm around Laura, the other stretched in front of him, elbow locked, he used it as a human battering ram and pushed into the crowd. With their ordeal less than two years ago, he had learned to despise the paparazzi. And that's what most of these people were. Even the serious press were paparazzi. The news was no longer the news. The news was opinion. He blamed CNN for that. When they launched the first 24-hour news station, they quickly realized they couldn't fill it with 24 hours of interesting news—there just wasn't enough happening in the world. So, they filled the gaps with opinion. Then they disguised the opinion as news, and now, thirty years later, you had a politicized news organization, pretending to be neutral. Then along came Fox. At least they didn't hide the bias. And again, opinion was disguised as news. To compete, all news organizations forgot their purpose. "Just the facts" was a phrase of the past. Who, what, when, where, why, and how were still practices, though the latter two had morphed into opinion. As an archaeologist and historian, he had read enough old newspapers to know what real news was. Read an old paper, and it was dry. It reported the facts. They had editorials, clearly labeled as such, but they occupied a small part of the paper. Now, even in fact-based articles, reporters interjected their personal opinions and beliefs at every opportunity, with speculation allowed in the articles rather than the editorials, and because of it, the notion of a free press was lost.

His fist impacted the chest of a cameraman. He grunted and stumbled back, cursing at Acton in Italian.

Curse in Latin, and I'd understand you.

He kept pressing forward, increasing his pace, those in front clearing out of their way. He caught a glimpse of the front gate to his left. He rapidly switched directions and continued mowing through the reporters until he reached the cordon of police surrounding the entrance to St. Peter's Square. He was about to tell the officer in front of him who they were when he saw somebody waving.

"Jim! Laura!"

Laura lifted her head. "Is that Hugh?"

Acton raised his arm and waved. "Can you get us through?"

Hugh Reading passed through the gates with a bald man he recognized from their previous visit, and both jogged over to their position. The bald one tapped the two officers in front of him and showed them his credentials. "They're with me."

The officers stepped aside and let Acton and Laura pass.

"Let's get away from these nutters," said Reading as they all followed the bald man through the gates and across the cobblestone of St. Peter's Square. The din outside the gates slowly faded, and Acton began to pay attention to his surroundings. There was a heavy police presence, outside and within. Sniffer dogs were leading their masters, examining bushes, trees, statues, walls. All were searched. He glanced up at the balcony, famous for its pontifical waves.

And shuddered at the memory.

"Have you told the public yet?"

The bald man gave him a look and Reading spun around, holding his finger to his lips. "Loose lips sink ships."

Acton kept his mouth shut until they were indoors. Reading turned to face them, as did the bald man. Reading gestured toward their escort. "I'm sure you remember Inspector General Mario Giasson, head of Vatican Security?"

"Of course I do." Acton reached out and shook the man's hand, as did Laura. "Good to see you again."

The man bowed slightly. "I just wish it could be under more pleasant circumstances." He extended an arm, pointing deeper into the complex. "Shall we? Time is of the essence."

"Indeed," agreed Reading, and the foursome quickly made their way to Giasson's office, Acton chomping at the bit to tell them about their ride from the airport. Once inside the office, they all took seats. Reading was about to speak when Acton cut him off.

"Did you send a car to meet us at the airport?"

"But of course! Why it would not have come through the side gate we kept clear for you, I don't know. Perhaps he was redirected by the police." Giasson eyed him. "Wait. Why are you asking me this?"

Reading leaned forward. "Yes, why?"

"Because the person who picked us up, in a stretch limo, replete with driver and Vatican flags, had a gun pointed at us the entire ride."

"Mon Dieu!" Giasson grabbed his phone and pressed a button. "Get in here!"

Through the window, one of the security staff rose and strode quickly to the door. He opened it and poked his head inside. "Yes, sir?"

"Find out what happened to the car we sent to pick up our guests. Apparently, they were picked up by someone else."

The man closed the door, rushing back to his desk. Giasson turned to Acton. "With the level of attention focused on us right now, I would never dream of sending you a limousine—it would draw far too much attention. We did send a diplomatic vehicle, however something lower key, as I think you Americans say."

"Only one Yank in the room." Reading winked at Laura. She was still too high-strung from their ordeal to respond. He leaned over and gave her knee a pat then looked at Acton. "Why don't you tell us about your ride."

"She said she was from the Order of the Blessed Virgin." This elicited a chuckle from Giasson. Acton eyed him. "What's so funny?"

Giasson waved at the air, as if dismissing his laugh. "I'm sorry, but the Order of the Blessed Virgin are just a bunch of harmless quacks who think we have hidden a book, penned by the Virgin Mary herself, stolen from them over a thousand years ago."

Acton nodded. "That's basically what she said as well."

"Why did they kidnap you two?" asked Reading.

"They want us to find this book, and return it to them."

Giasson still had a smile. "In exchange for?"

"Returning Chaney and the Pope."

All smiles were wiped from the room, Giasson's elbows hitting the desk hard as he lunged forward in his chair. "They have His Holiness!"

"They have Chaney!" exclaimed Reading.

"Yes, and they will kill them if we don't deliver what they want," said Acton.

Giasson grabbed his phone again, hitting an extension. "Get me everything we've got on the Order of the Blessed Virgin." He listened for a moment. "Yes, I'm serious." He slammed the phone into the cradle, tossing a glare out the window at a woman who had just glanced over her shoulder as she put her phone down. Her head spun back to her computer screen.

The man looking into the missing car and driver dashed the ten feet from his desk to Giasson's office. He threw open the door, not bothering to knock. "The Polizia just found the car at the airport in the charter terminal parking lot."

"Parking lot? Why would he—" Giasson stopped. "The driver?"

"In the trunk. Shot in the head."

Giasson made the sign of the cross, sinking back in his chair. "Get down there, see what you can find out."

"Yes, sir." The man left, closing the door.

"Perhaps not 'harmless quacks' after all." Reading's voice was subdued at the loss of another life.

Laura squeezed Acton's hand. He returned the acknowledgment, his heart beating a little harder with the fact their brief captor was indeed a killer. "So, why don't we just get this book, do the exchange, and get this thing over with?"

"Because, Professor, as I said earlier, the book does not exist."

"Then why are we here?" Acton's frustration level was rising. "If we're not here to find this book, then why did we fly all the way to Rome?"

Laura patted him on the hand. "James, no one knew about the book until tonight." She turned to Reading. "I'm certain you brought us here for a very good reason."

"Yes. We need you to break into a chest."

Acton's eyebrows shot up. "Break into a chest? Can't you?"

Giasson shook his head. "No, it is very precious, very ancient, and very secret. We need an expert we can trust to open it without damaging it, examine its contents to see how it might be connected to our current situation, then to reseal it, without revealing anything about its contents unless absolutely necessary."

"Naturally, I thought of you," said Reading.

The prospect of inspecting a Vatican secret wiped away Acton's frustration of moments ago. He leaned forward and Laura's grip tightened slightly on his arm as she shifted position in excitement. "What can you tell us about this chest?" she asked.

Giasson rose and closed the blinds, then pulled his chair around his desk so they formed a tight square. He lowered his voice to barely a whisper. "We know little. In fact, I knew nothing of this until last night. Apparently, on the first eve of a new pope's reign, a chest is brought to him. He is instructed to open it, read what is inside, then reseal it. It is then placed back in the Secret Archives." He leaned in even closer, the rest joining him. "Our man tells us that the last three popes he's delivered this chest to, have all remained awake through the night examining it, and are changed men the next day."

"What's inside?" asked Acton, his heart thumping in excitement.

Giasson tossed his hands out, palms open. "No idea. It's for a pope's eyes only." He waved his hands around them. "No one here would dare open this chest, but you"—he pointed a finger at Acton—"I trust. I trust you to keep the secret of the chest, no matter what happens."

Acton glanced at Laura then back at Giasson. "You mean, you trust *us*."

Giasson's eyes darted to Laura, then to Reading, who nodded. Giasson's eyes returned to Acton, dropping his head slightly. "Of course."

"Then what are we waiting for?" Acton leaped to his feet. "Let's get to work." He glanced around for his suitcase that contained his tool kit and his shoulders slumped. He turned to Laura. "Our luggage."

Her hand quickly touched her forehead then came to rest on her chin. She turned to Giasson. "Our luggage must still be at the terminal."

Acton cursed. "You're right, we got in the car and immediately left." He smacked his forehead then ran his fingers through his hair, pulling it slightly in punishment. "I can't believe I didn't pick up on that."

"Might have been the gun pointed at your head," offered Reading.

Giasson picked up his phone and selected an extension. "Contact the airport and have the professors' luggage delivered here." He hung up then rose. "Let's get this over with before something else goes wrong."

Papal Office Antechamber
Apostolic Palace, The Vatican

As they entered the antechamber of the Papal Office, a man in priestly garb rose from behind a desk. "All is prepared as requested."

Giasson nodded. "Father Morris, these are Professors Acton and Palmer. They will be examining—"

"They?" interrupted Morris, his eyebrows raised, eyes wide. "I thought there would be only one?"

"*We* work together." Acton lowered his voice. "We understand what is being asked of us. The trust you are putting in us."

The man didn't appear pleased, though opened the inner doors to the empty office. He led them in, then, as if scared to even look at it, pointed a shaking finger toward a chest sitting upon a table at the far end of the room. "There it is. When you are finished, please lock it, then let me know." He rushed from the room, closing the doors behind him."

Giasson didn't look at all, purposely placing his back to the chest. "I'll be in my office. Come see me when you're finished." He opened the door and glanced at Reading. "Coming?"

"In a few minutes. I just want to bring them up to speed on a few additional details."

"Very well." Giasson closed the door behind him and Reading spun around, facing the two professors.

"There's little time, so just listen. This has everything to do with the Triarii."

"How?" asked Acton.

Reading gave him a look, as if reminding him of what he had just said.

Just listen.

"They found a paper pasted to the outer wall after the Pope was taken. It was the Triarii symbol, with a red X through it."

"Does Giasson know?"

"He knows of the poster, but not what it represents." Reading took a quick glance at the door. "We're the only ones who know the Pope and Chaney are Triarii."

"Somebody else knows," said Laura.

"Apparently." Reading placed a hand on her shoulder, then Acton's. "Be careful. There's more going on here than just a book. These people are anti-Triarii, and have now killed at least two people, one within these very walls."

Acton's mind raced. There was something he should be remembering. He turned to Laura, and realized she too was thinking the same thing. She smiled, her jaw dropping just as he remembered as well.

"It's not them!" she exclaimed.

"It can't be!" agreed Acton.

"What the devil are you two going on about?" asked Reading.

"The woman in the limo. She had no clue who the Triarii were!"

"What?"

"When I mentioned the Triarii, she didn't know who they were. Never heard of them. And if they've never heard of them—"

"Then how would they know their symbol," completed Reading.

Acton walked over to where the chest had been placed and sat. "Are we on a wild goose chase?"

Laura joined him. "If the Order has Chaney and the Pope, then it suggests the anti-Triarii poster is a coincidence, and that, I find incredibly hard to believe."

"There's no way this is a coincidence," said Reading. "One dead, two kidnapped, including the Holiest man on Earth. That takes massive bollocks and a lot of planning. And how would they have known Chaney would be here? In fact, why take him at all?" He plunked down on one of the leather couches. "I get the distinct impression that this was not planned to take place on a certain date, but when a certain event happened. Which means they had people on the inside, ready to take action whenever necessary."

"If that's the case, then we don't know who we can trust."

"Do you trust Giasson?" asked Acton, already sure of the answer.

"Absolutely." Reading lowered his voice. "I ran a background check on him, just to be sure, and he's clean as a whistle."

"He could still have been recruited while here."

"Possible. But I've always been able to read people, and I sense nothing off about him." He grinned. "After all, I didn't arrest you two, now did I?"

"Hey, I distinctly remember being nicked and brought down to the Yard." Laura's voice was playfully indignant.

Reading laughed and dismissed her comment with a wave. "You were brought in for questioning, not nicked."

She shrugged. "Just sayin', it felt like it."

"Okay, we have to trust someone, and Giasson seems to be the man. If we assume the Order is not involved in the kidnapping, then perhaps they are just taking advantage of the situation."

Reading's head bobbed. "Perhaps. But they would need to know that the situation was occurring."

"They would have to have known we were called in, when we were arriving, when and what car was being sent to pick us up—" Acton stopped. "They have someone on the inside."

Laura agreed. "Perhaps someone in Security? They would have access to all that information."

Reading stood. "I'll talk to Mario and see what we can come up with." He pointed at the chest. "You two figure out what the hell"—he stopped and glanced up—"what the heck, that thing has to do with all this."

Acton grunted. "I'll need my luggage. It has my tools, otherwise you might as well just give me a crowbar."

"I'll have them sent over—"

There was a knock at the door.

Reading opened it and stepped back. "That was quick."

A young priest, accompanied by Father Morris, pushed a luggage cart into the room. "Your charter had already sent your luggage ahead when you left without it," explained Morris.

Acton rose and retrieved his Desert Storm canvas bag. He opened it and reached deep inside, his fingers grasping for the soft leather case containing his tools. Near the bottom, he found it and wrapped his fingers around the bundle, pulling it through the clothes. He held it up in triumph. "This is all I need." He looked at Laura. "You need anything, hon?"

Reading stared at the half-dozen suitcases that were a little more upscale than Acton's worn bag. "It looks like you brought everything you own."

Laura stood and walked toward them, hands on her hips. "I was packed for a one week visit with James' family. And with *our* track record, I never know what I'll need, or how long I may actually be away." She ran her fingers across one of the bags. "So, I pack for every eventuality."

"On the dig sites, we have a cabin just for her luggage," said Acton.

Laura punched his shoulder and he feigned injury. "Okay, okay. Do you need anything?"

"No."

He turned to the Father. "Can you just have these taken to our room, please?"

"*Your* room?" Father Morris distinctly eyed their ring fingers. "Are you two married?"

Acton blushed and stared at the floor, realizing his gaffe. "Ah, no."

"Then I shall have your luggage brought to your *rooms*."

The luggage was rolled out and Reading followed with a huge grin as he turned to close the doors behind him. Acton flipped him the bird, and when the doors sealed, he and Laura erupted into laughter. "Oops," said Acton.

"Maybe tonight I'll sneak over to your room and we can be the first people ever to have sex in the Vatican."

"Something tells me we wouldn't be the first."

She shrugged. "You never know."

Something down below tweaked at the thought, then he eyed the chest. "I know you find me irresistible, but first things first, my dear."

She feigned wounded pride with a pout, then smiled. They both sat in front of the chest, neither touching it. His heart pounded as he examined it. It was about three feet across, two deep and three high. It was clearly old. Very old. He reached out and tentatively touched it. The wood was dry, but smooth, with no telltale signs of degradation, no splinters, no splits. "Well maintained."

"If they keep it in the Secret Archives, then it would be climate-controlled."

"I wonder if this appears on the Archive's manifest."

Laura shook her head. "I doubt it. They claim the manifest is complete, however no one really believes that."

"What? The Church lies?"

They both stopped and looked around, then up.

"Remember where we are, dear."

He was struggling to filter his thoughts, filter the words coming from his mouth, but it was difficult.

Damned near impossible.

He did a mental shake of his head, admonishing himself, then lifted the case with a grunt. It was heavy. "About fifty pounds, give or take."

"It's not that big. The sides must be thick."

He raised it and examined the bottom. Other than the four solid, round feet, carved directly from the piece of wood that made the bottom, it was featureless except for an engraving on the front. He ran his fingers over one of the feet, then grasped it and gave it a slight tug. There was no give at all. "Solid, single-piece construction of the bottom."

"Meant to last."

"And never needing to be maintained. I bet if we asked, we would be told that it's given a ceremonial polish before being presented, and nothing more."

Laura agreed. He placed it back on the table and she knocked on the side. "Doesn't sound hollow. I'm guessing the cavity isn't that big."

"From the shape, I get the impression it's designed to store scrolls vertically."

"Possible." She examined the scene engraved across the front. An upside-down cross, with two ornate keys, themselves crossed over the top portion of the engraving. "Saint Peter's Cross."

"Interesting." The upside-down cross, signaling Saint Peter's wish to not die upright on the cross like Jesus, but rather upside down, as he didn't consider himself worthy of meeting his fate in the same manner as his friend and Lord. Streams of heavenly light burst from behind the carved cross, and below this, a man, prostrated in front, wearing the distinct papal miter, completed the artistry.

He ran his finger over the only words carved on the chest. "Unus Veritas."

"Latin. One truth?"

"Curious. What do you think it means?"

Laura pursed her lips. "I would assume the word of God, the Bible? Only one source of truth?"

"Makes sense." He examined the lock then reached over and untied his leather case, rolling it open, revealing a set of delicate tools, along with additional trappings of the trade. He retrieved a magnifying glass and peered at the mechanism. "Not very secure. I think this was more of a ceremonial lock than anything else."

"It probably wouldn't occur to anyone to try and open it, considering where it's stored and who it's meant for."

He agreed. "It looks like—" He stopped and held a knuckle up to the lock. "A ring maybe?"

"The Piscatory Ring perhaps?"

"The Ring of the Fisherman." He traced the outline of the opening with his finger. "It could be. This lock has a slightly odd shape to it that if memory serves, might just match the shape of that ring." He whipped out his cellphone and Googled the ring. Within moments, he had an image and held it up triumphantly to Laura. "You were right!"

"So, the ring is used to open the chest." She paused for a moment, running her thumb over the opening. "I wonder which came first."

"What do you mean?"

"Was the ring created to open the chest, or was the lock created to be opened by the ring?"

Acton tapped his chin. "That's a good question." He leaned back. "A *very* good question." He turned to Laura, excitement building inside. "The Ring of the Fisherman has been handed down for at least eight hundred years, and most think far longer than that. Some historians think it goes back to Peter himself."

Her hand ran over the carving of the cross. "My word, how old *is* this chest?"

"I'm not sure, but we could be dealing with something that goes back to the very founding of the original church of Christ. Not just the Roman Catholic Church, but to the Apostles themselves."

She leaned back, her hand on her mouth, her cheeks flushed, her eyes focused laser-like on the chest. "I've never considered myself very religious, but at this moment, I feel—" She paused, as if searching for the words. She looked at Acton. "Filled with joy."

He smiled, knowing exactly how she felt. His heart was shoving against his ribcage, and he was almost lightheaded. The thought of this predating the Church, predating everything that corrupted it after the deaths of the Apostles, excited him in a way he couldn't remember having been in the past. If this chest did indeed date back to Peter, then what it contained could be the true teachings of Christ, not those the Nicene Creed had deemed them to be. He gripped Laura's hand. "The original Bible?"

She gasped. "That would be brilliant," she whispered. "How do we open it though, without the ring?"

He smiled. "As I said, fairly primitive." He took a small compressed can of foam, and sprayed it into the hole, quickly filling it. He put the can down and stuck a small T-type socket wrench into the rapidly hardening foam. Within moments, it had turned solid. Looking at Laura, he paused, enjoying the anticipation on her face, then twisted the makeshift key. Bits of excess foam broke away, falling to the tabletop, as the key slowly turned. At forty-five degrees, something gave slightly, then at ninety there was a click and the lid popped open a sliver. He let go of the wrench and leaned forward, grasping both sides of the top.

"Here we go."

He lifted the top, both of them rising to their feet as it swung open. Laura gasped as the opened top revealed the hidden treasure inside.

"I wasn't expecting that!"

Neither was he. He was disappointed. Before them, sitting at the top of the box, was a jewel case containing a compact disc. "Ancient CD? Jesus was a DJ?"

She elbowed him. "Respect," she hissed.

He placed a quick kiss on her forehead, then carefully lifted the CD case and placed it on the table. Underneath where the CD had sat, was a wood insert with a leather clasp in the center. He gently pulled, and the insert lifted out. This time they gasped together, smiles exchanged. Below the insert was a stone tablet, the text mostly illegible, but one thing on the ancient stone was unmistakable.

A fish.

He pointed. "Saint Peter."

"I wonder what it said."

He pointed at several sharp edges. "Looks like a chisel was used to remove the words."

"I wonder why."

He shrugged. "Perhaps after we read what's inside, we'll know." He carefully removed the stone and placed it aside, revealing a honeycomb of several dozen slots, each numbered consecutively in Roman numerals. Inside the first dozen slots were carefully rolled parchments. He snapped on a pair of latex gloves. "Where to start?"

"Crazy idea. How about number one?"

"I." He said the Roman numeral like a pirate.

"Would you take this seriously?"

"Sorry, I get giddy when I'm excited."

"That explains a few things the first night we were together."

Acton blushed. "I was better the second time."

She kissed his cheek then patted it. "Yes, dear, you definitely were."

He stared at her for a moment, not sure if his manhood had just been insulted, when she winked at him. He decided his ego needed to take that as an acknowledgment of a joke. He reached inside and carefully removed the first scroll. Laying it on the table, he gently unrolled it then sat back slightly, each end held by his latex covered fingertips.

"That doesn't look very old."

"It isn't." He pointed to the bottom. "Look at the date."

"May twelfth, nineteen-eighty-one. Why is that familiar?" She pulled his cellphone off his belt and quickly

Googled the date. A 'this day in history' site appeared, and she found nothing of significance. She swiped her thumb to show the next day and smiled, holding it up for him to see. "It's the day before the assassination attempt on Pope John Paul the Second."

"That's too big of a coincidence." He pointed at the document. "That's the seal of the Ring of the Fisherman there, with his name."

"So, it would appear that recent events are not the only time violence has surrounded this chest."

He agreed, quickly reading the Latin text on the page, the hairs on his arms rising as he did.

Should we even be looking at this?

"What's it say?"

"My Latin's a little rough—"

"Stop being modest."

He smiled. "Well, here goes." He cleared his throat. "Your Holiness, let me begin by congratulating you on your new post. I, too, remember that day as if it were yesterday, the fear I felt in wondering if I was worthy, and the humbleness I felt in having been chosen by my peers to be their conduit to our Lord. On the eve of my first day, I was presented the chest now before you, with instructions to open it immediately, and read its contents. What I found, and what you shall find, shall shock you. The information contained herein is terrifying, and shall test your faith. But I know you are strong, or you would not be here today. It has served to strengthen my own faith, and to believe there is only one truth, and it is that taught by our Church.

"The documents contained herein are ancient, and thus fragile. I took it upon myself to have them scanned and transcribed by a trusted associate. They are contained within the box, and I urge you to use any currently available methods to preserve these contents, in secret, so they are not lost. For when secrets are lost, they are then bound to be found. And we cannot risk that."

Acton traced his finger across the signature. "Yours in God, John Paul the Second, May twelfth, year of our Lord, nineteen-eighty-one."

"What could possibly be in here that is so bad that it's worth killing for?" asked Laura, her arm now intertwined with his as she held herself close to him. She looked at him, a touch of fear in her slightly widened eyes. "I'm having second thoughts."

"Me too. But the answer to saving two people's lives, including someone who almost died to save ours, could be in here."

She squeezed his arm. "Of course, you're right." She stood. "I'll get the laptop." She quickly left the office, the doors closing behind her. Acton busied himself clearing out the foam he had squeezed into the lock, adding a neutralizing agent to break it down. He was just finishing when Laura returned, the laptop case slung over her shoulder. She closed the doors behind her, took a quick glance around the room, then joined him at the table. Moments later, the laptop was fired up and the CD inserted.

They found a series of directories, each labeled with the Roman numerals they had observed in the chest. Laura clicked on the first directory, labeled 'I,' and they found three files, one an image, the other two text documents. She opened the image, and a scan appeared of the page he had just read. She closed it, opened *I.doc*, and it proved to be the same text they had just read. The third file, *I-eng.doc*, was an English translation. They both reread it just to be sure.

Without looking, Laura gave him a quick elbow. "And you said your Latin was a little rough."

He didn't respond. His heart was pounding as her finger moved the mouse pointer to the second directory. A quick double-tap and they were inside. This contained what appeared to be a dozen files. She opened the first translation file. He closed his eyes for a moment.

"It's an inventory," whispered Laura.

He opened his eyes and read the first entry. It was meaningless. "Open the scanned image."

Laura complied and he pointed. "Look, much of the upper half of this page is missing, no wonder the text is gibberish. Whoever translated this had almost nothing to work with."

"What if what we're looking for is in a destroyed piece?"

"Then we're SOL. For now, let's just see what we find."

They read through page after page, many of the oldest in poor condition with entire portions missing. As they read through the list, each would comment, point, gasp, or otherwise express surprise at various entries. Most proved dull, simply texts considered heretical, others references to objects seized with demonic powers assumed. It was the descriptions that shook them both. Why each was seized, why each was considered heretical. The descriptions in some cases were terrifying, and he prayed they were interpretations of things today's science could easily explain. But for some, he could find no reasonable explanation. His mouth was dry, and every muscle in his body was taut, on edge, as if at any moment something might jump from the shadows of the darkening room.

Laura opened the next page and gasped. "Look!" She pointed to the first entry. "Gospel of Mary."

They both stared at each other in triumph.

"It exists!"

Their excitement lasted only a few moments as they pressed forward through the inventory. It was exhausting work, not only the tedium, but the emotional strain. The entries, each written by the pope who had made them, were filled with the emotional horror each of them had experienced when interring a new document or artifact. As he read each one, he descended down the rabbit hole, losing himself in the terror these men must have suffered centuries ago with no modern understanding of the world.

And as he shared in their terror, he questioned why he, a man of science, was succumbing. And he could find only one explanation. He believed. There were far too many things here that he simply couldn't rationalize. Perhaps with the object in hand he might, though right here, right now, with nothing but the written word of terrified men, he found himself drawn into their paranoia.

And it was exhausting.

Laura yawned and he mirrored her. They gave each other a knowing smile, his empathy statement from early on in their relationship flashing through his mind.

If I stop yawning when you yawn, then you'll know I don't love you anymore.

The few times he had loved in his life, and they were few, he had always known when it was over. He wasn't petty enough to break up with a woman because of a missed yawn, though if he noticed himself not yawning when she did, he began to analyze their relationship, and would always come to the conclusion that he had fallen out of love with the person, and worse, had fallen out of caring.

But sometimes it was them. If he noticed them not yawning when he did, he would discover they had fallen out of love with him.

He paused for a moment.

Which has happened more?

If he thought about it, probably the latter. He was a hard man to love. It was a lot to ask of a woman to put up with his gallivanting around the globe for weeks and more often months at a time. And where his dig sites usually were, it wasn't as if regular communications were easy. Sometimes he'd go days, even weeks, without talking to his latest partner. And more often than not, he'd find an icy reception on the other end of the line.

The few who had put up with it long enough to form a bond and fall in love, eventually demanded he change.

How can we make plans if you're never here?

Indeed, how? It was why he had given up on long-term relationships, especially in his thirties. Women in their thirties deserved to be in a relationship with a man with whom there was a future. They wanted to set down roots, have a family, have a normal life with a husband who was there when they needed him. And he could never be that man.

But Laura was different. She was in her mid-thirties, and he had fallen hard for her, and she for him. He was early forties, in the best shape of his life, or at least he told himself that, and here he was, with a woman in an age bracket he had said he would never date again. And madly in love. It had been well over a year, and their relationship continued to grow stronger, and he suspected this could be the one.

Marriage?

He had never thought it would be for him. Then again, he never thought he'd meet himself with breasts. They were so much alike, they understood each other. Understood the job. The sacrifices. And thrived on them.

He reached over and kissed her. Not a passionate kiss, just a long, lingering, gentle kiss. "I love you," he whispered in her ear.

"I know," she whispered back, squeezing the nape of his neck gently.

They sat there quietly for a moment, neither smiling, simply comforting each other as they contemplated the horrors they had just read. He broke the embrace with a forced smile, pointing at the screen. "Last directory."

Laura held his gaze for another moment then opened the directory, surprisingly revealing only a single file. She opened the image, and a map popped up on the screen, showing a set of chambers, and an X in one of them. At the bottom of the page was a diagram of the room, with a

BROKEN DOVE

piece of furniture the focus, with doors wide open. A note, in Latin, was written beside it.

"Enter wardrobe, close door, push up second hook from the left," said Acton.

"It must be the entrance to where all of this is hidden!"

"Must be." He pointed at the image. "Email this to our phones."

A few taps of the keys and the image was emailed. Both of their phones beeped moments later.

"Do you think we should copy this CD?"

He shook his head. "No. We were entrusted to keep its secrets, and after seeing that list, I can see why. There are things in there that still have the hair on the back of my neck at attention."

She squeezed his hand. "I'm glad it's not just me." She lowered her voice. "James, I'm scared. What we just read, what we just saw, we weren't meant to see."

He agreed. "Not like that. These are things that should be discovered over centuries, one at a time. What we've just learned, all in a few hours, is too much for anyone."

"Can you imagine what the popes must go through? There is so much in there that is evil, and so much that questions the doctrines they were just appointed to enforce. It must be overwhelming."

"Changed men."

"Now I see why."

He pointed at the laptop. "Let's put everything back where we found it."

She ejected the CD and put it back in its case as he returned the stone tablet and wood insert overtop the scrolls. She placed the CD on top, and he closed the lid, the click of the lock ending their journey through the past—for now. They would likely be experiencing the real thing before the night was through.

Papal Offices Antechamber
Apostolic Palace, The Vatican

Acton and Laura emerged from the Papal Offices shaken. Acton had his tool kit wrapped, gripped tightly in one hand, and Laura had the laptop shouldered in its case. Neither said a word. Father Morris rose as they cleared the doors, his face drawn, appearing as tired as Acton felt. Except for the eyes. The eyes, slightly wide, showed fear.

"Are you done?"

Acton nodded.

"And the chest…"

Acton knew what he was asking. He didn't want to see inside. "Is as it was."

Father Morris smiled slightly, conveying his thanks. He picked up his phone and was about to dial when he stopped. "You must not reveal anything of what you saw."

Acton came to a halt at the outer doors, meeting Father Morris' stare. "No more than what is absolutely necessary. Trust me."

The priest held Acton's gaze for several moments, then, as if deciding they could be taken at their word, turned his attention to the phone. As they left the room, the priest requested four guardsmen be sent.

They made their way through the twisting corridors, retracing their steps from memory, supplemented with the occasional request for directions from a passing resident, and soon found themselves at the Security Office. Entering, Giasson and Reading both turned and waved for them to come through. The woman manning the inner entrance was about to ask them their business when Acton pointed a finger toward Giasson's glassed office. She glanced over her shoulder then pressed the button under her desk to unlock the half-door keeping the riffraff out.

Acton held the door to Giasson's office open for Laura, then closed it behind them. They sat in their former chairs, not saying anything. Giasson avoided eye contact, as if nervous at what they might say, but Reading was having none of that. He stared at Giasson, then Laura, then Acton.

"Well?"

Acton glanced at Laura who nodded with a slight pursing of the lips. He gasped in a lungful of air and slowly exhaled.

What do I tell them?

The secrets they had read over the past several hours were never meant to be seen. He regarded Giasson. He was staring at him, his eyes wide, cheeks flushed, as if terrified at what he was about to hear. Reading seemed eager, as if ready to consume a Murdoch tabloid containing the latest sex scandal.

Tell them only what they need to know.

He shifted in his chair.

"Well, we made a commitment only to reveal what was necessary." He looked from man to man. "Are we still agreed upon that?"

"Definitely," said Giasson, a little quicker and louder than he might have intended. He leaned back and mopped the perspiration off his scalp with a handkerchief. "Nothing more," he added, this time quieter.

"But nothing less." Reading turned to Acton, clearly exasperated. "Come on, man, what did you find?"

Acton leaned forward, as did the room. "First, the Gospel of Mary is real."

Giasson gasped and made a sign of the cross. He gazed out at the bull pit then jumped from his seat. Acton's eyes darted to follow, and he saw the entire room of security personnel turn back to their desks as Giasson closed the blinds. Returning to his desk, he frowned slightly. "I think everybody knows you saw the chest."

"But I didn't think anybody knew about it."

"They do now, it would seem." He sat back down and leaned forward, elbows on the desk, chin resting on top of his interlaced fingers. He closed his eyes. "How do you know the Gospel of Mary is real?"

"Well, the chest contains an inventory."

"A what?" Reading was beside himself. "An inventory? I thought this was supposed to be some message from God, or something important like that?" He took a deep breath and looked at Giasson's horrified expression. Reading calmed himself by slowly exhaling. "So, what was in this inventory?" His voice was that of a schoolteacher asking what was in a note just passed secretly.

"It was a list of items collected over the past two thousand years that might harm the Church," explained Laura. "Writings, artifacts…" Her voice faded, her eyes clouding over. Acton sensed it too. As he thought of the list, of what was on it, he shivered. "Things man weren't meant to know," she whispered, her voice cracking.

Acton pulled his chair closer to hers and placed his arm over her shoulders, drawing her in. Her chest heaved as tears silently rolled down her face.

Reading leaned forward and gently squeezed her leg, his voice a whisper. "What was in there that was so bad?"

Acton shook his head. "The problem wasn't necessarily what was in there, although there was some mighty disturbing stuff. It was the sheer volume. If you encountered these items, if you were made aware of these things, one a year perhaps, then fine—your psyche has time to adapt. But we were just exposed to almost two thousand years' worth in just a few hours." He found his own voice cracking. "It's too much. Just too much to think about." He raised his eyes and met Reading's. "You don't want to know what we just read. Not if you believe in God."

Reading leaned back. "Are you saying it would make me question my beliefs?"

"Yes, but not in the way you're thinking."

Reading scrunched his eyes, deep lines creasing his forehead. "What do you mean?"

A tear rolled down Acton's cheek, unnoticed. "You'll believe. You'll believe in God. But you'll also believe in something else."

"What?"

Laura's head lifted off Acton's shoulder as she turned to Reading. "Evil."

The hair on the back of Acton's neck stood up.

Evil.

And that *was* it. He had been attempting to figure out the common thread through most of what they had read. It was obvious the items were things the Church feared threatened their doctrine. Yet it was more. And with Laura's one word, he knew what the purpose of this hidden archive was. It wasn't to protect the Church from blasphemy. It was to protect the Church, to protect mankind, from evil. As he had read the list of items and their descriptions, it was obvious these were considered a danger. Though it wasn't until Laura had said that one word that he realized why he had been on edge for the past several hours.

He believed.

He had always known there were evil people in the world. Hitler, Stalin, Khan, bin Laden. History was riddled with them. Yet the hundreds if not thousands of items he had just been exposed to were not people, but physical objects. Reading what they were believed to have done, or believed capable of, had shaken him to the core, and now that he realized why, that he now, truly, believed in evil, shook him further.

"Evil?" Reading's tone was doubtful, though still quiet out of respect for Laura.

"Evil." Acton stroked Laura's hair. "I don't know how to explain it, Hugh, but for the first time in my life, I believe in true evil. Perhaps in time it'll fade, but right now, I've never been so uneasy in my life. It's as if a force, a presence, I had never known was there, is all around us."

Laura gasped for air and continued her sobbing. Giasson rose, grabbing a box of tissues and rounded his desk. He held the box out for her. "Professor?" She looked up then reached out, pulling several tissues from the box, then sat straight in her chair. She blew her nose and wiped her eyes. Giasson put the box on a side table between Laura and Reading, then picked up the small garbage can near the door and held it out for Laura to put her used tissues in. He placed the can under the small table, returned to his desk, and retrieved a book. He made the sign of the cross and turned to face Laura. "Mademoiselle, when I need comfort, I always find it in this." He held out the leather tome with both hands, an offering from a spiritual man to the nonspiritual, the only thing a man in his position could offer, something he believed she needed, and judging from the trembling of his hands, and his tear-filled eyes, something *he* definitely needed.

Laura reached out with both hands and took the Bible, rather than reject it as on any other occasion she might have, not from disrespect, but simply refusal of something she didn't need. Though this time she took the book and hugged it to her chest, rocking back and forth slightly. At that moment, he wished he too had a Bible to hold. He had never been a religious man, yet today, he felt in more need of, and closer to, God, than ever before. Would today be their epiphany? A coming to God out of fear, rather than love?

Acton closed his eyes and breathed deeply, but images of the inventory kept playing across his eyelids like a movie. He opened them and blew the air out through pursed lips. "Okay, enough of that. If we keep dwelling on the nature of what we discovered, then it wins. And I for one am not going to let it."

Laura sat straighter, handing the Bible back to Giasson with a silent smile of thanks, then gave her nose one last blow. "You're right, of course, James. It's time to move forward."

Giasson turned and slowly rounded his desk, his Bible held tightly to his lips. He sat and returned it to its place of honor, and dabbed his own eyes with his handkerchief.

Reading hadn't said anything, apparently the only one in the room unaffected by this. And it made sense to Acton. Reading had been a cop for decades. He had seen the evil men do for years. The fact the rest of the room had just realized something he had always known, had no impact on him, though Acton could see in his eyes he had concern for his friends.

As if to make things easier for everyone, Reading spoke first. "So, the chest contains an inventory of writings and objects that the Church over the past two thousand years considered blasphemous or dangerous in some way." Acton and Laura nodded, but said nothing. "Each new pope gets this chest, reads the list, and probably, much like yourselves, finally, truly, believes in evil. An effective indoctrination tool, if you ask me."

Laura's jaw dropped and Acton's eyes widened.

Reading quickly backpedaled. "I mean, we really don't know how old this list is, how long they've been showing it to the popes, even if it's real."

"It's real," whispered Laura.

"And we know it's old. Ancient. Some of the documents had disintegrated with age."

"Or were made to look that way." Reading waved his hands in the air. "Please, understand, I'm playing Devil's advocate here." The entire room froze. "Sorry, poor choice of words, but you know what I mean." He leaned forward and counted out his points on his fingers. "First, we have no proof this list is real. It could be a work of fiction, meant to instill fear in those who read it. Perhaps in the event an unworthy pope was elected, this was a last chance effort to try and scare them straight." He shrugged. "Anything is possible. Second, this is an ancient list. Most of these items exposed to modern science would probably have innocent explanations, or be shown to just be on the list due to ancient superstitions. After all, we did have the Dark Ages. And finally, if there is this massive collection of artifacts, where is it? If this is an inventory, what is it an inventory of?"

Acton looked at Reading. "I won't argue your first point, but for number two, two items were added to the list by the last pope, so these aren't just ancient superstitions. And as to your third point"—Acton snapped his cellphone off his belt, bringing up the picture—"we have a map."

Reading glanced quickly at the screen then handed the phone to Giasson. His eyebrows shot up as he manipulated the image with his thumb and forefinger. "This is in the residence." He stared for a few more moments, then raised his head. "This is very near to DI Chaney's quarters, and not very far from His Holiness' chamber. If there's a secret entrance to the Vatican..." His voice drifted off as his eyes gazed into the distance, unfocused, as the ramifications of what this meant settled in.

"You have a security breach."

Giasson agreed. "Apparently so."

"But this is supposed to be known to no one but the Pope," said Acton.

"It would appear someone knows." Reading leaned back and crossed one leg over the other. "First, we have the Father, murdered in an unknown location, then placed in his chambers. We know he was murdered elsewhere, because there wasn't enough blood in his room for the murder to have taken place there. We also know he had his alarm set for four a.m., much earlier than normal, and he was dressed, so had obviously intended to go somewhere." Reading paused and pointed at the phone with the map. "Now I think we know where."

Giasson agreed. "It does make sense. Then for some reason His Holiness calls in DI Chaney to assist with the investigation. Since we know His Holiness knows of and where the chamber is, he most likely suspects as well that the murder took place there. He informs Chaney, who then enters this secret location, and he too is either killed or captured, if we are to believe this Order."

"But the Pope? Would he actually try and find Chaney?" Acton looked from Giasson to Reading then back. "The man is over seventy!"

"Faith gives strength." Giasson said it with a tone indicating he thought this should be obvious to everyone.

"Not to argue, but are we really saying that this elderly gentleman left his quarters in the middle of the night in search of Chaney?" Acton couldn't believe it, and it sounded more ridiculous as it came from his mouth, yet he could think of no other explanation.

Reading grimaced at Giasson. "It fits with what we know."

Giasson frowned. "Yes, yes it does. And it makes sense."

"What does?"

Acton glanced at Laura, seemingly back to her normal self.

"Two guards are supposed to be stationed at his door at all times, even when he is not there."

"Did they see anything?" asked Acton.

Giasson shook his head. "No. Apparently, His Holiness, after retiring, opened the door sometime later and dismissed them for the night."

"And I assume that is out of the ordinary?"

Giasson's head bobbed emphatically. "Completely!"

Acton ran both hands through his hair, gently pulling on the strands as they flowed through his fingers, then sighed. "I guess the question at this point is, did he do it because he was going to meet with Chaney, or did he already know Chaney was missing, and he intended to go looking for him?"

Laura tossed the last of her used tissues into the garbage can. "I still can't believe a man of that age would go looking in a secret chamber for someone. If he took the Father into his confidence, surely he would take someone else?"

"Who could he trust?" Acton waved a finger in the air as he spoke, his thoughts finally coming together. "The Father is murdered. He calls in Chaney, because he doesn't know who he can trust. Now Chaney is missing, and he knows for certain there is an even greater security breach. He can't risk anyone else's life, so he, being a man of God, puts his own on the line."

"But how did he know he could trust Chaney?" asked Giasson.

Acton made eye contact with Reading who gave a slight nod. They both looked at Laura and she shrugged. "I don't see how we have any choice."

Acton agreed and turned to Giasson, lowering his voice. "What I'm about to tell you can't be repeated to anyone. Ever."

Giasson glanced at the blinds to make certain they were closed, then leaned forward. "What is it?"

"The Pope, and Chaney, are—" Acton stopped and glanced at Reading for a dose of reassurance.

Giasson was turning red. "They are what?" he demanded.

Acton returned his attention to Giasson. "Triarii."

"What the hell is that?"

"Let me explain."

Corpo della Gendarmeria Office
Palazzo del Governatorato, Vatican City

It was hard to read Giasson. He appeared to have calmed down slightly from the initial shock of learning who the Triarii were, and that the current pope was a member. Acton feared he was now questioning his beliefs, his faith in the man now occupying the top position of a church he had devoted himself to his entire adult life. He hadn't said anything for several minutes, raising his hand to cut anyone off who dared speak.

Acton's phone rang.

Odd, since he was certain he had his cellphone set to vibrate, and it wasn't his ringtone. Laura gave him a look, as if she shared his confusion.

The other phone!

He reached into his pocket and grabbed the phone given to him when they were briefly kidnapped, and answered it. "Hello?"

All eyes, including Giasson's, were on him.

"Professor Acton, please report on your progress."

He clasped his hand over the microphone, and whispered, "They want to know our progress. What should I tell them?"

"Nothing!" hissed Giasson.

Acton removed his hand. "We've been making inquiries, but haven't had any success yet."

Reading waved his hand and Acton covered the speaker again. "Ask for proof of life."

"It would appear you do not take our threats seriously. Perhaps if we send you a finger, an ear, a *heart*, it might convince you."

Acton's own heart raced.

Are we sure they don't have them? Can we take that risk?

"No no no, it's not that. I believe you. But—" He paused.

How do you ask someone if they're full of shit, without getting someone else killed in the event they're not?

He took a deep breath. "Can we talk to Chaney, or the Pope, just to make sure they're all right?"

"I guess you don't take us seriously."

The phone cut off.

"No!" yelled Acton at the now dead line. He turned to the room. "They hung up. They don't think we're taking them seriously."

"We're not." Giasson's statement was matter of fact. And cold. Actually, emotionless. He seemed still in shock at what he had just learned about the Triarii and the Pope. He leaned back and Reading looked at him.

"Mario, are you okay?"

"I will be. It isn't every day you find out there's a two-thousand-year-old Roman legion guarding humanity from crystal skulls coming together, and that they have infiltrated the Vatican at the highest level."

Reading smiled slightly. "No, I guess that can be quite the shock. But remember, these people are good. We've had experience with them, my partner was one of them for years and I never knew it, and he always did the right thing. Your pope, he's a good man. I checked him out after we discovered he was Triarii, and he's a legitimate priest. The Triarii are a mix of all races and religions. They may have started as Romans, but now they are everywhere. They believe in the skulls, in that they are dangerous if brought together, and yes, some even worship them. But some are Christian, Muslim, Buddhist, Atheist. Just because your pope is a member, doesn't mean you should believe in him any less than you did an hour ago."

Giasson let out a burst of air he had been holding. "I know. He is a good man, and I've met him many times over the years. I believed in him then, I believe in him now." He shook his head then ran a hand over his scalp. "He and I will have to have a long talk when we rescue him." He sat up. "Okay, we have a map, and maps serve one purpose. My vote, and since this isn't a democracy, it's the only one that counts, is that we go to where this map indicates, and see what we find."

Acton raised his hand as Giasson and Reading rose from their seats. "Ahh, one thing."

They both sat.

"The instructions were clear. You weren't supposed to know the contents of the chest."

"So?"

"So, by extension, you aren't supposed to know about the map, or where the map leads."

"Bollocks!" exploded Reading. "This is a police investigation. We go where the evidence leads!"

"No."

Reading's head spun toward Giasson. "What?" He appeared dumbfounded.

"I said, 'No.' Professor Acton is correct. We are not meant to know what was in that chest. It's bad enough that *they* know. But I for one do not want to."

"But—" Reading stopped, his eyes darting between Giasson and Acton, as if searching for someone to be reasonable. "But how do we guarantee their safety?"

"Give us weapons, some flashlights, and some strong two-ways," said Acton.

Giasson nodded. "No problem. You're trained?"

"National Guard."

"Female on a bunch of third-world digs," said Laura. "And, we've been training for almost a year now."

"Training?" Reading's eyes narrowed. "What do you mean?"

"We've both been in weapons training, Krav Maga, basic and advanced self-defense."

"We're lethal weapons." Acton's voice was deadpan. Laura looked at him, dead serious as well, then they both howled with laughter.

"Are you two serious?"

"About the training? Yes. About being lethal weapons. Not yet."

Reading shook his head. "God help us all."

Laura turned to Giasson. "Yes, we're trained for use on most types of weapons."

Reading apparently wasn't satisfied. "When did you find the time for this?"

"At our digs. I've hired a former SAS guy to provide security for our sites in Peru and Egypt, and to train us. We usually get in at least a couple of hours a day."

"Must be nice to have money," muttered Reading. "Just don't think you're invincible and get yourselves killed. Training and the real thing are completely different." He jabbed his thumb at his chest. "I know, I fought in the Falklands, and when you come under fire for the first time, it's everything you can do not to fill your trousers and run the other way."

"I think between the two of us, we've been under enough fire the past couple of years to say we're past that point."

Reading chuckled, shaking his head. "You've got me there. You two have probably been under more fire than most civilians on the planet."

Acton grunted. "From handguns to nuclear weapons."

Giasson raised his head. "What do you mean nuclear weapons?"

Acton, Laura, and Reading all said in unison, "Nothing!"

Giasson frowned and Reading stared at him.

"Forget you heard that."

Giasson rose from his desk, shaking his hands. "Forget it all. I've heard enough today. I'll get you your equipment."

"One thing, and I won't compromise on this." The room turned toward Reading. "I want to be at the entrance, just in case. I don't need to go down with you, but I want to be close, just in the event something goes wrong."

Acton agreed. "Sounds fine to me."

Giasson stared at Reading for a moment then sighed. "Fine." He left then returned moments later with a box filled with weapons, utility belts, and two-way radios.

And body armor.

Reading held up one of the vests. "Body armor?"

Giasson shrugged. "Just in case."

Acton's eyes flitted between the armor and Laura. He could see the fear in her eyes. And the determination.

Why do we keep getting mixed up in these things?

Acton, Reading, and Laura donned the equipment as Giasson watched in silence.

"Sir, there's something you have to see!"

The door had opened without Giasson's permission, the young head that poked inside appearing not to care, his face flushed and pale at the same time, as if he were ready to be sick from terror.

"What is it?" Giasson's tone was unforgiving.

The man shook his head. "You have to see it."

They all rose and followed him into the outer office. The entire staff's attention was on the front desk where the young woman they had seen earlier was heaving into a garbage container, another person rubbing her back in an attempt to comfort her.

An open box sat on the counter serving as her desk, no one near it, as if it were contaminated in some way.

"What is it?" demanded Giasson as he neared the counter.

The man comforting the desk officer pointed. "Look inside."

Giasson leaned over the box and gasped, stepping back. Acton looked and a wave of nausea overcame him. Inside, on ice, was a bloody ear, with a note resting underneath it. Laura and Reading leaned in and Laura's hand darted to her mouth as she gasped.

"Maybe we should have taken them seriously," whispered Reading.

Giasson pointed at the box. "Get this to the police liaison. I need to know who this belonged to, and when it was cut off." He turned to one of his men. "Get them to DI Chaney's room—"

The phone rang in Acton's pocket.

"Silenzio!" yelled Giasson.

The room came to a standstill as Acton answered the call. "Hello?"

"Did you get our message?"

"Yes."

"Are you taking us seriously now?"

"Yes."

"Very good. We don't want to have to remove any more parts from our guests."

The phone cut off and Acton returned it to his pocket.

"Well?" asked Reading.

"They asked if we received the message, and if we were taking them seriously now."

"That's it?"

"Yes."

Giasson snapped his fingers. "Greco, make sure you get His Holiness' DNA profile to the police." Somebody wailed. In fact, the entire room remained frozen, the thought of the ear being that of their leader, too much. Giasson clapped his hands together. "Back to work people. Focus on your jobs. Do them well, and God willing, there will be nothing to mourn tomorrow." He turned back to their escort. "Get them to DI Chaney's room, then leave them there, alone." The man was about to open his mouth when Giasson cut him off with a finger. "No questions."

The man nodded and opened the glass door to the Security Office, ushering the armed party through.

Giasson continued to bark orders as the door closed
behind them, cutting off the sound.

Outside DI Chaney's Quarters
Apostolic Palace, The Vatican

Within minutes, they were in front of what had been Chaney's room, the young man who had escorted them unsure what to do.

Reading patted him on the shoulder. "Thank you, lad, you may return to your duties."

The man left at a jog and Laura watched after him.

"Everyone around here is walking on eggshells. I can't imagine what it must be like for them."

Acton grunted. "I can. When you were missing, I was going crazy."

She smiled and gave him a quick squeeze. "And you found me."

"Barely." Acton pulled his cellphone off his hip and brought up the map. He pointed at the bottom. "I assume we're here."

Laura and Reading peered over either shoulder, then Reading stepped back. "You're the archaeologists, I'll take your word for it."

Acton turned and pointed ahead. "We go this way."

Reading pulled his weapon and stepped forward, taking point.

"Is that really necessary, Hugh?"

Reading gave Laura an embarrassed smile as he holstered the weapon. "I guess it's not exactly appropriate in here." He raised his finger. "But, when we get to the room where this entrance is, you let me in first. And my weapon *will* be drawn."

"Agreed." Acton pointed down the hall with his chin. "Shall we?"

Reading gave his friend a half-smile and a knowing look, then led the way. After several twists and turns, they reached a dead end with a door to the left and one to the right. "Did we take a wrong turn?"

"No." Acton pointed at the door on the left. "This is it."

Reading drew his weapon and indicated for them to stand back. He knocked on the door and listened. There was no answer. He knocked again, then turned the knob. He glanced back at Acton and Laura who also had their weapons drawn. He gave them a look and Acton tilted his head to the side, raising his eyebrows and shrugging. Reading pushed the door open and reached inside, flipping the light switch near the door. The room flooded with light as he entered, Acton and Laura rapidly following him in, both branching to either side of the door as all three searched.

"Clear," whispered Reading.

Laura stepped from the bathroom. "Clear."

"Clear." Acton faced the wardrobe, his cellphone already having replaced his weapon.

Reading closed the door then holstered his own. "I thought I told you to wait?"

Laura shrugged. "What? You don't need backup?"

Reading chuckled. "I have to admit, you definitely have been paying attention to your training."

Acton bowed deeply, then in his best Elvis voice, said, "Thank ya, thank ya vary mawch."

Laura shook her head and joined him. "You and your jokes." She surveyed the wardrobe. "Is this it?"

"I guess so." Acton gripped the handle as Reading drew his weapon. Acton pulled open the door on the right, stepping to the side. Reading reached forward with his left hand and pulled open the other side, his weapon in front the entire time. "Clear."

They gathered in front and Acton summarized the instructions. "We enter, close the outer doors, push up on the second hook from the left, then whatever is going to happen is going to happen."

"What's that mean?" asked Reading.

"It means, it doesn't say what will happen. I'm assuming a door will open on the other side of this wardrobe."

Reading shook his head. "Or poison darts shoot at you, or the floor will drop out from under you."

"You watch too many Indiana Jones movies."

Reading lowered his chin into his chest, raised his eyebrows, and stared at Acton. "Excuse me? Kingdom of the Crystal Skulls?"

Acton chuckled. "Well, we all know which came first. Besides, I didn't see any aliens."

"Don't count on it. You just might find some on the other side of that door."

Acton and Laura exchanged glances, both knowing what they had read.

Some of those things very well could be alien.

Reading regarded them. "What?"

Acton shook his head. "Nothing."

"Don't tell me—"

Acton shook his head again. "Don't ask." He inhaled deeply. "Okay, we'll go in, you stay out here." Reading was about to protest when Acton cut him off. "We don't know what's on the other side, and you're not allowed to see anything, remember?"

Reading frowned but backed away. Acton stepped inside then held out his hand for Laura, who took it and stepped up into the large, though still cramped, wardrobe.

"Set?" asked Reading.

Acton snapped on his flashlight and Laura did the same. He glanced at Reading. "Set."

"Be safe." Reading closed the doors and the light from the room slowly sliced away, then as they clicked shut, they were left with the narrow beams of their flashlights, and the ambient light cast off the wood walls of the wardrobe. Acton reached up and pushed the hook upward. There was a clicking sound, then nothing. He pulled his weapon, as did Laura, then pushed on the wall. It gave way and they were met with a stone passage.

"You okay in there?" Reading's muffled voice didn't hide his concern.

"Yes, there's a passageway here. We're going in now."

"Radio check."

Acton retrieved the radio from his utility belt and squawked it twice. "Check one, two, three, check."

Two clicks answered, then Reading's voice, "Loud and clear on this end. How am I on yours, over?"

"Five-by-five. We're heading in now."

"Copy that. Keep your radios on and check with me every five minutes."

"Will do, out."

Acton stepped down into the passageway then helped Laura. He shone his light around, the beam playing off the stonework. "What do you think? Thousand years?"

"Probably older." She pointed at the floor. "Look. Footprints."

Acton used the beam to trace them until they were lost in the distance. "Several sets. Let's see where they lead." They followed the prints for several dozen feet, past what appeared to be a large pulley controlled platform, then to a winding, stone staircase. He raised his radio. "We're about to go down a staircase. Not sure if you'll be able to get a signal when we get down there, over."

"If you can't get voice, I might pick up a squawk. Two for okay, three for help, got it, over?"

"Got it. See you on the other side, out."

Acton shone the flashlight on his face and looked at her. "He worries too much."

She did the same with hers. "He means well."

He jerked his head toward the steps. "Shall we?"

"After you?"

"If you insist." He gave her a peck on the cheek, then with weapon and flashlight leading the way, began down the spiral staircase. It continued much farther than he had imagined it would, at least several hundred steps. Coming out at the other end, they both gasped. The chamber they found themselves standing in was massive, and went for as far as their flashlight beams could reach. Row after row of shelving, along with other objects covered by cloths, some ancient, some more modern, hiding their secrets from the naked eye. He found himself salivating at the thought of exploring this room of hidden treasures. Then he recalled what these were supposed to contain, and he shivered. Laura had her arm pressed against his and had obviously felt him shake.

"You okay?"

He nodded, then remembered she couldn't see him. "Yes. Just remembering what's supposed to be down here."

"I'm trying to forget."

He shone his flashlight on the floor. "The footprints go that way, let's follow them."

She gripped his arm. "Shouldn't you check in with Hugh?"

"Oops, forgot." He took the radio and pressed the button to talk. "Hugh, can you still read us, over?"

There was a burst of static, and a couple of syllables made it through, but nothing intelligible. He stepped closer to the stairs. "Can you hear me now?" The irony wasn't lost on him.

Bet you they never filmed the commercial down here.

Again, a burst of static.

"Looks like we're out of range."

"Too much rock over our heads."

Acton squawked twice.

Two squawks came back.

"Okay, at least he can still be reached if we need help." He clipped the radio to his body armor so it would be handy, then led the way, weapon and flashlight pointing ahead. Laura followed, slightly behind and to his right, walking backward, covering their rear. He moved forward slowly, careful to keep her always in his peripheral vision as he covered their advance. Two sets of shoeprints went up and down the shelves to their left, as if their creators had been searching for something. He continued ahead, and within moments reached a jumble of prints and a large pool of something dark. "Found something."

Laura turned to where his flashlight shone. "Blood?"

"Looks like it." He dipped the toe of his shoe in it. "Very dry."

"And a lot of it." She knelt. "There's too much here for anyone to have survived. If we're to believe that Chaney and the Pope are alive, then this must be where the Father was killed."

He took some photos with his phone, then pointed with his flashlight. "Look. Seems like someone was dragged this way." They followed the two solid lines and several sets of footprints back to the pulley system they had noticed earlier. He took some more photos. "This must be how they got his body back up there."

"Which means they know about the secret entrance."

Acton squawked twice. Two responded.

They walked back toward the scene of the crime then continued forward. He stopped again at another jumble of footprints and more drag marks. "Looks like another scuffle took place here, and somebody lost." Laura turned and her flashlight followed the drag marks off into the distance, deeper into the complex, rather than back toward where they had entered.

"This could be Chaney."

"Yup." He scanned the area with his flashlight. "No blood, so hopefully he's okay." Two clicks came over the radio. Acton reached up and squeezed twice in response. "Before we follow these, perhaps we should find this Gospel."

"Agreed. I'll start here, you go back to the start and begin there."

"I think we should stay together."

"If we split up, we'll be done in half the time." She stepped away then came back, grabbing his arm. "And only look at texts. I don't want some ancient curse or demon possessing you."

He laughed and turned toward the first shelf in the distance when she pulled him closer and whispered in his ear. "I mean it."

He embraced her head in his hand, pushing it against his chest and kissed the top. "We'll be okay." He let go and she walked away without saying anything, probably, knowing her as he did, to hide a fresh set of tears. He walked briskly to the first stack of shelves and began scanning them with his flashlight for anything resembling a book or parchment that might contain the Gospel in such high demand. His flashlight fell upon a small, leather-bound tome, gilded writing glittering slightly under the glare of his flashlight. He blew the dust off and translated the Latin on the cover. "The Word of Mary."

He picked up the book. "I found it!"

Laura screamed.

Not in excitement, but fear.

Acton rushed out from between the stacks and saw Laura's flashlight roll across the floor, highlighting two figures who spun toward him. He flicked his flashlight off and dove to the right, two shots ringing past where he had been just moments before. He raised his weapon and squeezed off two rounds at the figure on the left. They dropped as he rolled again, his muzzle flash having revealed his position. An ancient pot exploded with a gasp as whatever was inside experienced freedom for the first time in over a thousand years. He fired again, and the second figure dropped. He rushed forward and turned on his flashlight, revealing a third figure leaning over an unconscious Laura.

"Let her go." Acton pointed his weapon directly at the masked figure. "I have your book."

The figure stared at him, then Acton saw his eyes shift momentarily, as if looking behind him. He began to turn when cold metal pressed against his neck.

"What book, Professor Acton?"

Entrance to Hidden Chamber
Apostolic Palace, The Vatican

Reading heard gunshots and grabbed at the handles. The
doors wouldn't budge. He threw his shoulder against
them to no effect, then tried pushing the large wardrobe
aside. It wouldn't give. He pulled his weapon and shot
out the lock, then yanked the doors open and stepped
inside and through the hidden door that stood ajar. His
flashlight out, he raced to the stairs his friend had
described earlier and rushed down the steps, the spiral
construction leaving him slightly dizzy by the end. He
skidded to a halt just as he was about to burst into the
open. Flicking off his light, he listened, then poked his
head out.

Nothing.

Though in the distance, he could see what appeared to
be several flashlights, some moving. He quickly but
quietly pressed forward, weapon drawn, pointed at the
distant beams of light. As he approached, he slowed,
struggling to still the drumbeat in his chest.

He stepped on something, the scraping then cracking
sound echoing through the chamber.

The beams of light shone his way and several
gunshots rang out as he dove between the shelves. He
fired two shots in the air, not willing to risk hitting his
friends.

A man yelled something in what he assumed was
Italian, the tone suggesting he was urging others to hurry.
Reading peered around the shelf. The lights were no
longer pointing in his direction. He quickly advanced, his
weapon searching for a target. One of the flashlights was
lying on the floor, illuminating the scene, but he was still
too far to take a safe shot.

"Take him, I'll take care of her," said another voice in
perfect Queen's English. He saw one heave something
over their shoulder and start running, their flashlight

bouncing off into the distance as they struggled with their load.

The other one raised his weapon and pointed it at the body lying on the floor. Reading stopped and squeezed off two rounds. The man dropped in a heap, the beam of the other's flashlight disappearing in the distance. Reading raced forward, turning on his flashlight as he made sure no one else was there. All he found were two other bodies and Laura, lying in a heap, her would-be assassin bleeding out next to her. He dropped to his knees and checked her pulse. It was strong. He ran the beam of his flashlight across her body, searching for wounds, and found none.

He sprinted after the other light which he could no longer see. He followed the prints in the dusty floor and soon found they disappeared into a tunnel, a heavy door ajar, as well as a metal grate, several feet in, opened, the heavy chain that had kept it closed for generations unlocked.

Footfalls splashed through what turned out to be several inches of water farther in. Reading charged forward, and as he came around a bend, the flashlight was visible for a moment in the distance, then nothing. He ran headlong toward the next bend and a bright light cut through the darkness, as if a door to the outside had opened. A shot rang out and he dropped to the floor, his mouth filling with the rot of the storm sewer he now occupied.

He looked up and saw nothing. Climbing to his feet, spitting his mouth clean, he struggled forward, his body aching from the fall he had just taken. As the kinks worked themselves loose, he picked up speed, and arrived at the opening through which his adversary, and friend, had disappeared.

He poked his head out and saw a city street, the lights blazing. A shot ricocheted off the stone near his head. He dropped to one knee and pointed his weapon. A car engine roared, tires squealing as they gained traction. He rose and rushed outside, his weapon tracing the path of the vehicle, but not shooting.

He glanced behind him and saw a taxi. He waved it down and hopped in the passenger seat. "Follow that car!"

"Eh?"

Reading held up the gun, then pointed at the car as it raced away from them. "Follow!"

"Okay, I understand!" yelped the driver, putting the car in gear and flooring it. The car leaped forward as Reading yanked his cellphone off his hip, dialing Giasson's number. It was answered on the first ring.

"I'm in pursuit of a car, late model sedan, possibly dark green, partial plates Charlie Zulu One Four. They've got Jim. See if you can get me some local backup."

He could hear Giasson yelling orders then his voice cleared. "Where are you?"

"Here, talk to the driver."

He held the phone up to the man's ear as he turned a corner. He started talking, hopefully naming off streets as they passed them. Within minutes, however, it was obvious even to Reading where they were going. He looked up and saw a massive Airbus pass overhead, and he removed the phone from the driver's ear. "I think we're headed toward the airport!"

"I agree. We've contacted local authorities, but they won't be able to set anything up in time."

"Then it's up to us. Laura is down in that chamber. You've got to go get her."

"I'll take care of it." Reading could hear the reluctance in Giasson's voice. "I'm going to pass you on to Greco, one of my men. I'll tend to Professor Palmer personally."

The call was handed to someone and Reading pushed his phone against the driver's ear. "Rapido!" The driver gave him a quick glance then a sputtering of Italian as he pointed at the speedometer. Reading looked. 105kph. In city streets. He regretted looking, returning his attention to the other car in the distance. They hadn't lost them, but they hadn't gained on them either. They raced into the airport, the traffic light with it now well past midnight. The vehicle ahead weaved in and out of the few cars, heading deeper inside the massive complex, then screeched to a halt.

Two people ran up to meet the car with a wheelchair. The rear door flew open and a man climbed out, dragging a body behind him that he unceremoniously dumped into the chair. The rear backup lights activated, and the car raced backward, directly at them, as Reading watched the three men disappear with Acton into a building to their right. The cab driver slammed his brakes on as the car flew toward them. Reading threw his door open and stepped out, raising his weapon and emptying it into the rear window of the car. It veered to the right, hopping the curb and impaling itself on the concrete bollards designed to prevent car bombs from being driven into the terminal.

Reading ran forward, reloading his weapon, and as he rounded the driver's side, found him slumped over the wheel, a hole in the back of his head where Reading had shot him. He raced toward the building where Acton had been taken as curious onlookers and airport security gathered. Yells from behind him in Italian, some in English, ordered him to stop, but he ignored them. He darted into the building and out of the line of fire, rushing through what appeared to be a terminal aimed at the well-heeled. He raced past private charter kiosks lining either side and out onto the tarmac, security shut down for the evening. A Gulf V's engines whined as the steps retracted and it began to taxi.

Reading raised his weapon in desperation and fired several shots at the cockpit to no avail. He stopped, not wanting to risk hitting the fuel tanks.

It was over.

He had lost his friend.

He lowered the weapon in defeat, his shoulders slumping as he was quickly surrounded by dozens of armed security officers.

His radio squawked three times.

Ciampino Airport
Rome, Italy

Reading sat handcuffed in the back of a squad car as they verified his identity. His mind was unfocused, jumping from one crisis to the next. Acton had just been abducted aboard a private jet. They could be anywhere by now, and as far as he knew, nobody was looking into it. Laura was unconscious in an ancient hidden chamber, and he had no idea if Giasson had found her yet. Chaney was gone, likely injured, and perhaps even dead, as he couldn't see them cutting off the Pope's ear first.

Is Martin on the plane?

That was a good question. All three of them could be on the same plane, heading to jurisdictions unknown. He slammed the back of the seat in front of him.

There was a tap on the window.

He breathed a sigh of relief as he saw a smiling Giasson, his arm around Laura. Some words were said in Italian to the officer watching the car and the door opened. Reading climbed out and his cuffs were removed. Rubbing his wrists, he looked to Laura who rushed from Giasson's arms and into his. She quietly sobbed for a few moments, hugging him tight, then gently pushed away, wiping her eyes.

"Sorry, sometimes I'm such a girl."

Reading chuckled. "No need to apologize. Most men couldn't handle what you've been through today, let alone the past couple of years."

She smiled appreciatively at him as she wiped her eyes. He was almost twenty years her senior, and her natural beauty wasn't lost on him. She rarely wore makeup, not needing it, and when she did, it was only a slight application, unlike his ex-wife who would paste it on like icing. He smiled at the memory. He still loved her, though wasn't *in* love with her. She had given him a wonderful son whom he didn't see nearly enough, and enough bitter memories to cure himself of any thoughts of reconciliation. In fact, she had remarried years ago, but luckily for him, long after his son was old enough to ever call the man 'Dad.' That was reserved for him.

Laura finished drying her eyes as Giasson handed Reading his credentials. "Everything's been straightened out with the local authorities and you are free to go."

"The plane?"

"It's being tracked, but unfortunately has already left Italian airspace."

"Any idea who owns it?"

"It's a charter, apparently stolen."

"Stolen?"

"That's what the owner is saying. We're having him checked out. Apparently, he's known to police. It's just as likely that he took a large payment to say it was stolen."

"At least we know one thing though," said Laura.

"What's that?" asked Reading.

From behind her back, she swung a satchel hanging around her neck and opened the leather flap. Inside was what appeared to be an old book.

"Is that"—he stopped himself, looking around—"*it?*"

She nodded, concealing it once more. "James found it just as I was attacked. When Monsieur Giasson found me, it was lying by my side, which means the Order doesn't have James."

"What makes you say that?" asked Giasson.

"Because, if it were them, they would have taken the book, not him."

Reading agreed. "They were more concerned with taking Jim out of there than they were with any book. In fact, I don't believe the one I shot was even holding it."

"*If* we assume that is true, then we can ignore the Order. But, it's just as likely Professor Acton dropped the book without them knowing."

Laura shook her head. "You'd hear a pin drop in that place. If he dropped a book, they'd have noticed."

"You're most likely right, but I'm not yet willing to rule them out."

Reading had to agree with Giasson. His years of training as a cop told him not to jump to conclusions. Evidence could be misleading. His cop gut, however, told him they were dealing with two groups, as they had previously suspected, and he said so. "Regardless of who took Jim, we know we have two groups. The Order had no clue who the Triarii are, and we know their symbol was pasted on the walls after the Pope's disappearance."

Giasson pointed to a nearby car with Vatican plates. "Let's return to my office, I don't want to be away for too long. As to your point about two organizations, you may be right. On our way here, we received word that the ear belonged to our driver that was sent to pick up the professors. They were bluffing, hoping we would act before we knew the truth."

"So, either they didn't want to harm their prisoners, or they have no prisoners."

Reading helped Laura into the rear of the car and then joined her, Giasson in the front passenger seat, one of his men driving. Giasson turned to face them as they pulled away. "Considering they have killed, I see no reason why they wouldn't cut an ear off of someone like your former partner. I can understand not wanting to hurt His Holiness, but a police officer from London? I can't see them hesitating." He shook his head. "I don't think they have any prisoners."

"Agreed. I think we should assume they are merely taking advantage of the situation, and did not kill the Father, or kidnap Chaney or the Pope."

Laura cleared her throat. "You're forgetting one thing."

Both men turned to face her. "What's that?" asked Reading.

"They knew the Pope had been kidnapped."

Reading's head snapped toward Giasson. "When—"

"We didn't! There's been no press release on this, but we were forced to call the police in. Hundreds of our own people know by now, but the police have been bringing their resources inside, then informing them what's going on only when necessary, and not letting them leave. They've also been confiscating cellphones, so…" Giasson's voice drifted as he lost himself in thought.

"If the police have been sequestering their resources inside the Vatican, then the leak may be within."

Giasson looked at Reading. "Very few Roma resources are inside who have been informed. The K-9 units are searching, but they know not for whom, and most of the resources are outside, providing perimeter security. Crime scene investigators have been inside, gathering evidence. The first group processed the Father's room, which was no secret. A second group processed Chaney's room, which hasn't been made public, but they weren't told of His Holiness' disappearance. Only the third group of investigators who were allowed into His Holiness' chambers know he is missing, and they are the only ones who've been allowed to leave besides the liaison officers we've been working with. I've been assured they are all very trustworthy."

"All it takes is a slipped mention to a wife, mother, family member. This is news that is irresistible to share."

Laura pulled out her phone and began typing on the touch screen, and seconds later held it up, showing a BBC news report titled, "Pope Kidnapped?"

Reading cursed. "The story's out."

Giasson slammed his fist on the dash, his own string of profanity erupting before he made the sign of the cross, eyes tossed upward in apology. "This is not good." He turned to the driver. "Better take us through the back. We'll never get through any of the main gates."

The man glanced in his rearview mirror then changed lanes.

Reading turned to Laura, pointing to the satchel with his chin. "Is it wise to be carrying that around with you?"

Laura gripped it tighter. "Probably not, but this is a forbidden item, and we don't know who we can trust. I couldn't just leave it lying around."

Reading glanced at Giasson. "And you let her leave with this?"

"She insisted, we were in a hurry, and if it's a forbidden item, I don't want to even touch it." Giasson's eyes flitted to the satchel then away. He made the sign of the cross again.

Reading shook his head. "For a religious man, you're awfully superstitious."

The car screeched to a halt, throwing all of its occupants forward. Reading looked to see what had happened and saw a vehicle blocking the way. Four masked men climbed out, automatic weapons in hand. The driver slammed the car in reverse and floored it as they opened fire. Bullets ricocheted off the bullet-resistant skin as Reading tossed his body over Laura.

A cacophony of screeching metal jarred them to a halt. He twisted around to see what they had hit, and found another large SUV blocking their escape to the rear. Four more, dressed head to toe in black, exited, opening fire as a third vehicle pulled up on the driver's side. The rear end passenger side of the Vatican vehicle dropped several inches as the hot lead belching from the fully automatic weapons chewed away the run-flat-tire. Each of the other three tires were destroyed, leaving them stranded, though still safe inside. Giasson was yelling into his phone when the gunmen changed their focus to the driver and passenger side windows. As round after round pummeled the reinforced glass, it quickly became clear they would soon be through—the windows weren't designed for sustained volleys of gunfire, they were meant to stop the lone bullet of an assassin or crazed gunman. Not an unrelenting assault.

"Get us out of here!" yelled Reading.

The driver put the car in gear and pressed the gas. The car lurched forward on misshapen tires, but at least it moved. They slowly gained speed as the driver pulled onto the sidewalk, the exposed rims screeching on the cobblestone, barely heard over the continuing gunfire. Reading pushed Laura down behind the seats so she'd be protected by the much thicker doors of the car, then lay down prone on the back seat, his weapon pointing at the passenger side window that appeared ready to give.

Giasson pressed the button, leaning his seat back so he too could shield himself with the doors, the driver doing the same, pulling himself up with the steering wheel so he could see through the pockmarked windshield. "Give me your weapon!"

"Left shoulder!"

Giasson reached over and pulled the driver's weapon from its shoulder holster then, with a gun in each hand, took up position, covering the front windows as best he could.

Reading looked down and saw Laura flipped over, her head and back against the door opposite him, weapon drawn and aimed directly at the window above his head, determination on her face, fear nowhere to be seen. His admiration for her grew even more as he realized how formidable she was in the face of danger. She might let her emotions out when the situation permitted, but when the shit hit the fan, she was all business. This was the woman he had met in London two years ago. And this was the woman he could rely on to watch his back. He flashed her a smile, which she returned.

The window above his head exploded.

Yelling from outside had Laura's eyes widening slightly, then two rounds roared from her weapon. There was a scream directly on the other side of the door, then two more shots from Laura's weapon silenced them. The window above her head shattered and Reading prepared himself. One of the attackers raced forward, gun in hand, flame belching from the muzzle as bullets rained over his head. He squeezed the trigger, placing a bullet in the hostile's forehead, and he dropped out of sight.

Laura fired twice more as the rear windshield shattered. Giasson rolled over in his seat, the weapon in his right hand jerked up several times as he fired, leaving Reading almost deaf. He saw a hand reach inside the car, grasping for the door handle. They found it and pulled. Laura yelped as she fell backward. The car, still moving, albeit slowly, bounced up on the left-hand curb, swinging the door open, leaving most of the upper half of Laura's body hanging out of the car. Reading lunged forward and grabbed her by her belt as her arms swung over her head, clasping her gun in both hands. She fired two shots and he saw a body collapse to the ground as the open door revealed what only she could see from her upside-down position, mere inches from the pavement. He yanked with all his might and dragged her inside. The car bounced up another curb and the door slammed shut.

The driver's side window was the next to go and their driver cried out as he shook from multiple gunshots slamming into his chest. His foot pushed on the accelerator as the car careened out of control and into the side of a building. Giasson squeezed off covering fire as Reading reached forward and attempted to put the car in reverse, the engine still revving.

There was a loud bang and smoke billowed from the engine compartment, briefly filling the entire area with acrid fumes. Reading leaped across the back seat, poking his head through the shattered passenger side window, and could see no one. He opened the door, grabbed Laura, and pulled her along with him. Giasson's door open and Reading reached out for him. Together, the three moved forward and emerged from the smoke seconds later, much to the surprise of one of their attackers.

Reading put a bullet in the man's head then pushed Laura forward. A line of parked cars along their side of the street provided them with some cover as he shoved Laura between two of them, he and Giasson taking up covering positions on either bumper. Gunfire erupted from their former position, concentrating on the car they were hiding behind, the unreinforced windows shattering instantly. Reading and Giasson squeezed off several rounds, quieting the enemy, though only for a few moments.

"Can you fit under this?" Reading pointed at the car behind them. Laura checked and nodded. "Then go, as far as you can, as fast as you can." She was about to open her mouth to refuse when he shook his head. "Go! Now!" She dropped and slid on her belly under the car.

Giasson squeezed off another round. "I'm getting low on ammo."

"Last mag for me," replied Reading. "Make them count." Heeding his own advice, he waited until he could see one of the black-clad attackers before shooting, dropping him in a heap, and sending the others ducking for cover. Yet each time, the attack resumed, and they kept getting closer. It was only a matter of moments before they would be out of ammo and helpless. Giasson fired two more rounds then ejected the empty mag.

"I'm out."

Reading fired again and ejected his mag too. Bullets continued to rain down on the car as the three remaining attackers sprayed the area with bullets, lack of ammo apparently not a problem for them. Suddenly, from the other side of the street, three distinct shots rang out and the three attackers dropped, bathing the area in silence. With his ears still ringing, he slowly raised his head, and through the smoke and haze, he saw Laura slowly rise from behind a car on the other side of the street.

"Are you two okay?"

"Yes!" yelled Reading. "Keep down, there may be more!"

Laura dropped back down, moving forward one more car, her weapon still pointed in the direction of their attackers. But their guns remained silent. Reading rolled out from behind the car and looked at the shredded mess that had been a much-maligned British sports car. The last few shards of the rear window collapsed inside, a piece of cardboard with writing and a phone number the only thing left.

At a crouch, he ran forward and grabbed the weapon from the nearest dead attacker and spotted Giasson doing the same on the other side of the car. Together, with Laura on their flank, they advanced. After finding several bodies, Reading heard one moan. He rushed forward and kicked the man's weapon from his hand. "I've got a live one here!"

He grabbed a plastic tie from the utility belt he was still wearing and flipped him over, tying off his wrists and ankles.

He's awfully light.

Reading flipped the man back over and tore off his mask. And gasped. The fiery eyes of a woman glared at him. She spat then winced in pain, muttering curses in Italian. "Miss, don't waste your breath on Italian curses. I don't understand a word of it." He stood, taking note of his companions' positions. "This one's a woman!"

"So's this one!" Giasson bent over another writhing form. Reading tossed him two ties and advanced. He reached their car and shook his head. It appeared as if it had been through a warzone, the outside riddled with hundreds of dents and gouges, most of the windows torn out. He saw Giasson check the driver then shake his head at Reading, making the sign of the cross.

They continued forward then raced for cover as they heard the squeal of tires. The rear SUV that had blocked their escape pulled a 180 and tore away from the scene as the three of them emptied their weapons into the back of it. It careened around a corner and out of sight. Sirens wailed in the distance, and the road filled with the flashing blue lights of the Polizia Municipale arriving just after the nick of time.

All three of them raised their hands, Reading and Giasson holding up their identification as the police poured from their vehicles, shouting orders as they took in the carnage before them. All three of them slowly lowered their weapons to the ground, then stood, waiting to be searched.

It didn't take long for their identities to be sorted out, and as a gurney with one of the wounded women passed, a hand reached out for Laura.

"Do you have it?" she gasped.

"Yes."

"Please, let me see it."

"You try to kill us, and you expect favors?"

"Please, I'm dying. It is everything I have lived for."

Laura looked at Reading who shrugged. She flipped the cover of the satchel open and Giasson spun on his heel, turning his back to her. She pulled the book out and held it so the young woman could see the cover.

Tears filled her eyes then poured down her cheeks, her lips rapidly moving in silent prayer. The paramedics resumed their push to the ambulance. The woman forced her head up so she could see Laura. "You are a woman. Read it. You will understand why we did what we did." Her head collapsed in exhaustion as the gurney came to a sudden stop, the paramedics yelling in Italian as one began to perform CPR. They all watched as one of their attackers became a little more human, and died.

Laura stared at the book still in her hand, then returned it to the satchel. "I don't know how I feel about that," she said to no one in particular.

"Come, let's rest." Reading put a hand on her shoulder and guided her away from the scene. The three of them moved down the road then sat on the rear bumper of the car that had proven to be their last stand. Reading smacked the trunk. "I never thought I'd say anything positive about one of these, but this lassie saved our lives."

Giasson agreed. "She certainly took a beating, but"—he reached over and pulled the sign out of the back window—"I think you'd be alone in saying anything good about her."

"Why, what does it say?"

"Well, roughly translated, it says, "For sale. As reliable as my ex-husband. I got this piece of shit in the divorce. I wanted the dog."

They all burst out laughing, the tension of the past half hour slowly easing. A car with Vatican plates roared up beside them, a man erupting from the driver side causing everyone in the area to spin toward him, weapons drawn.

"Scusa! Scusa!" he yelled, realizing what he had just done.

Giasson waved off the locals and approached the man. "I'll lecture you tomorrow. Today, just get us back home."

The man nodded, returning to the car, waiting for his sore and tired passengers to moan and groan their way into their seats. Minutes later, they pulled into the garage of a building situated a couple of hundred feet from the massive wall surrounding the Vatican. The door closed behind them. The driver reached up and pressed a button, revealing another garage door in front of them. It slowly rolled up and they pulled through. He pressed the button again, closing the second door, then a series of lights turned on, stretching ahead of them.

"Bloody hell! What's this?" asked Reading.

"Secret entrance. We rarely use it, but I think today is a good day for it."

They drove the short distance and came to an interior gate opened by a pair of saluting Swiss Guards. Moments later, they pulled into a secluded courtyard, the driver parking near the entrance of one of the buildings.

Reading climbed out then helped Laura. Giasson said something to his driver, then he too left the vehicle. Screams of delight came from the building, causing them all to spin toward the source. Two small girls raced through the doors, followed by a striking woman. The two girls rushed toward Giasson who knelt down, his arms outstretched, a huge smile spreading ear to ear.

"Jade! Zoé!" he cried as he grabbed them in his arms and picked them up, placing big kisses on both their cheeks. "What are you doing here?" he asked in English, no doubt for the benefit of his guests.

"We heard the news, and figured we wouldn't be seeing you for some time," said the woman as she approached, giving Giasson a tender kiss on the lips, her gloved hand gently touching his cheek. He lowered the children to the ground and turned to Reading and Laura.

"May I present my wife, Marie-Claude, and my children, Jade and Zoé. These are my friends, Agent Hugh Reading of Interpol, and Professor Laura Palmer of University College London. They are helping me on"—he paused, then shrugged—"the case. I guess it isn't a secret anymore."

"No, the entire world knows now," said his wife. "I brought you a couple of fresh changes of clothes, plus some meals you can reheat, and some toiletries, just in case you don't get home tonight."

"Most likely."

She pulled both children close, covering one ear with her body, the other with her hands. "Was that gunfire I heard?"

He glanced at the children. "Yes."

"Were you—"

"Yes. But we're okay, so don't worry."

156

She gave him a cheek. "Don't tell me not to worry, it's my job. You certainly won't."

He chuckled and gave her a kiss. "Don't worry, ma chérie, I'm okay, and with these two crack shots"—he motioned to Reading and Laura—"I have no need to worry about any ambush."

Marie-Claude's eyebrows shot up as she stared at Laura. "I thought you were a professor?"

"I am. But I lead a violent social life."

Everyone started laughing except, at first, Marie-Claude, who finally joined in, waving her hand in the air. "I don't want to know! I don't want to know! As long as my bébé is safe." She patted the children on their backs. "Now, say goodnight to Papa, and we'll go home so he can work!"

The two children gave their father hugs and kisses, then were led off by their mother, waving until they were out of sight. Giasson wiped a tear from the corner of his eye, watching them until they disappeared.

"You have a beautiful family," said Laura.

"Merci. They are my most valuable possession."

Reading found himself thinking of his son, a twinge of regret at not being there for most of his life racking his heart.

A man rushed through the door and ran up to Giasson. "Sir, they've intercepted the plane!"

"Who?" asked Giasson as they followed the man through the doors.

"The Turkish Air Force."

Over Turkish Airspace

"This is Turkish Air Force Flight Izmir Four-Three to Gulf Five Flight out of Rome. You have illegally entered Turkish airspace. Acknowledge, over."

Again, Major Erten was met with nothing but static. He glanced over to his wingman. "I'm going to see if I can get a look in the cockpit."

"Copy that."

Erten pushed ahead on the throttle, adding a little speed, and peered over at the cockpit not fifty feet from him, a shaft of moonlight breaking through the clouds overhead, briefly illuminating the pilot's position.

Is he…?

He flipped his F-16C Fighting Falcon on its back, positioning himself so he was staring directly down and into the unauthorized flight.

"He's asleep!"

"Izmir Four-Three, Command. Repeat your last transmission, over."

"Command, Izmir Four-Three. He's asleep, I repeat, the pilot is asleep, over!"

"Izmir Four-Three, Command. Confirm your last transmission, did you say the pilot is asleep, over?"

"Command, Izmir Four-Three. Confirmed, he is asleep. Or dead. There appears to be a hole in the canopy. I will try to get a visual on the passengers, over."

He righted his plane and took up a position off the left wing, his wingman doing the same on the other side.

"See anything?"

"Negative, I can't see anything. Most of the blinds are closed."

Erten leaned over and squinted, peering through the windows, but with the cloud cover, could see little. He descended slightly, and for a moment, another shaft of moonlight illuminated one of the windows, revealing a passenger, head slumped against the glass, then nothing as the cloud cover returned.

"I've got one, asleep or dead. Let me call it in." He activated his comm. "Command, Izmir Four-Three. We've confirmed at least one passenger asleep or dead, no other activity detected, over."

"Flight Izmir Four-Three, Command. Continue surveillance and await further instructions, over."

"Command, Flight Izmir Four-Three. Roger that, over."

Erten advanced for another view of the cockpit, to see if there had been any change, yet in the pit of his stomach knew there wouldn't be. Obviously, something had gone terribly wrong, and the plane was without oxygen.

And all aboard were doomed.

Corpo della Gendarmeria Office
Palazzo del Governatorato, Vatican City

Reading held the door open for Laura then nodded at Giasson behind his desk. All had showered and changed after their ordeal, but were still sore and tired. Reading glanced at his watch. *3:37am.* Giasson was on the phone, speaking in Italian, then slammed the receiver down, the vein near his temple throbbing.

"What's wrong?" asked Reading.

Giasson sighed, his hands clasped over his head. His eyes rolled up to look at Reading, his chin remaining down, only inches from the desk on which his elbows rested. "The plane is not responding."

Laura sat. "Well, that's not exactly unexpected, is it?"

Giasson shook his head as he leaned back. "No, you don't understand. The Turkish Air Force challenged them, and there was no response, so they took a closer look and it appears the pilot is passed out or dead, along with the passengers."

"James!" cried Laura, her hand darting to her mouth, tears filling her eyes.

Reading reached out and squeezed her arm. "You mean they depressurized?" he asked softly.

"Most likely." Giasson rose and rounded the desk, kneeling in front of Laura. "I'm sorry, but there's nothing they can do but let the plane continue until it runs out of fuel." He glanced at Reading. "And hope that they survive the crash."

"You mean there's still a chance?"

"They're at about six thousand meters—twenty thousand feet. They could have just passed out from the thin air if they depressurized. The human body can survive in that state for a while, but with no one to fly the plane..." Giasson clearly didn't want to finish the thought.

"But why wouldn't the pilot have gone on oxygen?" asked Reading.

Giasson rose and returned to his desk. "I don't know. Apparently, there's a hole in the canopy, which may explain it."

Reading's chest tightened and his voice cracked. "It's my fault."

Giasson and Laura looked at him. "What do you mean?" asked Giasson.

"I took a few shots at the cockpit before they took off. I must have damaged it."

Laura patted his arm. "You were trying to save him. Don't blame yourself."

Reading put his hand over hers and squeezed. "I know, but still…"

I killed my friend.

He sighed and looked at Laura, giving her a weak smile. "Quite the day we've had."

Giasson cleared his throat. "You do know that with Professor Acton confirmed on board, in all likelihood DI Chaney and His Holiness are as well."

Reading frowned. "I realize that. And I grieve with you at your loss, at the world's loss, but forgive me if I focus on my friends, first."

Giasson dropped his head in acknowledgment, closing his eyes. He yawned then glanced at the clock on the wall. "I need sleep. We all do." He rose. "I'll have you shown to your quarters and wake you as soon as I hear any more news. They think it will only be a couple of hours. Apparently, the plane wasn't fully fueled. I guess they were expecting a short run."

Laura said nothing, still in shock. Reading rose and helped her up by the elbow, then they both followed Giasson into the outer office where there wasn't a dry eye in the place. Reading knew from experience what was going through their minds. He had been on enough kidnapping cases during his career that had ended with the death of the victim. You felt helpless, you felt sick.

You felt like a failure.

Vatican Guest Quarters
Apostolic Palace, The Vatican

Reading woke with a start, his ears straining to hear what had disturbed him. There was a knock at the door. "One moment!" he called as he rolled out of bed, throwing his shirt on and shoving his legs in his pants. He walked to the door in bare feet then opened it.

Giasson stood there, subdued. "It is time."

Reading sighed. "I'll get Laura and meet you in your office."

Giasson turned and left as Reading walked down the hall and knocked on Laura's door. There was no response. He knocked a little harder and he heard a faint, "Come in."

He turned the knob and opened the door slightly. "It's me, can I come in?"

"Yes."

He stepped inside and found Laura still lying under the covers. "It's time."

She stared without saying anything.

"Five minutes in the hall?"

She nodded.

Reading closed the door and returned to his room, making a rapid toilette, then hurriedly finished dressing. He stepped out into the hallway to find Laura already waiting for him.

How the bloody hell did she finish before me, and look that good?

"How are you holding up?"

She shrugged as they walked toward Security. "As good as can be expected, I suppose. It's not every day you know when and how the one you love is going to die." Her voice cracked and a tear rolled down her cheek. She brushed the back of her hand across her face, ridding it of her heartbreak. They hurried through the corridors and finally to the Security Office, Giasson standing in the pit, a large television screen surrounded by most of the staff. Reading looked at the screen and saw they were watching a CNN feed showing a plane, and a banner highlighted in red: *Plane About to Enter Iranian Airspace.*

"What's the status?" asked Reading.

"They're about to enter Iranian airspace, so the Turkish escort is about to break off."

"Any estimate on fuel?"

"No more than an hour left, maybe minutes."

They all returned their attention to the screen.

"For those of you just joining us, you're watching live footage of a Gulfstream Five plane, allegedly stolen from the Rome international airport late last night. It entered Turkish airspace approximately two hours ago and has not responded to repeated hails. The Turkish Air Force has issued a statement indicating they believe there has been a depressurization of the cockpit and cabin, leaving the passengers and flight crew, including the pilot, unconscious. Some of you may remember the tragic loss of golfer Payne Stewart in a similar incident in 1999. As this is a stolen plane, we have no idea who is on board, however with news the Pope, the head of the Roman Catholic Church, has been kidnapped, it is feared he may be on board, and this is a kidnapping gone terribly wrong."

"What have the Iranians said?"

Giasson indicated for them to follow him into his office, and closing his door, took a seat on the edge of his desk. "They're threatening to shoot it down as soon as it crosses the border."

"What?" Reading looked at Laura, her face flush with anger. "Don't they know who could be on that plane?"

"They're claiming it's a CIA plane, and the story of it being out of control, and possibly having His Holiness on board, is Western propaganda, designed to make Iran look bad if they defend their sovereign airspace."

Laura shook her head. "That's just ridiculous. God help us all if nutters like that get the bomb."

164

"Agreed." Reading never concerned himself that the Iranian's would use the bomb officially. They knew they'd be wiped off the map, and though millions of them believed they'd be heading straight to Paradise, their leadership would hedge their bets and remain on Mother Earth as long as they could.

But that was the problem, as he saw it. There were enough of them that *were* nutters, and what would *they* do with the bomb? Would it be "stolen" and given to the likes of Hezbollah who were certifiable? Would the terrorist groups they supported be supplied with weapons to wreak havoc on the West, on Israel? People pointed to Pakistan as an example of a Muslim nation with the bomb that didn't use it. But what happened? The scientist who developed the bomb for them promptly sold the information to Iran, North Korea, Libya, and others. And the only reason the bomb hadn't been used by Pakistan was that the military still essentially controlled that country. Why else would the United States send billions of dollars a year to a country providing safe haven to the Taliban? Because they couldn't risk the country collapsing, and nuclear weapons falling into the hands of the fanatics that made up a significant portion of the population.

Reading sighed.

What a screwed up world we live in.

A round of cheers rose from the other side of the glass.

Iranian Airspace

"This is Angelfire One to Iranian aircraft. Break off or we will be forced to open fire, over."

There was no response, not that Lieutenant Colonel Braddock was expecting any. At least not at first. Scrambled from the USS Abraham Lincoln Aircraft Carrier two hours ago, and refueled over Iraq for possible extended combat, they were on a Hail Mary mission, a name he found ironic if the reports were true and the Pope was indeed on this plane about to be shot down.

"Angelfire One to Iranian aircraft. We are on a rescue mission. Break off or we will be forced to open fire. This is your final warning, over."

Again, no response.

He switched channels. "Hornet's Nest, Angelfire One. Requesting permission to engage, over."

"Hornet's Nest, Angelfire One. Permission granted, over."

Braddock's pulse quickened slightly as the reality of combat took over. "Okay boys, let's splash 'em." He glanced at his wingman over his right shoulder. "Full House, you're with me, we've got the two on the left. The rest of you, break 'em down by the numbers, left to right. Let's get this over with quick, and watch your threat alarms for SAMs."

He jerked his stick to the left as the acknowledgments came through, the rest of the wing of twelve planes breaking off to line up their attacks. They were dealing with six targets, all ancient MiG-29s, no match for their F/A-18 Super Hornets.

This will be over in seconds.

Braddock lined up with the rapidly approaching targets and marked the first from the left, then the second. "Angelfire One, targets marked, preparing to fire."

"Angelfire Three, targets marked, preparing to fire on your command."

"Angelfire Five, targets marked, preparing to fire on your command."

"Angelfire One to Angelfire Three and Five, fire on my mark." He took a breath, flipping his weapons selector to his AIM 9 Sidewinder missiles. "Fire!"

There was a slight jerk as the two missiles dropped off his wings then sped forward, their propellant igniting. A quick glance to his right showed four other missiles streaking toward their targets. The Iranians scrambled, breaking off their approach, but it was too late, the missiles having acquired their heat signature. The contrails in the air drew paths to destruction as each missile adjusted its course, closing inexorably on their targets like unstoppable juggernauts. Within seconds, all six missiles made contact, erasing their targets from the sky, thick black smoke all that remained as the airframes of the MiGs dropped to the barren ground below.

Braddock checked his scope and found everything clear. No SAMs had been launched, and with the jamming gear they were using, he crossed his fingers they would be all right. "Hornet's Nest, Angelfire One. The road has been cleared, I say again, the road has been cleared. Deploy Dove Collector, over."

He looked at the scope and saw Dove Collector appear behind them.

There's no way this is going to work.

To Captain Shaun Richards, it sounded stupid.

Dove Collector? Sounds like some wacko who hoards soap.

There was an entire group of people who all they did was generate cool sounding names for ops, and often they managed to have them fit the spirit of the mission.

Who the hell ever expected the Pope to be kidnapped and held in a plane with no oxygen?

He shook his head.

But Dove Collector was the best they could come up with?

"Two minutes!" yelled the crew chief over his mike. Richards gave the thumbs-up and double-checked his harness. He watched the grappling crew take knees as the rear door of the C-17 Globemaster III opened. Wind whipped through the cargo hold and the cold bit at his exposed skin. His heart raced as the excitement of the moment took over. He had never done this before, but the principle was simple. This was just something for which pilots never trained.

He glanced over his shoulder at the two other pilots behind him. They both acknowledged him, the closest slapping his shoulder in respect. He would be first. And if he failed, there were only two more tries aboard this plane, and judging from what the fuel situation should be, there would be no time for additional tries.

They had to succeed.

"One minute!"

He checked his chute, something he was more familiar with from training, and took a steadying breath. He pushed against the wind, and his nerves, as he approached the door. The tail of the Gulf V appeared to the left, slightly below them, as the engines of the C-17 strained to overtake her. The grappling crew knelt at the far corner to get the best angle on their target. One, a corporal, held what appeared to be a rocket launcher on his shoulder, with a shell protruding from one end, attached to a long coil of metal cable lying on the floor behind him. His partner, a sergeant, sat to his side, a second shell at the ready.

"Execute when ready!"

The young man—Richards put him at no more than twenty—shuffled forward on his knee, getting the best angle he could, then suddenly a loud sound drowned out the howling wind and screaming engines for a split second as the hydraulic launcher fired the round at its target.

They all strained to see what happened, but it was obvious by the shaking of the young corporal's head. His partner loaded another round, and this time the corporal moved much farther out onto the ramp, his harness stretched to the limit. He took a much sharper angle, compensating for the several hundred mile per hour winds it would hit the moment it cleared the fuselage.

He fired.

Richards was close enough to see the round leave the launcher and disappear to the left, the long coil of cable streaming after it rapidly. The round reappeared and smacked the side of the plane, just three feet from the cabin door, the aerodynamic housing of the shell shattering, the hardened arrow it had been covering piercing the skin of the aircraft then unfurling inside the fuselage. The sergeant grabbed the end of the line, already secured inside the C-17, and cranked the cable tight. With most of the slack removed, Richards shuffled into position. The sergeant hooked him up as the order was given for the plane to rise.

He grabbed the cable stretching between the two planes and, hand-over-hand, moved to the edge of the platform, accompanied by the grappling crew who gripped him on either side. Outside, he watched the Gulf V drop from his perspective as the C-17 rose to let gravity do its job. His heart hammered, adrenaline fueling him with the courage necessary.

"Get ready!"

Richards turned around, lowering himself so the two lines hooking him to the cable took most of his weight. His hands still grasping the cable, he hooked his feet over the line and, freed from the deck of the plane, his full weight pulled on the cable. He lowered his head so he could see out the back of the plane. The Gulf V was out of sight, below his field of vision for the moment.

"Go! Go! Go!"

Richards gulped.

And the grappling crew let go.

And nothing happened.

He had expected to slide, but he didn't. He pulled with his hands, and whatever friction had been holding him in place let go and he began to move. The deck of the ramp disappeared, and all he saw was the ground below. He raised his head slightly, seeking his destination, and quickly found it, racing toward him as he slid rapidly down the cable.

"Shit!"

He squeezed the handbrake, slowing slightly as gravity did its job—too well—hurtling him toward the large piece of metal in the sky. His pulse roared in his ears, his breath rapid as the Gulf V quickly filled his view. He saw the door, then where the hook had pierced the fuselage.

Please, God, let this work.

He had talked to his wife and newborn just this morning. It was supposed to be a routine day. He wasn't even scheduled to fly. And now here he was, twenty thousand feet in the air, sucking oxygen through a mask, a performer in the ultimate high wire act.

I love the Air Force!

The cable jerked and he was whipped up then back down. His eyes focused like lasers on the other end of the cable.

Did it come loose?

170

He was sure it had moved. He let go of the brake. He had to get off this line fast. He raced toward the plane, the wind buffeting him, tossing him to and fro, as he desperately hung on.

He slammed against the fuselage.

And it hurt.

The pain shocked him for a moment and he lost focus, the elbow and kneepads protecting his joints, but not the rest of his body.

"Hit the brake! Hit the brake!" yelled the crew chief through his comm.

He remembered where he was.

Sliding down the side of the Gulf V, toward the engines at the rear.

"Shit!"

He squeezed the handbrake as hard as he could, bringing himself to a halt. Repositioning his knees so the suction cups attached to the pads could do their job, he looked forward at the door now twenty feet away. And he swore he could see one of the prongs of the hook holding his life in the balance now outside of the fuselage. Grabbing onto the cable in front of him, he pulled then released the brake, repositioning it ahead. He repeated this procedure, advancing inches at a time, his muscles screaming, his body protesting as the wind flowing down the aerodynamic skin of the plane slammed into him, tossing his battered and bruised body against the unforgiving aluminum.

He was getting closer. Only feet away now. But with each tug, he could see more of the hook that had pierced the fuselage revealing itself, signaling it could let go at any moment.

Who the hell came up with this plan?

He pulled again and the grappling hook jerked loose some more, and in a panic, he released the brake to take off the tension. He slid down the side of the aircraft then regained his senses and gently squeezed the brake, coming to a jarring halt as the suction cups on his elbows and knees grabbed hold. He looked up and saw the hook was still holding, though for how long, he had no clue. He lowered his head to his chest, calming himself.

And gasped.

Right in front of him was a label that read, "ESCAPE WINDOW RELEASE PUSH." He looked and found a panel with more instructions. "OPEN DOOR. PULL HANDLE UP PUSH WINDOW IN." He grasped at the panel, and with both hands now in the housing he had just revealed, the pressure was now off the cable. He pulled forward and saw the handle. He grabbed it and pushed up. Above him, he could see the window move slightly. He freed his right hand and reached up, pushing on the window.

It budged.

Just half an inch. But it fueled him with hope. He pushed again and managed to get his fingers inside. He inhaled deeply and let go of the handle with his left hand, swinging his arm up as hard and as fast as he could, shoving the fingers into the tiny crevice of hope he had found. His feet were now dangling behind him, the slack taken off the cable, his fingers screaming in agony. He pulled with all his might and got his helmet even with his hands, then pushed with his head against the window.

It gave.

And continued to give. The opening became wider and wider, and his head pushed through when suddenly he had a view of an empty seat. He pushed with his arms and dropped inside and onto the floor.

He flipped on his back, unhooked the two lines still attached to the cable, and instantly the metal lifeline whipped out the window.

He caught his breath then activated his comm. "I'm inside, retract the cable!"

"Roger that!"

He pushed the window closed then peered out as the expandable grappler contracted then sprung loose, whipping clear of the fuselage as it rapidly coiled back into the C-17. He looked about him, finding several people in their seats and no signs of life. He rushed forward toward the cockpit, stripping off his knee and elbow pads, not wasting any time on checking if the passengers were alive. None of them would be if he couldn't land the plane.

He punched in the code for the reinforced cockpit door, provided by the owner of the plane in Rome, and yanked it open. Inside, the pilot was still sitting in his seat, his head lolled to the side, no oxygen mask on. He moved forward and saw why. The cockpit window had exploded, and it appeared something had hit the pilot in the head, a large lump and a lot of blood indicating he was probably out cold from the moment of the emergency.

Richards dropped into the empty copilot's seat and strapped in. He quickly oriented himself, then jacked into the plane's communications.

"Hornet's Nest, Pegasus One, I'm about to take control, over."

"Pegasus One, Hornet's Nest. Copy that, over."

He flipped the switch to take control from the pilot, then disengaged the autopilot. Gripping the controls, he gently banked to the left. Out the cockpit window, he saw the C-17 turning in the opposite direction, back toward Iraqi airspace. He was heading back to Turkish airspace, the closest airstrip within thirty minutes of his position. He looked at his fuel gauge.

Oh shit!

Corpo della Gendarmeria Office
Palazzo del Governatorato, Vatican City

Cheers, tears, and hugs were exchanged. Laura simply collapsed in her chair, exhausted. Reading placed his hands on her shoulders and she reached up with one hand and squeezed his. The ordeal had been indescribable. When they had received word of what was happening, the US Air Force arranged for the Vatican to receive a feed of the live audio communications between the rescue crew. None of them could believe what they were hearing, and when the Americans shared the video feed with the press, shot from the tail section of the rescue aircraft, her heart had been on a rollercoaster of hope and despair. When it looked like all was about to be lost, with the pilot sliding down the side of the plane toward the engine, she had turned away, unable to watch, knowing if he were sucked in, not only would he be dead, so would everyone on the plane.

But he hadn't died.

And he was now in control, heading back to Turkish airspace.

"I've got bingo fuel, say again, I've got bingo fuel, over."

The room was silenced.

"Say again, Pegasus One?"

"I have bingo fuel. What's the nearest safe location to ditch, over?"

Reading's grip on her shoulder tightened.

"Pegasus One, Hornet's Nest. Negative within five hundred klicks of your position. You're east of a mountain range. Confirm insufficient fuel, over?"

"Hornet's Nest, Pegasus One. That's a negative. Onboard computer is estimating fuel exhaustion within twenty minutes, over."

"Pegasus One, Hornet's Nest. We have a level area outside the Green Zone, eight-zero klicks from your

174

current location, bearing two-eight-zero. Can you make it, over?"

"Hornet's Nest, Pegasus One. Confirmed, should be able to make it. Have rescue standing by, over."

"Pegasus One, Hornet's Nest. Rescue standing by inside Green Zone, moving to intercept, over."

"Copy that, Hornet's Nest, Pegasus One, out."

The radio fell silent, the entire room turning its attention back to the screen. The Gulf V was now only a dot on the horizon highlighted by a superimposed circle as the rescue plane headed back to Iraqi airspace. Moments later, the talking heads replaced the live feed with replays of the rescue being analyzed and dissected by a flurry of ex-military commentators and civilian reporters ignorant of how risky and incredible a rescue had just taken place, likely disappointed it had succeeded, a spectacular failure a better ratings grabber.

Murmurs then chatter filled the room as the collected security and Papal staff who had converged on one of the few rooms with a large screen, and initially the only room with the live feed, debated what would happen next.

Laura took a long breath. "Where will they take the bodies?"

Reading let go of her shoulders and rounded the chair. "They're not dead yet."

Laura smiled at him, knowing he was just comforting her. "I know. But we all know the chances of them surviving this are slim to none." She turned back to Giasson. "Where would they take"—she paused—"*them?*"

Giasson shook his head. "I don't know, but I'll find out."

"Very well." Laura stood. "Have my plane readied, and we'll go there to meet them." She walked toward the exit. "I'll be in my room packing."

"Don't you want to wait—"

"I do not want to be witness to James' death." Her voice cracked. She stepped through the door, holding her breath, as if letting the air escape would allow that last piece, that last bit of control, to flee with it. She strode with purpose, with resolve, not making eye contact with anyone, navigating the winding corridors as if on automatic pilot, finally reaching her room. She closed the door behind her, pressed her back into the wall, and slid down it, her head buried in her hands as tears, long held back, gushed forth.

"Oh, James!"

48 Miles Outside the Green Zone
Iran

Richards gripped the controls, the plane in a steep dive as he rid himself of nearly twenty thousand feet of altitude while at the same time trying not to gain too much airspeed. An impossible task. For now, he decided getting rid of altitude first was the best bet, then he could worry about airspeed. He just had to get low so he could hunt for the level area referred to by Command.

He wondered if anyone was even alive behind him. Had any of this been worth it? Was he going to die with a few already dead people behind him, or was he at least dying from a failed attempt at saving the Pope? He closed his eyes for a moment, picturing his parents, and how hard they'd take the news.

His eyes shot open.

I wonder if they're watching this at home.

They were supplying the feed to the news organizations so they would have some ass-covering material when the Iranians bellyached to the UN about their airspace being violated, but when he had volunteered for the mission, he hadn't even thought of the fact his parents might watch his own death.

I'm so sorry.

Though he wasn't dead yet. If he could just find this level area, without too many rocks, he might just land her on her belly and skid to a halt. He wasn't too worried about breaking up. He might survive that. It was burning alive that worried him more.

8000 feet.

He ripped his oxygen mask off and gulped in some fresh air. It was still a little thin, but breathable. If anyone were alive back there, they might just come to. Hopefully, they'd have the sense to stick to their seats.

Should I make an inflight announcement?

6000 feet.

He decided against it. Anyone with half a brain should realize they were in a steep dive and it was an emergency situation. He looked at the horizon and his heart leaped. The rocky terrain below him appeared to level out in the distance.

4000 feet.

"Hornet's Nest, Pegasus One. I think I have a visual on the level area, ETA three minutes, over."

"Pegasus One, Hornet's Nest. Copy that, rescue is already inbound, ETA your location ten minutes, over."

2000 feet.

He pulled back slightly on the stick, leveling out his descent. Easing off on the power, he applied some flaps to lower their speed. He reached for the landing gear, then thought better of it. The last thing he needed was the nose gear collapsing and sending them head over heels. As the rock-strewn terrain below him whipped by, he could clearly see the level stretch ahead, and it was huge. There would be no problem coming to a stop, but from this distance, he couldn't tell if it was clear of rocks.

1000 feet.

He activated the internal communications. "If anyone is alive back there, buckle up and assume crash positions. We'll be landing inside of two minutes." He thought about what he had just said.

Could have chosen something more formal.

He chuckled.

Kiss your asses goodbye, we're goin' in!

500 feet.

With the slight down angle, he still had a good view of the ground, and it was level now for as far as the eye could see. In fact, if he didn't know better, it appeared to be farmland. The morning sun, just rising behind him, cast long shadows across the landscape, shadows that indicated something he could hit. And they were everywhere.

250 feet.

He had no choice now. He was going in whether he liked it or not.

Please, God, if there was ever a time to answer a prayer, this is it.

He pulled up gently, his aim to land with the nose slightly more up than usual to try and use drag to slow them even further. He eased back on the throttle some more, and adjusted the flaps. He eyed his airspeed.

Fine for a traditional landing.

100 feet.

He took in a long breath and gripped the controls. "Hornet's Nest, Pegasus One. I'm going in, over."

"Copy that, Pegasus One. Good luck."

"From your lips to God's ears."

50 feet.

He pushed forward slightly, leveling the aircraft so the tail didn't hit at too sharp an angle, and as he did, the ground came into view on either side of him, but not in front.

25 feet.

He powered down and applied more flaps, killing his speed some more. He wasn't concerned about stalling or proper procedure. He just needed to land as slowly and as gently as possible. The nose leveled and he could see ahead again.

Oh shit!

He pushed the stick forward and threw his engines into reverse, applying full flaps. The plane slammed into the ground, not as gently as he would have liked, yet he didn't care. All he was focusing on was the huge stone pillar, at least thirty feet high, standing directly in his path. He eased off on one of the engines, attempting to steer the now skidding aircraft as it bounced at over one hundred miles per hour down Mother Nature's runway. He checked his speed indicator and the numbers were rapidly ticking down, though not enough. His manipulations of the engines had his view changing slightly, but not his direction. Without landing gear, he had no control. He slammed both engines back into full reverse.

There was an explosion and a fire indicator lit up on his panel as the engines sucked in whatever crop he was gliding through, his left one finally having enough of the forced feeding. He cut the fuel and looked up as the huge stone whipped by his cockpit on the right. The plane jerked as the wing smacked into the unyielding stone, shearing from the fuselage. He leaned over and glanced back in time to see the wing shred into thousands of pieces, many of them tearing through the still roaring right engine.

It erupted in a fireball as the plane spun in circles.

Richards continued to grip the controls as the plane whipped around and came to a halt. He reached to unbuckle his shoulder belts when a screeching sound, as if Hell had opened a door just for him, erupted from behind him. The entire plane vibrated, and moments later flame whipped past the cockpit window, superheating the air and devouring any oxygen it could find.

Richards gasped, searing his lungs, and shut his eyes as the explosion blasted the cockpit door off its hinges, sending it through the window as it escaped the flames behind. He took a deep breath and ducked. Flames licked at his clothing, at his skin, but his fireproof flight suit did its job, keeping him alive.

Long enough to suffer the pain.

He screamed in agony as the flames dissipated as fast as they had come, the small amount of fuel flaming out spectacularly, though quickly. He attempted to open his eyes but they were sealed shut. He reached up with his hands, every nerve at maximum, his pain receptors on overload. He touched his eyes and could barely sense anything. He had almost no sense of touch. None in his fingers. Some on his face. He pulled his fingers away, the skin tacky, as if partially liquefied.

BROKEN DOVE

Oh God, kill me. Please kill me!

Fifteen Miles Outside the Green Zone
Iran

"There!"

Captain Joshua Riggs looked to where Sergeant Kerrigan, ten years his senior, was pointing. "Hornet's Nest, Rescue One. We have a visual of the target, over."

"Rescue One, Hornet's Nest. Copy that. Be advised, we have hostiles closing on the area. Consider your LZ hot, over."

"Hornet's Nest, Rescue One. Copy that, our LZ is hot, over."

Riggs turned to the Lieutenant in the back leading the ground rescue. "Did you copy that?"

Lieutenant Hornby nodded. "Yes, sir, hot LZ. Got it."

Riggs returned his attention to flying his UH-60 Black Hawk, banking slightly toward the plume of smoke just ahead. He glanced up as four Super Hornets roared past to take up position around the crash site, they or a Predator drone likely having spotted the Iranians on their way. He glanced back at Hornby. He was young, though his face had experience written all over it. And so did the sergeant's. They were both battle-hardened from Iraq and Afghanistan. Sometimes it was hard to remember that America had been at war longer than in World War II. The tough veterans that had returned from the wars of old commanded respect now due to their advanced years, but they were no different than the boys and girls now fighting, fighting because their country asked them to, some dying, more wounded, even more scarred psychologically for life. These soldiers, these brave men and women, had seen more than most could ever imagine, whether twenty-five, or forty-five.

Why don't we just buy our oil from Canada instead of this Godforsaken place?

Something pinged off the skin of the Black Hawk.

"We're taking small arms fire," said Kerrigan.

Riggs nodded as they flew over a small convoy of military vehicles rushing toward their LZ. "Hornet's Nest, Rescue One. Be advised, we're taking small arms fire from a convoy of hostiles just west of our position, over."

"Rescue One, Hornet's Nest. Copy that, dispatching cover, over."

Ahead, he saw two of the Super Hornets bank sharply and race toward him, dropping to the deck. They roared under him, and at only a few hundred feet above the ground himself, the turbulence they caused buffeted the Black Hawk slightly.

"Did they get them?" he called to the crew in the back, most of whom he could see were hanging out the open side door.

"And did they!" The team in the rear exchanged fist bumps, then Kerrigan leaned forward. "Tore the shit out of the convoy and the road."

Riggs smiled, then as soon as the muscles in his face had completed the move, he frowned. He had his first view of the crash site, and it didn't look good. The plane had scarred the field it had landed in, the fuselage ripping across the surface revealing the rich, dark soil underneath, contrasting sharply with the golden-brown of the crops now felled. The right wing had disintegrated, along with most of the tail section. The wing impacting a large, unmovable stone, had whipped the plane around, and it lay slightly on its side, resting on the one remaining wing.

And the entire thing smoldered.

A thick black smoke still rose from the fuselage, evidence of any large fires now gone.

"Sixty seconds!" He slowed the mighty craft down, clearing the final knoll. Killing his airspeed, he descended rapidly. Ahead, he could see the two Apaches take up covering positions, and to either side of him, the other rescue choppers descending toward what might turn out to be a recovery mission rather than a rescue mission, judging from the view he was getting. The wheels touched the ground and he reduced power to take the edge off the wind whipped up by the 53-foot long rotors. He glanced back and the team was already out, racing past his cockpit toward the smoldering wreckage. "Hornet's Nest, Rescue One. We are on the ground, I repeat, we are on the ground, over."

From his vantage point, he had a clear view of the operation. A platoon of Marines was spread out, providing cover, two Apaches were in the air to provide close ground support, and at least half a dozen Super Hornets were circling overhead at varying altitudes. If the Iranians tried anything, they'd be wiped out instantly.

Small puffs of dirt erupted from the ground in front of him, followed by the distinct sound of a fifty-caliber machine gun belching rounds. He couldn't tell what direction it was coming from, but one of the Apaches tilted forward and raced to his left. Leaning for a better view, he watched the gunship tear across the landscape, belching fire from its 30mm M230 chain gun, and about half a mile out, a vehicle with a rear-mounted machine gun erupted in flames. Several more crested the same hill, along with two troop carriers, their men pouring from the rear and spreading out, diving to the ground as the Apache tore into them. A quick glance at the Marines showed those covering that side were also peppering the new arrivals with rounds.

"Hurry up, boys," he muttered. He examined the plane. The entrance near the cockpit was now open and the rescue teams were inside, stretchers handed in. He saw movement in the cockpit and a minute later the first stretcher came down the ladder, a sheet covering the entire body. Two more stretchers emerged, both covered, then a fourth, fifth, and a sixth. All covered. He glanced back at the cockpit. The movement had ceased, but his mental tally suggested there were still some of his crew aboard. Moments later, a stretcher appeared, uncovered, and its two bearers raced toward his chopper. As they rushed by the cockpit, he caught a glimpse of the pilot's face.

Charred pork.

He turned away quickly, gagging. The stretcher was shoved into the rear as the team piled in.

"All clear!" yelled the Lieutenant.

Riggs powered up and within moments they were airborne, racing back to Turkish airspace, the few Iranians that had survived still taking fire from the Apaches covering their escape. "Hornet's Nest, Rescue One. We're on route to Rendezvous Point Alpha, over."

He glanced back at the writhing figure on the floor, screaming in pain as the medics cut off his flight suit. From what he could see, the flames had traveled up the arms of his suit, and down the neck. His face was unrecognizable, the skin sagging, bone exposed, his eye sockets seared shut. Riggs sucked in a quick breath and his mouth filled with bile at the taste of the air. "Can't you give him something?"

"No, he's not stable enough to risk it. It might kill him."

Riggs looked back as a charred hand reached up and grabbed the medic by the arm, pulling him closer. Riggs couldn't hear what the poor bastard was saying, but the medic shook his head.

"Please!" the man screamed in one last burst of strength.

"What did he say?"

"He wants me to kill him."

"Then do it."

The medic's jaw dropped. "I can't do that! I could be court-martialed."

The sergeant leaned forward and put a hand on the young medic's shoulder. "You've never been in combat before, have you, son?"

The man—scratch that—boy, shook his head. Riggs recognized the hints of innocence, of the raw recruit on his first mission, who still thought the world was mostly good, and that if you were good, then good things would happen to you.

And that killing one of your own was wrong.

The sergeant glanced at the young but experienced lieutenant who nodded.

The pilot's hand still gripped him by the arm as he repeated, "Please!" over and over, barely a whisper now.

"I can't," cried the medic, tears rolling down his face. "I can't!"

"Let me give him something for the pain, son."

The medic reached into his equipment and pulled out a syringe, filling it with the fluid from one of the many vials revealed in a small case.

The sergeant pointed at the bottle. "More."

The medic stared, then acquiesced, continuing to fill the needle.

"Is that enough?"

"Y-yes." He handed it over. "Just inject him in the leg."

The sergeant took the needle and without hesitation plunged it into the thigh of the crying carcass that was once a proud member of the United States Air Force, and a loving son with a wife and newborn. His pleas stopped, his lips still moving. The sergeant leaned forward and whispered something in the man's ear. His hand dropped from the medic's arm, and the writhing stopped.

The sergeant rose to his knees and snapped to attention, as did the rest of the rescue crew. Without words, they saluted, then slowly lowered their arms, along with their heads, eyes closed, in silent remembrance of their fallen comrade.

"Rescue One, Hornet's Nest. Do you have any survivors, over?"

Riggs tore himself from the scene and activated his comm. "Negative, Hornet's Nest, no survivors, over."

Diyarbakir Airbase, Turkey

Laura stared out the window of the chartered Gulfstream V as they taxied to their debarkation point. Reading sat across from her, doing the same, and Giasson sat next to him. A separate plane was bringing the Vatican delegation, but Giasson had "volunteered" to go with Laura and Reading, thus granting their plane diplomatic status, and permission to land at the military airfield. Giasson had indicated after they were in the air the biggest benefit to traveling with them—they would get there far faster than the other plane. Apparently, organizing a dozen cardinals and bishops took far too long for Giasson's liking. It had also allowed them to bring the owner of the crashed plane, to see if he might identify the original pilot, though in mid-air they had been informed he had been identified, and the owner was no longer necessary. Reading had whispered something about letting the known smuggler out at thirty thousand feet, but neither Giasson nor Laura seconded the motion.

The rescue operation, or, as it was now called, recovery operation, had finished less than three hours ago. There were no survivors. Laura had steeled herself against the news, knowing it was coming.

But inside, she had died a little.

She had never loved anyone as much, and as hard, as she loved her James, and at this moment, was convinced she could never love again. If the loss of a love, so intense it was worthy of marriage, hurt so much, she didn't want to ever go through that again. But she didn't want to think about the future. She wanted to think of her present. To remember her beloved James. His laugh. His smile. His smell. Tears welled in her eyes and she quickly blinked them away.

The plane came to a stop.

Their flight attendant rose and opened the door, the stairs dropping slowly to the ground as the engines powered down. She was aware of the reason for the flight, and didn't bother with the customary, "Welcome to Turkey!" announcement one might usually expect.

Giasson rose and pointed at the smuggler. "You stay here."

Laura unbuckled her lap belt and followed Giasson down the stairs and onto the hot tarmac in front of a hangar, its massive doors opened about ten feet. A Turkish officer, along with an American Colonel, saluted, the American stepping forward first.

"I'm Colonel Babcock, in charge of the recovery operation. This is my colleague and Base Commander, Colonel Tansel. I trust your flight was uneventful?"

"Yes," replied a subdued Giasson who shook the proffered hand. A quick round of handshakes followed, and Babcock stretched his arm toward the hangar.

"Shall we?"

They walked briskly toward the massive structure and through the towering doors. Inside was an assortment of vehicles and other equipment that Laura recognized in passing, but ignored. Her focus was on the line of gurneys laid out in front of them.

Five.

Babcock looked at Laura. "Ma'am, you might not want to see this. There was a fire." He paused, as if searching for the words. "It isn't something I'd want to see."

She shook her head. "No, I have to see—" Her voice cracked, and she stopped, knowing she wouldn't maintain control if she continued.

Babcock, jaw squared, nodded.

They approached the first gurney and a young man in a crisp Air Force dress uniform snapped to attention, saluted, then slowly rolled down the sheet covering the body, revealing the upper half of the victim, badly charred, unrecognizable.

Laura turned away for a moment then forced herself to look back.

Babcock pointed. "We believe this one is His Holiness, the Pope."

Laura watched, as if a spectator in a theater, as Giasson and Reading stepped forward. Giasson pointed to the papal ring, the Ring of the Fisherman. "This is him." He made the sign of the cross and stepped away, pulling his cellphone from his pocket as he did.

They moved to the next gurney, and another young man, repeating the rituals of respect for the fallen, revealed the body. "We believe this to be Detective Inspector Chaney. He was several inches shorter than Professor Acton. We'll confirm this when our forensics team arrives."

Reading stared at the badly charred body, then pointed. "That looks like his watch, though I'm not sure."

"It's most likely him, but forensics will confirm."

They moved to the third body. He looked at Laura, his eyes focused on her, as if beseeching her to reconsider.

"Are you sure?" he asked gently.

No, I'm not.

"Yes."

The ritual was repeated, and the body revealed. "Based upon height, we believe this to be Professor Acton."

Laura was on autopilot as she found her feet carrying her forward, whether she wanted to or not. Her nostrils filled with the smell of scorched meat, sickly sweet, her mouth, filling with bile, ready to betray her as her stomach churned. She grabbed her left wrist and shoved her thumb hard into the bundle of nerves on her arm, just above the wrist, and slowly made a circular motion as she steadied her breathing. The repeated massage of the nerves slowly steadied her nausea, and she was soon herself again, focusing on the body.

Unrecognizable.

How am I supposed to know?

There was nothing left. It was all meat on a tray. The clothes were unrecognizable. There was no undamaged skin left. Where a watch might have been there appeared to be part of a strap embedded in the skin, though nothing else. Her eyes traveled up his chest then she stopped, her hand darting forward. She pinched her fingers around what she thought she had seen, what she hoped she had seen, for if she were wrong, she feared what she might be yanking.

Yet if she was right, she was terrified at what it meant.

Babcock gasped and Reading stepped forward, but she waved them off. She pulled, and the sickly sound of tearing, melted skin, filled the hangar, though it was only her imagination. Her heart slammed a horror-filled beat as the rush of painful discovery filled her ears. She pulled harder and finally revealed what she had hoped.

And what she had feared.

A gold chain.

She continued to pull at it, and soon several inches were revealed, then finally a pendant popped out from a patch of greasy skin.

"What is it?" asked Reading.

"Saint Helena, patron saint of Archaeologists."

"And that was his?"

She dropped it back onto his chest. "I gave it to him on our first anniversary."

She was about to absentmindedly wipe her hand on her blouse, when Reading handed her a handkerchief. She flashed a smile and wiped her fingers, then handed it back. Reading carefully folded it, and placed it in a different pocket.

"And these two?" asked Reading.

"We presume they're the kidnappers. Neither fit the height profiles we were provided with. We have one more on ice that was found in the cockpit, so obviously not one of the three that concern you."

"Men or women?" Laura caught the surprise on the Colonel's face at her question.

"Men."

Reading gave her a glance then turned away from the final two covered bodies, returning to those of his friends. He lifted the sheet covering the legs of Chaney and waved off the honor guard member. "No, let me." He slowly covered his partner and friend of over ten years.

Laura stepped over to her beloved James, tears filling her eyes, and pulled the sheet over him, covering the grotesque husk that remained, then collapsed on top, sobbing, her broken heart pounding as her chest heaved, her body racked with sobs. A foot scraped the ground behind her, then hands on her shoulders gently pulled her away.

"Come." It was Reading. She let go and turned around, burying her head in his chest, the tears she had held back now flowing rivers of pain, burning her cheeks. Reading didn't say anything, simply holding her, caressing her head as her sobs slowly waned.

Then she stopped.

She drew a deep breath and gently pushed away, Reading releasing her from his arms.

"You okay?"

She shook her head. "No, but I will be." She reached into her satchel and removed a handkerchief of her own, wiping the tears from her eyes and giving her nose a quick blow. She took one last look at the gurney that contained the man she had hoped to marry, and closed her eyes. "Take me out of here."

With a hand on her arm, Reading guiding her toward the hangar doors. Her eyes remained closed the entire short walk until she sensed the warmth of the sunlight hitting her face. She looked about. The others had followed them.

"What's next?" asked Reading.

Babcock stepped forward. "A forensics team will be arriving within the hour. They'll confirm the identities, then the bodies will be returned."

"We'll wait." Her voice was barely a whisper.

"We can have the body transported back to the States for you, ma'am."

She shook her head, her chin buried in her chest. "No. He's coming with us, in my plane. I need to bring him back to his parents."

Oh my!

She lifted her head and looked at the Colonel. "Did you contact them yet?"

Babcock shook his head. "No, not until positive identification."

"Okay, let me do that."

Babcock nodded and stepped away to talk to Giasson who had just finished on the phone.

"It's my fault."

"Pardon me?"

She glanced at Reading. "It's my fault."

"How the bloody hell do you figure that?"

"He was trying to save me. If we hadn't split up—"

"Now listen here. Don't be getting any daft ideas that this is your fault. If it's anybody's fault, it's mine."

Laura looked up at Reading. "And how do *you* figure that?"

"I'm the one who shot at the plane. Obviously, I'm the one who caused it to eventually lose pressure."

"*That's* daft. You were trying to save him."

Reading harrumphed. "Yeah, by shooting at him."

Laura finally sighed. "It's not our fault, it's theirs."

Reading leaned against a nearby forklift. "The question is, who are they? If we presume all of the Order are women, then this is definitely a different group."

"They'll pay," whispered Laura.

"Absolutely."

The pain turned to anger inside, a fire in the pit of her stomach igniting, a hate building the likes of which she had no recollection of ever feeling. "I want them dead."

"I know how you feel. But *justice* will prevail."

"Screw justice—"

Her phone beeped with a message, interrupting what was about to be a tirade she would later regret. She reached into the satchel and held the phone up to her face, the facial recognition software unlocking it for her. She pressed the screen to view the message, and fainted.

Rome
8 Hours Earlier

Acton's head throbbed and his entire body ached. Tossed to the side, he impacted something soft with a grunt. Not his, but someone else's. Another jerk and he was thrown to the other side, this time slamming into something harder. His senses regaining function, he quickly realized he was in a car. And judging from the rapid up and downshifting, constant hard turns, and panicked Italian chatter from the front, they were being pursued.

Someone had hit him over the head. He remembered that. Or at least the pain from it. Nothing else from then until now.

Laura!

He risked opening his eyes slightly to see if the body he had hit a moment ago was hers.

Definitely not.

A man, dressed in black from head to toe, stared out the back window. Acton snapped his eyes shut as his captor's head swiveled back toward the front.

"Rapido!"

They careened around another corner, another surge of acceleration pressing him into his seat before the car screeched to a halt. Doors opened, all four it sounded like, then rough hands were on him, grabbing him under his armpits. He played possum, forcing them to drag him. His feet bounced on pavement, smacked against something, probably a curb, then he was dropped. He gasped for a moment until his backside pressed against something soft rather than hard concrete. He was tilted back then had the sensation of movement.

A wheelchair?

Tires squealed then gunshots cracked followed by the sounds of a vehicle crashing into something.

Then someone yelled.

Hugh?

194

He was tempted to call out, but if it were Reading, then it was no doubt him who had chased them, so there was little point. He was still wearing his body armor, and had been disarmed, but a thought occurred to him.

Did they get the radio?

He took a deep steady breath to calm his nerves, then opened his eyes slightly. And discovered what his nose had already told him.

He was in an airport.

The distinct smell of jet fuel was unmistakable. The line of check-in counters and seats only confirmed it. But there was no one around, likely due to the late hour. They breezed unchallenged through a security checkpoint.

This makes no sense.

They shoved through a set of automatic doors and into the night, the black tarmac lit by the surrounding yellow lights filling in the last piece of the puzzle.

This was a private terminal.

Jet engines powered up, and he caught a glimpse of what appeared to be a Gulfstream V, its stairs down, less than one hundred feet away. He jerked to a stop near the ramp, then again was grabbed under the arms, and this time by the feet as well. They carried him feet first onto the plane, the experience unsettling.

The door sealed shut and the plane rolled forward, followed by half a dozen cracking sounds that if he didn't know better might have been gunfire. He was tossed in a seat, his head smacking the hard wall of the cabin. He opened the eye nearest the wall and looked down. His radio was still clipped to his vest. Slowly reaching up, he grasped it and clicked three times.

Someone grabbed him by the collar and whipped him around.

"Awake, are we?"

He opened his eyes to see a large hand reach down and rip the radio from his collar, the clip making a loud snapping sound as it broke off. The man turned off the radio and tossed it aside.

"Let's see what else you have here."

Acton took the opportunity to look around as he was patted down. Across the aisle from him sat an old man, praying, who Acton recognized as the Pope. A slight turn of the head revealed Chaney, staring directly at him, then behind him were six others, all in black.

Scratch that.

A seventh man left the bathroom in the back, and his searcher made eight, plus the pilot, and copilot if there were one.

We're not getting out of this.

He stared again at the bathroom, familiar with the layout of the plane, having just flown on Laura's private charter.

This cabin is smaller than it should be.

The man stood. "He's clean. Wait a minute." He leaned forward and the man's fingers reached under Acton's collar then pulled out his Saint Helena medallion. "Take it off."

"Please, let me keep this. My girlfriend gave it to me."

The man stared down at him, visibly angry, his nostrils flared, his ears red. "You dare ask to keep a medallion of a holy saint, around the neck of an infidel?"

"Infidel?"

Are they Muslim?

"You deny that you assist this man"—his arm swept toward the Pope—"a pretender to the crown?"

Acton decided not answering was best.

"Your lack of protest proves your guilt."

Acton remained silent.

"You deny that you live in sin with the woman who gave you this?" He grabbed Acton by the hair, pulling his head forward. The chain lifted from his skin then pulled through his hair. The man tossed Acton's head back against the padded leather seat. He held the chain in front of Acton, triumphantly, the cabin lighting glittering off the gold figure. "You are not worthy of wearing this." He put it around his neck and tucked it into his black tunic. "I, however, *am* worthy."

Acton glared at the man as the medallion given to him by Laura on their first anniversary, disappeared from view. "And just who the hell are you?"

The man's eyes narrowed and the back of his hand swiftly smacked Acton across the cheek. "Blasphemer!"

The sting filled Acton's senses, but he held on enough to make sure his eyes never broke from his captor's, and as he regained control, he decided on a different tact. "Obviously you're a very religious man." His captor nodded. "Then I apologize for my poor choice of words." The man again nodded, some of the tension in his eyes relaxing. "May I ask, then, who you are, and why we have been taken?"

The man stepped back. "I am Sir Battista, second in the Keepers of the One Truth, established by Saint Peter himself. Have you heard of us, Professor Acton?"

"You know my name?"

"Of course we do. We know of you, we know of the Triarii"—his hand indicated Chaney and the Pope—"and we know of how you assisted them in the past."

"I wouldn't exactly say I assisted them."

"You gave them the false idol, did you not?"

Acton glanced at Chaney, who slightly shook his head. Acton looked back at Battista. "I don't know what you're talking about."

The man chuckled, his long, shoulder-length hair dangling in midair as he tossed his head back. He pointed at Chaney. "Don't think I didn't catch that." He turned to Acton. "I know the Triarii are naïve enough to think they are invulnerable to infiltration, but do *you*?"

Acton shrugged. "I hadn't really given it any thought." He leaned forward. "To be honest, I'd kind of like to not have any involvement with them, after what happened last time."

The man leaned on the back of the seat in the next row. "I don't blame you. Do not worry, Professor, if it were our intention to kill you, you would be dead. There is only one person here today who may die, and I think you know who that is."

"I am prepared to die, my son."

Everyone turned toward the Pope, still sitting, hands clasped in front of him, eyes closed, head bowed. Acton noticed his fingers were bare, the Ring of the Fisherman missing.

"So, it speaks."

"Indeed, *I* do." The old man opened his eyes and stared at Battista. "Why do you say I am a pretender?"

"You are Triarii."

"Indeed I am. What of it?"

Battista's jaw dropped as his shoulders raised and his palms turned upward. "What of it?" He looked at his companions. "What of it? Isn't it obvious?"

"Apparently not."

Battista rose to his full height, his head nearly grazing the ceiling. "You cannot have two masters, not in your position."

"I have but one, and that is our Lord our God."

"Yet you worship the skulls."

"I do no such thing."

"You are Triarii."

"Again, what of it?"

"Triarii worship the crystal skulls. This is known by everyone who knows of them."

"That may be what is known by those who know of them from without, but not those who know of them from within."

Battista gave him a look. "What?"

Even Acton had to repeat that a few times in his head to get it. And the old pontiff was right. Even within the

Triarii, there was debate on what the skulls meant, and only some, albeit a large portion, apparently worshipped the skulls. But many were Catholics, Jews, Muslims, Buddhists, and Atheists. The Pope was obviously one of those who was a Catholic.

"Your Holiness, perhaps if you were to explain what you believe?" offered Acton.

"With pleasure, Professor." He turned to Battista. "I'm a Catholic. I was born to two Catholic parents, and was raised a Catholic. I was an altar boy, and joined the seminary after college. I have been a faithful servant of God my entire life. My father, upon my graduation from the seminary, revealed to me the truth of the Triarii, something he had been a member of since he was a young man through his own father. I agreed to listen, and eventually, I joined after reading the history. Not because I felt the skulls were something to be worshipped, but because I believed they were dangerous, something evil that had been placed upon this earth to destroy it."

"That makes no sense," said Battista. "You think the skulls are evil, yet you protect them?"

The old man shook his head. "No, you misunderstand, my son. Do I believe the skulls are evil? Yes. Do I protect the skulls? Yes. But I protect *mankind* from the skulls, not the *skulls* from mankind. The Triarii are the only organization on Earth that I believe are purely motivated by a sense of duty in protecting mankind from the dangers of bringing the skulls together, which is when I, and others, believe the evil is released. By keeping them separate, scattered across the globe, we protect mankind from the evil that could be unleashed."

Battista was silent for a moment, then leaned toward the elderly man, jabbing his finger at him. "You talk a good game, Your Holiness, but I don't believe it. Do I believe you are a good Catholic? Yes, I do. But as I said before, you cannot serve two masters. Should the choice come between serving our Savior, and serving your Triarii masters, where would your loyalties lie then?"

The old man regarded his captor. "I don't believe they could possibly conflict."

Battista stood and flicked his hand at the Pope, as if ridding the air of their entire conversation. "And that is all I needed to hear. The fact you cannot give a direct answer tells me you are conflicted. And a conflicted man cannot serve the Lord in the capacity you have been granted the honor to do so. You will renounce your position, or die. This will not be over before white smoke again graces the roof of the Sistine Chapel."

Acton attempted to cool things off. "So, who, or what, are the Keepers of the One Truth?"

Battista returned his attention to Acton. "We preserve the integrity of the Vault of Secrets."

"The vault underneath the Vatican?"

Battista nodded.

"'Preserve the integrity.' Does that mean you kill anyone who enters?"

Battista shook his head. "Of course not. It means we make sure the pope"—he glanced over at the old man—"does his job, and nothing more. The Unus Veritas Chest is an agreement between the new pope and Saint Peter. These secrets are to be preserved, forever, never to be looked at, never to be studied." He paused, this time staring at the Pontiff then Chaney. "Or removed."

"So, you're saying Saint Peter created your group?"

"Yes."

What is it with me and two-thousand-year-old cults?

"So, for two thousand years you've been, what, just hanging around the Vault, making sure no one takes anything out, or looks at anything?"

"Essentially. We are brothers, we hold vigil, we pray, we train, we recruit the next generation. We are eternal."

Acton huffed. "It sounds to me like you're judge, jury, and executioner."

There was a crackle overhead then the voice of what Acton assumed to be the pilot interrupted. "We're at twenty thousand feet. Better get into position."

Suddenly there was a loud noise over the speaker, then it went dead. Wind whistled and anything loose tumbled toward the cabin door behind which the pilot sat. Oxygen masks dropped from the overhead compartments. As if one, they all reached forward and grabbed their masks. Acton placed it over his mouth and inhaled.

Nothing.

He tried again, yet came up empty, finding himself gasping for air. He threw it away and grabbed another.

"They won't work!" yelled Battista, not to him, but to his companions. "The emergency oxygen is all routed through the containers!" He dropped to his knees and pulled at a latch, lifting part of the floor. "Help me!"

The others rushed forward and they removed a segment of the floor covering the aisle. Acton looked over and saw a small ladder descending into the hold below. Battista grabbed him then pointed into the hole. "Get in!"

Acton shook his head.

"Get in if you want to live!"

Acton took a breath of the now frigid, thin air. He'd die if he stayed here, and apparently there was oxygen below. He rose, stepping over the hole, then descended one rung at a time until only his torso was above the floor.

"Move to the back!" The man grabbed the Pope, urging him forward. Acton crouched, the hold only a few feet high, and crawled forward several feet.

"He's dead!"

"What?"

Acton turned around so he could hear the conversation more clearly.

"The pilot, he's dead!"

Battista muttered something, probably blasphemous. "Then who's flying the plane?"

"Looks like autopilot."

"Who will eject the pods?"

Acton couldn't see who asked the question, but Battista appeared stunned.

"Does anyone know how?" he asked, looking among his companions.

Apparently, no one knew.

Battista looked back. "Get them in the pods, then I need four volunteers to stay with me."

"Why?"

"There is only enough air in those pods for one hour for four people. This plane will be in the air for hours." He coughed, his voice now laboring against the lack of oxygen, his words freezing in the air as he spoke them.

"Why you, sire?"

"This is my mission, it is mine to die with. I will stay!"

"Then so will I!"

"And I!"

"And I!"

Acton counted and figured all had volunteered. He watched Battista smile at his comrades. "You are all good servants of the Lord, and I am certain we are all destined to sit by His side in the Kingdom of Heaven. But not today, at least, not for all of us." He pointed at three of his companions. "You take charge of the captives, and deliver them to our brothers." Hands were shaken and hugs were exchanged. Battista smacked one of them on the back. "Tino, you go with the professor." Acton was quickly joined by Tino in the cramped confines, and the two crawled to the rear of the plane to find three containers occupying a full-height hold.

This is why the cabin seemed so much shorter!

A door to the container in front of him was opened, and he was shoved inside to find two pairs of bunk bed style cots lining either side. "Strap in, take an oxygen mask," ordered his captor.

Acton, gasping for air, didn't need to be asked twice. He lay down on the lower bunk on the left side and reached up, grabbing the mask attached to the underside of the cot above him. He placed it over his mouth and drew a breath, his heart straining, desperate for air. His lungs filled and he sighed with relief before gasping a few times. He steadied his breathing as his companion took a few lungsful of his own, then closed the door, sealing them inside.

Acton closed his eyes against the cold and reached down, pulling a blanket he saw rolled at his feet over his shivering body.

You're alive!

Acton glanced at his captor as he too retrieved a blanket.

And now there are only three.

It was three against three now. Too bad they were in a plane about to crash, otherwise they might just get out of this.

Diyarbakir Airbase, Turkey
Now

Reading leaped forward, catching Laura just before she hit the ground. The Colonel and Giasson rushed over and the three of them helped her back to the plane, sitting her in one of the deep leather seats. Reading directed the air nozzles on her, then looked for the flight attendant who had just rushed in the cabin from the back. "Get me some ice water and a cold cloth!" She disappeared, returning moments later with both. Reading took the cold cloth and placed it on Laura's forehead. "Laura, can you hear me?"

She moaned, her head tossing back and forth, then her eyes fluttered open and she gasped. "James!"

"Easy now." Reading gently pushed her back into her chair. "Here, take a sip." He held the cool liquid to her lips and she took a drink.

"Where's my phone."

Giasson stepped forward, holding it out. She took it then tapped the display several times. Her eyes widened.

"Look!" She held the phone out for Reading. He took it and gasped.

"What's it say?" Giasson leaned forward with the Colonel, peering at the display.

Reading held up the phone. "It says, 'we are alive.'"

"How the hell is that possible?" asked Babcock.

All eyes turned to the owner of the hijacked plane still sitting at the back. He twisted in his seat and stared out the window.

Reading marched toward him and leaned down. "That was your plane that crashed! What aren't you telling us?"

The man turned toward Reading, his eyes cold, as if he had no interest in what had been going on around him. He said nothing, though his look said everything.

You bore me.

Reading's hand darted out and gripped the man by the throat. He squeezed. Hard. The man's eyes bulged and he raised his hands to try and break the hold, but it was useless. Reading, fueled by rage and over thirty years of police knowledge that grip was everything, refused to let go.

"Okay," the man gasped.

Reading loosened his grip. Slightly. "What haven't you told us?"

The man gasped in several breaths then glared at Reading. "I might not have told you about the special alterations I had made to the plane."

Unknown Location
4 Hours Earlier

They were turning. There was no mistaking it. And they were turning sharply. It flashed across Acton's mind they had finally run out of fuel. That this was it. Then the plane leveled out.

Somebody's at the controls!

He glanced over at Tino, who remained as silent as he had their entire voyage, but the exchanged glance conveyed the excitement he too felt.

We might just get through this alive.

Could they have managed to get the oxygen in the cabin working? That made no sense. It had been hours. Anybody up there would be out cold by now, possibly dead. He racked his brain.

Could you remotely fly a Gulf V?

He didn't think so. There was no way the FAA would allow that. Terrorists would have them flying into office towers daily.

No, somebody above them was alive, and in control.

Acton closed his eyes and pictured Laura.

I just might be coming home, babe.

He reached for his Saint Helena medallion, forgetting it had been taken.

Bastard.

He made a mental note to retrieve it when they landed, then found himself drifting off, the thought of dying pushed away now that someone was in control. He sank rapidly into a deep sleep, the drone of the engines only lulling him faster into slumber.

Something woke him.

He wasn't sure what, though it might have been his feet sliding into the edge of the container as they were now pressed against the wall, the plane in a steep dive. He glanced at his companion and found him holding onto the bed above him with one hand, the oxygen mask with the other. Acton reached up and tentatively lifted the mask off, taking a breath. It was thin. He put it back on.

Airtight?

One of them had mentioned ejecting earlier.

Over the water?

If these were watertight, then they'd be airtight. Guaranteed to float. He looked about again. These containers hadn't been hastily thrown together. And if they could eject them, this plane had definitely been modified.

Human smugglers.

It was the only explanation. But high-value humans. This was not a fifty thousand dollar a head operation. Those were jammed into sea containers and the back of trucks. This was a private jet, with a state of the art transport system. This was meant to avoid customs, to get their cargo *from* Point A, but Point B was not the final destination of the aircraft. It was the destination of the cargo containers.

Visions of Gadhafi's family played through his head. He could picture them lying in these cots, fleeing the onslaught of the revolution.

How many dictators' families escaped in this very plane, in this very container?

He heard something. A voice. It was faint, from above, probably the pilot. He couldn't make out the words, though they were leveling out. He drew a deep breath and closed his eyes, saying a silent prayer. He thought of the other passenger behind him.

He'll probably have more success getting through.

The plane continued to descend, just not as rapidly. Then the nose pulled up, tipping him slightly backward. He slid, his head smacking the metal of the container.

Then they hit.

The jolt sent him bouncing up, the lap belt he had discovered earlier and secured, holding him in place at the waist, the rest of his body free to jerk around. He glanced over at Tino who hadn't been as wise, his belt still unfastened. He was reaching up with both hands, protecting himself from the bed above, as blood flowed freely from a cut above his eye.

Seatbelts save lives.

The plane continued to bounce, then there was a terrific jerk and they spun before coming to a halt. A roaring sound filled the container and the walls began to smoke. Acton reached out and touched the side nearest him. Hot. Incredibly hot. He gripped his mask, debating if he should pull it off or not. If the oxygen were to ignite, it could send flame shooting through the tubes feeding him.

He gulped in a breath and pulled the mask off his head, still holding it in his hand. The roaring outside died down, both engines now out. He slowly exhaled and took a tentative breath. Acrid, and still thin. Apparently, some of the container's skin on the inside had melted, and no fresh air was getting in. his lungs finally gave out and the air he held burst forth. Covering his face with the mask, he inhaled deeply then sighed in relief they still had oxygen. He lay there for a few minutes, catching his breath, his companion apparently out cold from a blow to the head.

Acton unclasped the lap belt and swung his legs off the bed, sitting up, still hunched over from the bed over his head. As his ears adjusted to the eerie silence, he thought he heard something. He jumped up and pressed his ear against the wall and yelped, the metal still hot. His second approach was more cautious. He placed his ear mere inches from the metal and listened, willing his heart to stop pounding in his ears. There were definitely sounds.

A helicopter?

His heart leaped. His experience had indicated that was rarely good.

Then there was yelling. There was no doubting that.

Then gunfire.

Gunfire?

But it sounded distant. Not as if it were coming from the plane. He raised his fist to pound on the container when something pressed into his back. He spun his head and saw his companion, his captor, standing beside him, his weapon pressed against Acton's back, and a finger over his lips.

Acton frowned then sat back down, listening to the sounds of footsteps and yelling inside the plane, gunfire and explosions outside. He eyed Tino.

Could I jump him and get the gun before it's too late?

As if reading his thoughts, the man shook his head, raising his gun to point directly at Acton's face.

And then it was over.

The shouting stopped, the footfalls disappeared, the gunfire died down, then the unmistakable sounds of helicopters leaving.

Then nothing.

Diyarbakir Airbase, Turkey
Now

Reading bound down the few steps to the tarmac then ran inside the hangar, the Colonel and Giasson following. Flipping the sheet covering Chaney's body aside, he grabbed the wrist and removed the watch. Underneath was perfectly preserved skin.

And no tattoo.

The Triarii tattoo on the underside of his wrist, covered by his watchband for all the years he had known him, was nowhere to be found. Giasson and Babcock jogged up as he held the wrist in the air. "This"—he shook the arm—"is *not* Chaney."

"How can you be certain?" asked Babcock.

"He had a tattoo under his watchband, on his wrist. It isn't there."

Both men leaned in and Babcock pursed his lips. "Okay, if we presume they're alive, then where the hell are they?"

"Perhaps they were never on the plane?" suggested Giasson.

"That's possible." Reading put the arm back on the table and reached for his handkerchief, remembering at the last moment he had given it to Laura, and what she had used it for. "I saw who I assumed was Jim getting on the plane. It might have been someone else."

"You're forgetting one thing, gentlemen." They all turned to Laura as she walked up behind them, handing Reading a clean handkerchief. "The medallion was on him when he was captured at the Vatican. This leaves two possibilities that I can think of. One, the medallion was taken before this man"—she motioned to the body of the man they had thought was Acton—"boarded the aircraft, or two, the medallion was taken after this man boarded the aircraft."

Reading agreed. "So, the man could have taken it from Jim then boarded the plane himself, leaving Jim behind, meaning he is alive somewhere, most likely Rome."

"Or it was taken from him on the airplane, which means James was in that crash, and somehow survived."

"If it were option number one, then we would be assuming that they had time to not only search him and take this medallion, but also to confiscate the radio he had with him. And I know for a fact I heard three clicks come from the radio."

"Meaning?" asked Babcock.

"Meaning James was on that plane," answered Laura. "That was the SOS signal we had arranged with Hugh if something went wrong. Two clicks, we're okay, three clicks, we need help."

"If he was able to send that signal, that means he hadn't been searched, which means they wouldn't have taken the medallion."

Babcock completed the thought. "Which means he was on the plane."

Giasson held his chin, pinching it between his thumb and forefinger. "Colonel, is it possible they were missed?"

"Absolutely. Our rescue party was not looking for people hidden in a smuggler's customized cargo container. They were looking for people sitting in passenger seats."

"We have to go back," said Laura.

The Colonel shook his head. "Impossible. That place will be crawling with Iranians by now."

"We need to let the Iranians know that we know they're alive."

Giasson stepped forward. "Professor Palmer is correct, Colonel. If we don't let them know, then they can just kill them out of hand, and be answerable to no one. If we let them know that we know, the Iranians wouldn't dare kill His Holiness and his companions."

"I'll make some calls," said Babcock. "This is in the hands of the diplomats now."

"God help them," muttered Reading.

Giasson sighed. "Indeed."

Reading wasn't sure if the sarcasm had been caught.

15 Miles Outside the Green Zone
Iran
4 Hours Earlier

Tino yanked at the handle then pushed against the door. It opened slightly. He pushed against it again and it gave a little more, though he appeared exhausted from the effort. Acton was content to let him continue, to weaken further, but there was one thing foremost in his mind.

Who had the rescuers been fighting?

The rescue had clearly been rapid and under fire. It meant they weren't in Italy anymore.

But where?

Being the Mediterranean, there were far too many possibilities to narrow it down without at least seeing their surroundings. And first, they had to get out of here and away from whoever prevented their rescue only minutes before.

"Let me."

Tino looked at Acton and nodded, stepping back and aiming his weapon at Acton's chest.

"How about you point that thing somewhere else so you don't accidentally shoot me?"

Tino just flicked the weapon at him, urging him on.

Has he even said a word since he got in here?

Acton pushed, wedging a foot between the frame and the door. He slid his back toward the opening and managed to get a shoulder in. Shoving with his back, shoulder, and hands, he made enough room to squeeze his entire body through and clear. The pressure on his chest relieved, he stood, hands on his knees, gasping for breath. After a few lungsful of air, he stood and examined his surroundings. They were still in the cargo hold, but the right side of the plane was missing, exposing the hold to the outside. Sunlight poured in through the opening, revealing what had been blocking the door—a chunk of the wing, or some part of the fuselage, was wedged between the two containers.

There was a tapping sound.

Acton looked and saw Tino's gun pointing through the hole.

"Yeah, yeah, I didn't forget you, I was just catching my breath."

He grabbed hold of the piece of wreckage and pulled. It gave a little, and with some effort, he hauled it the several feet necessary to clear the door. His companion squeezed through, then gestured for Acton to move to the next container. They both navigated down the narrow walkway to the next pod. There they found it tipped against the one in front.

Tino knocked three times.

Someone inside knocked three times back.

"Get us the bloody hell out of here!"

Acton smiled as he recognized Chaney's voice.

He's alive, and he sounds strong.

"Give me a minute, I've got to tip your container back in position. Go to the far end, your weight will help."

Acton and Tino each took up position on either side of the container, shoving with their hands and shoulders. The crate rose several inches, but fell back when Tino let go, exhausted.

"Give us a minute. I'm going to try and open the other container and get help!"

"Okay!" yelled Chaney.

Acton stepped over Tino, who waved the gun weakly at him, his wrist limp from exhaustion. "Don't worry, I'm not going anywhere without my friend."

Again, the man said nothing.

"You must be a hit on the party circuit."

Tino eyed him, confused.

Doesn't get it.

Acton rounded the final container and smiled, finding His Holiness standing silently, praying, without a mark on

214

him from all outward appearances. His captor, a young man Acton had only caught a glimpse of leaving the bathroom earlier, sat, exhausted, his head between his knees, his chest heaving as he caught his breath.

"I need a hand opening the other container."

The man raised a finger, bidding Acton to wait. "We ran out of oxygen in the last ten minutes. Give me a minute."

"Okay, but I wouldn't take too long. Whoever the rescue team was fighting will be here any minute."

The man frowned then pushed to his feet, waving with his hand for Acton to lead the way.

At least that confirms one thing.

Whoever the rescuers had done battle with were not part of the kidnapping operation, otherwise this man wouldn't have gotten up so quickly. Acton rounded the container, nodded to Tino, and all three of them positioned themselves.

"On three!" called Acton. "One, two, three!"

He shoved with his shoulder as hard as he could. He could hear grunts from the other two men as all three strained. The container tipped an inch, then two, then several more. He quickly repositioned himself lower for better leverage, and shoved with all his might. Then the load crested. Gravity took over and the container tipped the rest of the way by itself, smacking the metal of the cargo hold floor with a massive rattle sure to draw the attention of anyone within several hundred feet.

He grabbed the handle and pulled. The door swung open easily, and with the light from outside pouring in, he saw Chaney and his captor huddled against the back wall. Acton waved at Chaney, holding a hand out for him. "Let's go. We're about to have company, and I don't think they're friendly."

Chaney stepped forward, taking Acton's hand. His captor followed, and soon all six men were standing outside in the sun. Acton stretched every which way he could think of, hoping to prevent any future knots that might slow him down. Now that the odds were greatly evened out, he had every intention of getting out of this alive, with his companions.

He scanned their surroundings. Farmland, dark soil, wheat, sun low in the east, still cool.

"Which direction were we heading when the cabin decompressed?"

He was answered with silence.

"Listen, if I can figure out where we are, then I can figure out where we need to go to be safe."

"East-north-east."

It was Chaney's escort who answered.

"Thank you. And you are?"

"Nazario."

"Are you in charge?"

He nodded.

"Okay, judging from the position of the sun, the time of day, and the landscape, I'd say we're in northwestern Iran or northern Syria."

"And how did you reach such a conclusion?"

"We headed east-north-east from Rome. Along that flight path, we would have Italy, Greece and Turkey. None of those countries would fire on a rescue mission. Which leaves Iraq, which wouldn't fire either, or Syria and Iran, neither of which we want to be in right now." Acton turned to Nazario. "You're Catholic?"

The man nodded.

"Then I don't think you or your companions want to be caught here either."

The man nodded again.

"Stellar conversation, Nazario." Acton pointed to the north. "Looks like some military units took a beating in that direction. We need to head northwest if we hope to reach Turkey. And that's without knowing how far into either country we may be." He peered again at the horizon then stepped over to Nazario, pointing. "Look."

"At what?"

"It looks like an abandoned jeep. Let me go check it out."

Nazario shook his head.

Acton put his hands on his hips. "Listen, I told you, I'm not going anywhere without my friends. And there's no way in he—." He stopped himself, glancing at the Pope who smiled slightly. "In *heck*, I'm going to leave them in the hands of the Iranians or Syrians. So, let me go see if that jeep is running, and get us out of here before more arrive."

Nazario had cracked a slight smile at Acton's near slip, and subsequent correction, to his language. He looked about. "Federico, go with him."

The young one from the bathroom nodded then jogged a few paces behind Acton as they raced across the field and to the ridge several hundred yards away. As they crested the rise, Acton dropped to his stomach and surveyed the landscape. Several vehicles had been destroyed, the remains still smoldering. Bodies were scattered about, some moaning in pain.

Something flashed on the horizon.

"Did you see that?"

Federico shook his head. "No."

"I saw something flash, like binoculars or something. Reinforcements are on the way."

Acton crawled over to the vehicle he had spotted and climbed in the vacant driver's seat. He turned the keys and the engine roared to life. He put it in gear and drove it down the hill slightly so it would be out of view from anyone in the distance.

"Get in!" he yelled to Federico.

Federico rounded the vehicle, opened the door, and grabbed the shirt of the dead passenger.

"Wait!" Acton grabbed the collar. "Revolutionary Guards." He let go and Federico tossed the body to the ground then climbed in.

"What does that mean?"

"It means we're in Iran."

5 Miles Outside the Green Zone
Iran
3 Hours Earlier

The engine sputtered. And not for the first time. Acton pumped on the gas, but it was no use. Another sputter and it died.

They were out of gas.

"That's it, folks. From here on out we walk."

They had managed to get about an hour out of the vehicle, which was better than nothing. The roads had been rough and winding, and they hadn't made good progress. Perhaps ten miles as the crow flies. The midday sun was high in the sky, blazing down on them. Fortunately, the vehicle was well provisioned. They had plenty of bottled water, enough food for several days, and with the exception of Tino, were in good health.

Acton glanced at the Pontiff.

He's old, and will definitely be slow.

He looked at Chaney who appeared to be thinking the same thing, and helped the old man out of the jeep. Acton glanced at the sun, then his watch. He pointed ahead of them. "We need to go in this direction. It's the only way we can be certain to hit Turkey." He checked behind them. There was no evidence of pursuit, but there would be no hiding that a vehicle had driven down to the wreckage and away.

They'll be coming.

"We'll need to keep off the roads as much as possible. We'll have company probably within the hour."

Nazario nodded and they headed out, Acton in the lead with Nazario, Chaney helping the Pontiff, with Federico and Tino bringing up the rear. They walked in silence for about twenty minutes before Acton finally decided he had to speak.

"Why don't you tell me what this is all about?"

Nazario said nothing.

"Okay, I'll start." Acton stepped around a large rock and pushed on one knee as he climbed up a steep berm. "You are a member of the Keepers of the One Truth. There's only one other place I've heard that term, One Truth, before. Unus Veritas?"

Nazario's head spun toward him. "What do you know of it?"

"Perhaps more than you."

Nazario turned back to watching the ground ahead of him. "If you do, that may not be good for you."

"Why?"

"What is it you Americans say, 'Curiosity killed the cat?'"

"It's my nature to be curious. I'm an archaeologist."

"I respect archaeologists. They seek the truth as well."

"Yes, we do."

Finally, he's talking!

Acton pressed. "And what truth is it that you seek?"

"None. I already know the truth."

"And what's that?"

"It is that written by other's hands, in the name of Matthew, Mark, Luke, and John. It is the truth contained in the Gospels."

Acton played it careful, not wanting to offend the man, and potentially silence him. "A noble truth."

Nazario's lips pursed as if satisfied with Acton's evaluation. "Indeed."

Acton smiled slightly at the word, one he often heard from his friend Reading. "What do you make of the Order of the Blessed Virgin?"

Nazario snorted. "Those fools? They are truly dangerous, but they know not why."

"What do you mean?"

"They believe there is a fifth gospel, written by the Christ mother herself, in her own hand, no less!"

"And you don't believe them?"

"Oh, I know it exists, our ancestors liberated it from the Order over fifteen hundred years ago, and protected it until the Vault was established."

"You established the Vault?"

"Of course. The Vault of Secrets was built by us over two hundred years, secretly, under the very church we protect to this day."

"And this was built without anyone's knowledge?"

"People knew, but no one knew the purpose, then with time, no one remembered. Everyone was simply told they were building an extension to the Secret Archives, and when finished, tradesmen go about their normal lives, thinking they expanded the Pope's Archives in service to their Lord, and die never knowing the secret. Within the Church, it was never spoken of, and over centuries, was forgotten to all but the few who needed to know."

"The popes."

"And a few of us who work from within, to make sure the Unus Veritas Chest is delivered to His Holiness on the night of his election."

"And you have your own way into this vault?"

"As you witnessed."

Acton regarded him and his eyebrows lowered.

The man chuckled. "Sorry, I forgot you were out cold. Yes, we have our own means of entering and exiting unnoticed, and we have monitored the Vault for over one thousand years, making certain its secrets remained undisturbed."

"But why? Surely much of what's in there can be exposed as superstition today."

"What you consider superstition, others may consider evil."

Evil.

Just the word sent a shiver down his spine, and a cold sweat formed on his forehead as he thought of what he had read earlier.

"I see you have faced evil."

Acton returned Nazario's stare.

Nazario stopped. "Indeed, you have. You have looked upon the face of evil, and it has marked you." He resumed walking. "Do you not see why we must never let out that which has been locked away? Even you, a highly educated man, a man who most likely doesn't even consider himself religious, has been shaken to your very core knowing what is in the Vault."

Acton nodded. He *was* still shaken. He could only imagine how Laura was suffering. She likely thought he was dead, just after having such a life-altering experience.

I have to get her a message.

Acton eyed Nazario's belt. A satellite phone was clipped to it.

"Why don't you call for help?"

Nazario's hand dropped and touched the phone without looking, as if making sure it was still there. "It would give away our position."

"True, but at least people would know we were alive. They could mount another rescue."

Nazario shook his head. "No, once we are across the border, I will make a call. We have people throughout Turkey who can help us. In Iran"—he shrugged—"not so much."

Acton decided not to press. "Why threaten to kill the Pope? And for that matter, why didn't you just kill *me*? You killed the Father."

Nazario made a sign of the cross. "That was an accident. An overzealous youngster"—he glanced back at Federico—"who doesn't know his own strength, and the frailty of old men. As soon as Sir Battista was informed of the death, he and I personally returned the body to the Father's quarters so he could receive a proper burial. A man of the cloth should never be killed on consecrated ground."

"And now that we are not on consecrated ground, what of us now?"

"Sometimes knowing too much can be a dangerous thing."

Acton reflected on that statement for a moment.

We're going to die.

He was sure of it. These were zealots, and he and Chaney knew a secret they weren't supposed to, and the Pope was a pretender to the Crown in their minds.

"Is there a crystal skull in the Vault?"

Nazario turned to Acton then grabbed his left wrist, peeling back his watchband. He threw the arm back. "You're not Triarii?"

Acton shook his head. "Definitely not."

"Then what concern is it of yours?"

"I know they seek it."

"So?"

"Well, if they were given it, then they would leave the Vatican, never to return."

"You believe so?"

Acton glanced back at the Pope, who Chaney was almost carrying now, the old man's arm over his shoulder, Chaney's arm around the man's waist. "Yes, I do."

"You might be right, however the skulls have been declared heretical, and anything concerning them is to forever be contained in the Vault."

"And there's no removing it, even if the Triarii were to promise to lock it away?"

"They would never agree to lock it away. They seem to think having these things free to wander the earth is in mankind's best interest."

"Doesn't that prove they aren't heretical?"

"How do you mean?"

"Well, the Church has known about these skulls for quite some time, and many I'm sure are quite easy to steal with the Church's resources."

"What of it?"

"Well, if they let them roam the planet, doesn't that mean the Church no longer considers them heretical?"

Nazario grunted. "You may have a point, but you don't know what I know."

This caught Acton off guard. He paused, evaluating the statement. "What is it you know?"

Nazario shook his head. "Nothing. I have said too much already." He surged forward. "Enough of this talk."

Yet Acton wasn't done. "What of the Gospel of Mary? You said it's real."

Nazario growled, but answered. "It's real, but not what they think."

"What is it then?"

"What's with all these questions?"

"Like I said, I'm an archaeologist."

"And remember what I said about the curious cat?"

"I'd rather die knowing why I died, than ignorant."

"You may just get your wish." Nazario looked back at the Pontiff. "And he may be the next pope lost because they interfered with the Vault."

Papal Procession of Pope John VIII
Via Sacra, Rome
AD 855

The crowd cheered as the procession passed, filling the Pope's heart with joy if but for a moment, the fear of the present situation quickly consuming that joy and tossing it aside. Another cramp, this the worst so far, and only moments after the last, doubled the Pope over in pain.

We must go faster.

Faster, to the safety of the Papal chambers, otherwise the terrible secret would be revealed. *Her* terrible secret. For *she* was not the *he* the world thought. She was a member of the Order of the Blessed Virgin, nearly wiped out 500 years previous, though re-established by the final surviving member, Sister Joanna, after she had tracked down the priest who had stolen the last known copy of the Word. Unfortunately, it had been too late. He had already delivered it to Rome, yet he had kept his promise. It had been locked away, not destroyed. And Sister Joanna had sworn that it would someday be retrieved.

And that day was supposed to be today.

She had been pope for almost two years, the fools of the Roman clergy having chosen her, her androgynous features, her soft-spoken way, and her towering intellect and faith in God winning them over. When she had arrived in Greece from England, she had taken on the persona of a man, and schooled in religion since her youth, quickly rose through the ranks of the Church, and eventually, to the Papacy, a sin that, if revealed, would cost her life. Though she would gladly pay it to deliver the Word to the people again, and prayed the Blessed Virgin would forgive her this sin, and grant her access to worship for eternity at her side in Heaven.

She doubled over again.

"Are you not well, Your Holiness?"

She winced as she breathed through the pain.

It isn't time. This shouldn't be happening.

"I'll be fine, just get me home, quickly."

Few knew her secret, of her being a woman. In fact, outside of the inner circle of the Order, only two people were aware. One was Cardinal Martino, who had discovered her secret years before, yet had kept it to himself. The two had become close, and on occasion, too close. Including eight months before.

The horror at knowing she was pregnant was one thing. But as the baby grew inside her, she had become attached to it, and if she failed to accomplish her mission before the birth, she would be forced to give up the baby and continue her charade until she did succeed. And that was why today was to have been a glorious day. She had found the book in the Vault, locked away for over five hundred years, just as the priest had promised. It had taken almost two years of searching, yet she had found it. And it now rested, locked in the Papal offices. Tonight, she was to receive a visit from the Mother Superior of a nearby convent.

But it was merely subterfuge. The book would be handed over to the Mother Superior, a member of the Order, then taken to safety. She would make her own escape, dressed as a nun, and simply walk from the premises. No one would challenge a woman leaving.

One more day, and it would all be over.

She cried out.

The carriage came to a halt as the coachman called for help. She was in too much pain to protest, to tell them to move on. Her water had broken just as they had started the journey. Her limited experience in these matters told her that she had hours, plenty of time to reach her chambers before the baby would be born, and by then she could have sent for trusted help.

Yet something was wrong.

The baby was a month early. And it wanted out. Now.

She screamed in agony.

Oh, Blessed Virgin, was it so with you? Was there this much pain?

But she knew the answer. She had read the scriptures. There had been no pain.

Oh Lord, please take this agony away from me!

The head of her guard climbed onto the side of the carriage. "Your Holiness, what is wrong?" Then he gasped, staring at the floor of the carriage, covered in blood, the pure white robes soaked from the waist down. She looked at him and he knew. He knew by the way she held her stomach, he knew from the expression of pain, he knew because he was a father himself.

He knew. And he stared at her in horror.

"You're a—" He stopped, apparently unable to say the word that would change everything.

She confirmed his discovery with a nod. "You must remain silent. Get me to my chambers." She screamed as she felt something between her legs. Something she shouldn't be feeling. She pulled her robes up, revealing her blood-soaked legs. The guard turned away for the sake of modesty as she confirmed what she feared.

A foot.

"Your Holiness, sir, I mean, ma'am, I must call a doctor."

And before she could stop him, he had jumped off the carriage, running to the rear where the Papal Physician rode, forever accompanying his charge. Within moments, Giovanni, the doctor for the past three popes, was in the carriage, and as she winced in pain, she could tell he was aghast at what he saw, his jaw dropped, his eyes wide in horror.

"But this cannot be!"

"But it is, Giovanni." She grabbed his arm. "And no one must know."

His eyes still wide, Giovanni shook his head. "No, I cannot keep this a secret. This is"—he paused, as if searching for the right word—"blasphemy!"

She hiked her robes again, revealing the footling breach in progress. "You are a physician, save this child, for it is a child of God and deserves to live, regardless of the shame that brought it into the world."

Giovanni snapped back to reality as he saw the wiggling foot. He nodded, then did the one thing she hadn't expected, and would set her on a course of no return. He stepped down from the carriage and ordered two of the guards to lift her to the street. The remaining guards created a cordon around them, pushing back the gathering crowds as two of her aides held their robes open as wide as they could in an attempt to block the view. She sensed the doctor between her legs, manipulating the baby, and she began to slip away, the crowd growing distant, the shouts of Giovanni a faint echo, telling her not to push until he said so, cursing that there was too much blood.

The world around her grew dark.

"Push!"

The word cut through everything, and brought her back with a roar. She screamed as she pushed with everything the Blessed Virgin provided her. The crowd, now massive, knew what was happening, and knew their pope was a fraud. Anger mounted and fear gripped her heart. She struggled to block it out, to block out the hate, when a searing pain tore through her shoulder as something hit her.

"One more push!"

She ignored the pain in her shoulder, the pain racking her entire body, and pushed. Then the tiny child slipped out and a wave of relief spread through her like a stiff shot of spirits. She fell back on the ground, gasping for air. A smack and a cry signaled the entry of a new life into God's creation.

"Is it healthy?"

"Yes, *he* is."

228

A rock smacked the doctor on the back and he fell forward, nearly dropping the baby. He reached into his bag and pulled out a knife, cutting the cord and tying it off, the final separation of mother and bastard complete, her sin now on his own in a world that would never accept him. Another rock narrowly missed them, ricocheting off the wheel of the carriage.

"We must get out of here!" yelled Giovanni.

She looked around for the first time and saw the throngs shaking their fists, screaming in hate, eyes bulging, vengeance on their minds. Chants of "blasphemer" and "false father" filled her ears, echoing off the cobblestone and surrounding buildings. Her guards, always loyal, always willing to lay down their lives for her, held back the crowds, but all to a man stared at her over their shoulder, their shock and confusion—and anger—plain to see.

More rocks, the stones of the very street she lay on, were thrown as the crowd tore up the ground they stood on to exact justice at the affront they had just discovered.

"Save the baby!" she pleaded to Giovanni. "Leave me now, and get the child to safety. My life is forfeit. Take my guards, take my carriage, I do not care. But save my son."

Giovanni put a hand on her shoulder. "I do not know what to say, this"—he waved his hand over her female form—"is too much for me to comprehend at this time, but"—he paused—"but may God have mercy on your soul."

She smiled then beckoned him to leave. He rose, climbed in the carriage with the child, and yelled for the procession to continue. The carriage lurched forward and the guard shifted to clear the crowd from their path, leaving her alone on the street, covered in blood, the crowd divided between chasing the procession and surrounding her. The hate-filled eyes, burning red with rage, closed in on her, but through their feet, she caught a glimpse of something on the far side of the road. A group of robed figures, standing shoulder to shoulder, their hands clasped in prayer as they stared at her. She caught the eye of one and recognized her. The Order was here. The Order was with her. And she wept at the opportunity lost, and at the knowledge she alone had gained in reading the Word, and how wrong they had been.

She closed her eyes and clasped her hands, praying to the Blessed Virgin for deliverance as the blows of stone and feet rained upon her body until she could feel no more.

5 Miles Outside the Green Zone
Iran
Present Day
30 Minutes Earlier

Every bone, every muscle, in Acton's body ached. He looked at the aged Pontiff and could only imagine how he must be suffering. Yet he never complained. He simply walked, accepting the assistance of Chaney or Acton without comment.

His faith gives him strength, but how long will it last?

It was only a matter of time before the well he had been tapping would dry up and he would collapse. The farmland was behind them, the terrain now covered in rocks, or rock itself, slowly ascending. It was late afternoon, and the rocks strewn across the area cast long shadows, providing occasional refuge from the heat, though also concealing hidden dangers.

Acton fell to the side, his foot finding another rut in the rock. His arm darted out and he saved his footing by pushing on a nearby boulder. He stopped.

"We have to stop for the night, otherwise one of us is going to break an ankle."

"Your ankles are no concern of mine," said Nazario.

"No, but your own might be."

Nazario's eyes took on a distant look as if debating what Acton had just said.

Time to press.

"If you break an ankle out here, you won't be moving anywhere. You might as well start walking straight back to the Iranians."

"Very well. We will rest for the night." He looked about and pointed to a collection of several massive boulders nearby, their peaks touching as if God had been building a house of cards with them eons ago. "We can rest in there, and light a fire without being seen."

Acton considered the hollow then nodded, stepping back and helping Chaney with the Pontiff. Once inside, Acton cleared a small area of rocks, and helped lower the old man. He gave a weak smile to both of them, then closed his eyes. Acton knelt and looked at the man's feet. He was wearing a simple pair of slip-on shoes, shoes not designed for this terrain. Acton reached forward and cupped the old man's heel, gently slipping off the first shoe.

The Pontiff winced with a gasp, his eyes squeezing shut, his head turning to the side. His feet were cut, bloodied, the bottom of the shoes sliced in several places from the terrain, the socks he wore soaked a dark red. Acton removed the other shoe and found the same.

"We're going to have to do something about this."

Chaney knelt beside Acton, examining the feet.

"Weren't you a doctor in a previous life?"

Chaney chuckled. "Almost. I quit med school to become a cop."

"Any regrets?"

"None." Chaney gently removed both socks, placing them to the side. "These will need to be washed if possible, his feet absolutely."

Acton reached into the bag he had been carrying and pulled out a water bottle.

"What do you think you're doing?" asked Nazario.

Chaney pointed at the bloody stubs in front of him. "We have to clean his feet before they become infected."

"You're not wasting our water on him."

"He can have mine," replied Acton.

"And mine," said Chaney.

Nazario shrugged. "Suit yourselves. But"—he pointed a finger at them both—"one bottle each, and that's it."

Acton bit his tongue, uncapping the bottle and handing it to Chaney. "First, let's clear some of this away." He poured some of the now warm water over both feet, the old man gasping again as he gripped a cross

232

hanging around his neck. Chaney frowned, lowering his voice and leaning toward Acton. "It's worse than I thought. There's no way he can walk tomorrow."

"There's nothing you can do?" Acton's voice was barely a whisper.

Chaney shook his head. "I can clean the wounds, bind them with whatever we find in the medkit, and make him comfortable. Other than that, he needs rest and time to heal."

Acton turned his head slightly to see their three captors talking among themselves, one of them pointing at Nazario's satellite phone.

"Looks like there may be a little dissension in the ranks."

Chaney glanced over at the three. "That could be good, but it could also be dangerous."

"I lean toward dangerous. They're just as likely to decide to shoot us here and save themselves. There's no way they'll agree to staying long enough for his feet to heal up."

"I fear what they might do in that case."

"Either we're going to have to carry him, or they're going to shoot him."

"Hand me the med kit."

Acton pulled the medkit from the nearby sack. Nazario glared but Acton ignored him. Nazario returned to his increasingly animated discussion, their hands raising the volume their lips did not.

"Better hurry, I don't know how long they'll let us use this."

Chaney took the kit and unzipped it. He removed a pair of tweezers and cleaned the wounds of any bits of sock and rock that were embedded, then, rejoicing with a big smile aimed at Acton, removed a bottle of iodine, which he poured generously over the wounds. The Pontiff gasped again, writhing in pain for a moment, then passed out.

"That's probably for the best."

Acton agreed, glancing from the corner of his eye at their captors. It appeared the conversation might be winding down. "Hurry."

Chaney took some gauze and dried the wounds as best he could. Leaning in, he inspected them. "Doesn't need stitches, they're just surface wounds, but they'll hurt like bloody hell for days." He removed a roll of gauze and wrapped first one foot, then the other, taping them off. He sat back on his haunches. "That's the best I can do for now."

"Best we don't tell them how bad he is. That should buy us until morning."

"Planning something?"

"I've got to get that phone. If we aren't rescued, or the roles in this play aren't reversed by morning, one or more of us is going to die."

Chaney frowned. "You're probably right. Let me know how I can help."

Acton motioned to the old man now sleeping restlessly. "Just take care of him." He stood and turned to their captors. "I need to go to the bathroom." The conversation stopped, hands in midair as they all turned to Acton. "Sorry to interrupt, but I really need to go."

Nazario turned back to his companions, said something, then stepped forward, waving Acton from the hollow. Acton stepped outside. The sun was very low on the horizon, and the heat radiating from the rocks would soon dissipate, leaving their refuge cold if they didn't do something soon. He was content to let their captors freeze, but the Pontiff needed the heat.

"We should start a fire as soon as possible. This heat will be gone within an hour."

"You and your friend can collect firewood when we get back."

Acton scanned the area. The pickings were slim, though there was enough brush for them to gather and keep a good fire through the night.

"This is far enough."

Acton shook his head. "It's a number two."

"So."

"So, never shit in your own campground?" Acton looked about. A large boulder the size of a small house was a couple of hundred feet away. He pointed. "I'll go behind there."

Nazario nodded and they continued, picking their way around the stones.

"You said earlier that a pope died because of the Vault."

"Yes."

"Which one?"

"Joan."

Acton stopped. "Really! That's remarkable! Do you have proof of this? She's little more than a rumor, doesn't make any of the official lists of popes of course, and the Catholic Church would have us believe she's a myth."

"She was real. She was a member of the Order of the Blessed Virgin. Very intelligent, very, how do you say, not looking like a man or woman?"

"Androgynous."

"Exactly! She arrived in Greece from England, made her way to Rome, and manipulated her way up the ranks of the Church, taking her blasphemous position as pope in 851, all in the hopes of gaining access to the Vault. It took her two years, but she found what she was looking for, and managed to smuggle the text out. Unfortunately for her, she was pregnant, and the pressure of the situation sent her into labor in front of a crowd, who once they discovered she was a woman, attacked her. She gave her baby to the Papal Physician who fled in her carriage, leaving her behind. The crowd stoned her, nearly to death, but she was rescued by a group of our people."

"Why?"

"We needed to know where she had hidden the book, and under threat of destroying it if we had to find it ourselves, she told us. We released her and she was placed in prison, where she lived out her days until her son, the baby born that day, was old enough, and powerful enough, to convince the authorities to have her jailed in his facility, where she remained until her death."

"I thought you said she died because of the Vault?"

"No, I said a pope was lost. The position, not the man, or in this case, woman."

"Fascinating. And you have proof of this?"

"It is written in our archives. But all the proof you need is in the street name of where it happened."

"What do you mean?"

Nazario motioned for Acton to continue walking. "There's a street in Rome called the Via Sacra. Do you know what the locals call it?"

"Between the Coliseum and St. Clement's Church? Isn't it nicknamed the Shunned Street?"

"It was renamed after the Pope Joan incident. This street was part of the usual route taken by the Pontiffs when journeying through the city, but even to this day, they never travel on it. I doubt they even know why anymore."

"That I'd believe. They've destroyed the history to avoid the embarrassment, and have probably been forbidden to speak of it for a thousand years." Acton stopped, staring up at the rock. "Here we are."

"Do your business, and"—Nazario raised his weapon—"no funny business."

Acton nodded, rounding the rock slowly, all the while searching for some means of escape. His eyes examined every rock, every crevice, every—.

He stopped.

On the other side there was a hollow, carved by ancient waters. He grabbed a fist-sized stone from the ground, squeezing it in his palm, then stepped inside. It went deep, almost all the way through to the other side, and was so dark he had to grope his way forward. Near the end, he found a recess to the side, deep enough to conceal a man.

Perfect.

He squeezed in the alcove and held his right hand over his shoulder, gripping the stone.

And waited.

His heart pounded as adrenaline fueled him with courage. This had to work. It was their only chance. He had to get that phone. He had to let someone know they were alive, and where they were.

A sound, from the front of his little cave.

Or was it?

He strained to hear through the blood rushing in his ears. He knew what he needed to do, yet was terrified of what would happen if he failed.

If I don't come out on top, we're all dead.

But the thought of killing someone with his bare hands horrified him. He had been forced to kill before, though it was with a gun, at a distance. This time, he'd be close enough to smell them, to feel them as they died.

Maybe I can just tie him up.

That was a possibility, but only if he knocked him out first. He couldn't approach this from that viewpoint. He needed to attack to kill. If the opportunity presented itself not to kill, then he'd take it, though he had to steel his resolve and approach this the only way he was likely to survive.

"Professor Acton. I said no games."

Acton nearly crawled out of his skin. The voice sounded only feet away, inches perhaps.

How did he get so far in without me hearing?

The rush in his ears answered him. He peered into the darkness, but could see nothing. He was sure he had had enough time for his eyes to adjust, and as he stared, he thought he could make out the opposite wall.

Something stepped in front of him, between him and the other side of the hollow. There was no doubting it. Acton raised the stone and stepped forward. His shoe scraped on a rock and he heard more than saw the figure in front of him whip toward him.

Acton dropped his fist hard, aiming at where he hoped the head would be. He made contact and heard a grunt, yet it was lower than he had expected.

Shoulder?

He rushed forward, his left hand extended, and the fabric of Nazario's tunic filled his hand as he raised his other for a second blow. A raging pain flashed through him, originating in the ribcage as Nazario landed a blow. With the breath knocked out of him, the second blow with the rock only glanced Nazario, maybe in the arm. Acton let his hand gripping the tunic slide up, searching for his opponent's throat, his right hand swinging out to the side and back. His left hand found Nazario's neck in time for him to adjust his swing slightly. The impact was solid, hard, Nazario's head jerking to the side, his jawbone touching Acton's hand that now gripped his throat. Nazario slumped slightly but recovered before Acton had a chance to take advantage of the situation.

Something clattered to the ground.

His gun!

There was no way to retrieve it, not in the dark, though at least now he wouldn't worry about getting shot. He pushed hard and shoved Nazario against the wall, his hand still gripping his opponent by the throat, squeezing off the oxygen. His right hand landed blow after blow on the man's ribcage and arm. He was winning. It was only a matter of time.

He heard a sound he had heard before.

And it fueled him with panic.

A knife had just been unsheathed. A long knife.

238

In his excitement at having what he thought was the upper hand, he had neglected Nazario's right arm.

His opponent hadn't.

Now Acton was facing a knife, with no way to see it. He removed his hand from Nazario's throat and dropped his arm, praying he would find his captor's right arm before the blade found him.

Something shoved into Acton's outstretched hand, and he closed his fingers around it. It was narrow like a forearm, which meant he now had control of the hand. It would be a battle of strength if he let it, but thoughts of his Krav Maga training kicked in. Strength wasn't the key. Leverage was. He pulled down on the arm then yanked it forward as he stepped aside, dropping the rock and shoving Nazario's shoulder with his right hand, sending him into a spin, his knife-wielding arm now twisted around and behind him. Acton shoved up hard, the hand with the knife now safely held against Nazario's back.

Acton pushed up again.

Harder.

Nazario cried out and the knife clattered to the ground as the pain proved too much. Acton reached around with his right arm and wrapped it around Nazario's neck, placing the crook of his elbow tight against his throat. He let go of Nazario's now disarmed limb and jammed his elbow down on Nazario's left shoulder. He interlaced the fingers of his right hand on his left arm then wrapped the fingers of his left hand around the back of Nazario's neck.

And squeezed.

Nazario's arms flung about, struggling to free himself from the viselike grip, occasionally landing a blow or a scratch, yet Acton kept pressing. Just a few more seconds and he would have his opponent out cold. Nazario dropped to his knees, jerking Acton forward and down.

He maintained his grip.

Nazario's hands slapping on the ground didn't concern Acton until he realized what was happening.

He's looking for the knife! Or the gun!

Metal scraped rock. And it didn't sound like a knife. He squeezed harder. A shot rang out, unaimed, but it sent the message.

Acton pushed forward with his left hand, reinforced by his own chin pressing into the back of Nazario's head. Another shot. He winced from a stinging sensation on his side, as if something had just bitten him. It wasn't painful enough to have been a direct hit, yet he was pretty sure he had just been grazed. He took a breath and jerked his viselike grip tighter while pushing on the back of Nazario's neck. He cringed at a sudden snap, Nazario's head noticeably moving forward as the crack of bone echoed through the small cave.

Nazario went limp.

Acton dropped the now lifeless body to the ground then fell upon the cold stone himself, exhausted, eyes filled with tears as he realized what he had just done. He had taken a life with his bare hands. In Peru, he had been forced to kill, yet it was at a distance, with a gun. He had just reacted, and it was over in seconds. He had then proceeded to save the life of his other attacker.

But this.

This took minutes. This took his bare hands. His victim's sweat was on his hands, his arms, his clothes. He spat, certain he could taste his victim.

He was going to kill you. He was going to kill all of you.

He had done what was necessary. He had done the right thing.

And now he couldn't let it go to waste.

He groped around the floor and soon found the knife and gun, tucking both into his belt. Grabbing Nazario's body, he rolled him over and pulled the satellite phone off his belt, then yanked the belt free, removing the sheath for the knife. He looped his own belt through the hole on the sheath, slid the knife into place, then searched Nazario's pockets. He found one extra magazine, pocketed it, then hurried to the entrance of the hollow. Looking about, he found no one, and, rather than return to camp, he rushed north of it, toward an outcropping of rocks where he could survey the entire area without being seen, and in a direction from which he would likely not be expected.

Hidden, he flipped the antenna up and sent a text message to the one person who needed it the most.

we r alive

Base Commander's Office
Diyarbakir Airbase, Turkey
Now

"What's happening?" Laura rose as the colonel and Giasson entered the room they were now waiting in, the office of the Base Commander one of the few air-conditioned spaces on the base. Laura didn't know how to feel. For hours, the love of her life was dead. Then he wasn't. But he could be again. She growled in her head.

I just need answers!

Her outward expression was a little calmer, and probably seemed perfectly so to those who didn't know her.

"The Iranians have been contacted, and they are sending a rescue team in," said Giasson.

"Can we trust them?"

Reading beat her to it. It was what they were all thinking.

Babcock shook his head. "Frankly, no. But will they kill them? I don't think they would kill the Pope now that it's been confirmed he's alive on the ground. If they did, they wouldn't have to worry about the Israelis hitting them, they'd have to worry about every Catholic country out there. Shit, Poland and the Philippines would probably declare war."

"But you expect problems?"

"Yes. Two things. One, we don't know how many hostage-takers are alive with them. They most likely *don't* want to be 'rescued'"—the colonel created his own air quotes—"so there could be gunplay, and two, once they do rescue them, you can be almost guaranteed they'll milk the situation for as long as they can, with only the Pope being released after photos and video are taken of him shaking the hands of every murderous cleric in the country, then they'll probably hang on to everyone else, put on some sort of show trial, sentence them to death, then in exchange for some concession, release them to even more fanfare. It could take months, maybe years, before we ever see them in person again."

Laura sat back down and the others in the room took their seats. "Perhaps it's time to try and send a message back? To warn him?" It had been agreed not to send a reply, just in case James had managed to send a message surreptitiously, unbeknownst to his captors. She had never bought into that line of reasoning. It didn't seem likely to her that he might get a phone from them without them knowing. He either had always had it, found it in the crash—which meant they didn't know he had it—or he had taken it from them in a successful escape.

"We'll have a Predator over the area in minutes, then we'll have a better idea of what's going on."

"How do you know where they are? It's been hours."

"Because he made a call, and we pinpointed his location."

Laura and Reading both leaned forward.

"Who did he call?"

243

3 Miles Outside the Green Zone
Iran
15 Minutes Earlier

Acton watched from his vantage point as Federico emerged from the cave and began to search for him and Nazario. Not knowing where to look, he was calling out Nazario's name into the increasing darkness. This was Acton's opportunity to eliminate a second hostage-taker, but he'd have to do it silently. That meant either the knife, or hand to hand again, and the way Federico was holding his weapon, even the knife couldn't assure a silent takedown. One squeeze of his finger and shots would be fired, even if it were in a death spasm.

I need help.

He was sure the Iranians would be here soon. They must have figured out by now they were missing a jeep. And he didn't trust them as far as he could throw them. Yet he couldn't leave to seek help either. He was, after all, in Iran, so there would be no help to find, and more importantly, he couldn't abandon his companions. Once they couldn't find Nazario, who knew what they would do with the hostages? From all outward appearances, Nazario was the only one holding things together among the three.

His eyebrows shot up as a possible answer to his problems flashed through his mind. A smile etched across his face as he thought about it, then, nodding to himself, he slowly made his way farther from the camp and out of earshot. He dialed his good friend, and boss, Dean Gregory Milton, at home. It rang twice before a tiny voice answered.

"Milton residence, how may I help you?"

Acton's smile grew at the sound of Milton's daughter Niskha. "Hi sweetheart, this is Uncle Jim. Is your daddy home?"

"Uncle Jim! Daddy, it's Uncle Jim! Uncle Jim, Daddy walked all day today without his wheelchair! Daddy, it's Uncle Jim!" Acton had to laugh as he pictured Niskha talking into the phone to him, then screaming for her dad with the phone still positioned directly in front of her mouth.

Another voice came on the line. "Jim, is that you?"

A wave of relief washed over him at Milton's voice.

"Bye, Uncle Jim!"

"Bye, sweetheart."

There was a click as the phone was hung up, and the two college buddies were left alone to talk. "Jim, what the hell—"

"No time to talk, just listen. Got a pen and paper?"

"Yes, go ahead."

"Okay, take some notes, but I have no doubt this call is being recorded, so here goes. This message is for Delta Force Command. I need to get a message to BD, Big Dog, head of Bravo Team. I need help. Professor James Acton, the one who was involved with the crystal skulls in London, the one who was involved with the nuclear bomb issue last year, needs your help. I was on the plane that crashed, and I, along with the Pope, the head of the Roman Catholic Church, and Detective Inspector Chaney of Scotland Yard, are still alive, and being held captive by terrorists. We also have Iranian military units closing on our position. Trace this satellite call. I estimate we are near the Turkish border, one hour's drive and five hours walk northwest from the crash site. Whoever is examining this call on Echelon, I need help. I don't know what other keywords you need to flag this for immediate attention, but how about terrorist, bomb, hijack, anthrax, and I'm going to kill that infidel of a president you have."

He took a deep breath.

"Done?"

"Hopefully that will get their attention."

"What do you want me to do?"

245

"Call my folks, tell them I'm okay, just in case they heard something to the contrary, then call Fort Bragg and keep calling Fort Bragg, repeating as much of what I just said to them until they put you through to someone."

"Will do. And Jim?"

"What?"

"How the hell do you keep getting yourself into these situations?"

"Someone wants to make a movie out of my life, and needs good material?"

"I'll call Hollywood so maybe karma will back off for a bit."

"I wish someone would." Acton peeked around the corner of the rock and couldn't see Federico anywhere. "I've got to go. Hopefully I'll be talking to you soon."

"Good luck, my friend. Be careful."

"Will do. Oh, and Corky."

"Yeeessss."

He smiled at the way Milton drew out the word—his friend hated the nickname. "Great news on the walking."

Acton hung up before becoming all teary-eyed over his friend's progress regaining his mobility. He still blamed himself for Milton being in a wheelchair, and until he saw his friend walking about like the old days, he would never forgive himself.

"Don't move."

His heart leaped into his throat at Federico's voice, directly behind him. He stood slowly, but left his arms down.

Never put your hands up unless they ask you to.

His SAS instructor's voice echoed through his head. He calmed himself with slow steady breaths.

Your body may be a prisoner, but your mind isn't. It will be your key to escape.

He had a gun, he had a knife. He couldn't see any way to use either at the moment.

"Turn around, slowly."

Getting at his gun would be impossible, so he offered it up. If Federico saw it on his own, he was liable to shoot first. "Do you want my gun first?"

"Yes."

"Okay, take it easy, I'm going to remove it from my belt in my back with two fingers, and drop it to the ground. Then I'll kick it to you."

"Okay."

Acton reached behind his back and lifted up his shirt, revealing the gun tucked into his belt. He gripped the handle with his thumb and forefinger, deliberately shuffling his feet counterclockwise, so he could turn his head to the left and look at Federico as he did so. He pulled the gun slowly from his belt as he reached down with his now hidden right hand and slowly drew the knife from its sheath. With the gun free from his belt, he dropped it to the ground and continued to turn, positioning his left foot to kick the gun toward Federico. Still hidden behind his torso, his right hand gripped the handle of the knife, his index finger on the top of the dull side of the blade, the hilt tucked into the palm of his hand. His shoulders, now perpendicular to Federico, hid his insane plan.

"Here you go."

Acton flicked the gun as hard as he could. Federico flinched, his eyes on the "ball" as it clattered across the rocky landscape. It slid to a stop at his feet. He bent over to pick it up, and as he did, he swung his Beretta PM12-S2 submachine gun behind his back.

Acton readied himself, stepping back and raising the knife level to his still hidden shoulder, wrist cocked.

Federico picked up the weapon and stood. Acton turned, squaring his shoulders with his opponent as he stepped forward. Federico's eyes bulged as Acton's right hand whipped over his shoulder, the blade glistening in the last of the day's sunlight. His finger slid along the top of the knife as his hand gently loosened its grip, sending the blade hurling toward its target, the angle only changing slightly as it sliced through the air, his instructor having taught him spinning knife throws were only in the movies. Federico reached for his weapon, his eyes, and Acton's, on the blade.

Federico turned, and as it became clear what was about to happen, Acton leaped forward. The knife buried in Federico's shoulder. He screamed out in pain, the blade sinking at least a couple of inches into the fleshy target. In seconds, Acton was on him, placing his foot behind Federico and shoving his enemy's body over the leg, knocking him to the ground. Acton dropped down, pushing his knee into Federico's gasping stomach, then punched him in the throat. He pulled the knife from the shoulder and wiped it clean on the man's tunic, then, removing the man's belt, flipped him over and bound his wrists together with it.

And it was over.

It had taken less than sixty seconds. His instructor would have been proud, and he managed to avoid killing this time, although that was more luck than anything else. If Federico hadn't turned, the knife would have buried in his chest, likely killing him.

He quickly scanned his surroundings, making sure they were still alone, and for a brief moment, spotted something on the horizon. Federico groaned and Acton fished a handkerchief from his pocket and stuffed it in the man's mouth, silencing him as best he could. Acton perched behind a nearby rock, peering in the direction from which they had traveled earlier. It was now dark.

Except for the bobbing headlights in the distance.

At least three vehicles, possibly four, were approaching.

They probably got a bead on the call.

There was no time for regrets. He had done the right thing. The call was their only hope of rescue from friendly forces. And if he knew his friend, he wouldn't stop until he had satisfaction.

Come on, Greg, work your magic!

Milton Residence
St. Paul, Maryland
Now

"Sir, I must insist you stop calling, otherwise I'll be required to report you to Homeland Security."

"Good! Do that!" Milton took a long breath. "Listen to me. You know and I know that the Delta Force operates from your base. This is no secret. The world knows it. It's all over the Internet. Can we at least agree on that?"

"Sir, I cannot confirm or deny anything with you. Now I'm terminating this call."

"Please, listen to me, and I'll stop calling."

There was a pause.

"Are you Catholic?"

"I'm sorry, sir—"

Milton cut her off. "I'm sorry, I shouldn't have asked that." He lowered his voice. "Have you been watching the news, about how the Pope was kidnapped, and the plane crashed, and he's dead?"

There was silence.

"I'll take your silence as a yes. Well, my friend, my best friend, Professor James Acton, was on that plane as well. So, let me ask you this. If they're all dead, why did I just get a call from him less than an hour ago?"

"I-I'm sorry, sir, but—"

"Yeah, yeah, I know, you have to terminate the call. Can I ask you one question?"

"Yes, sir."

"If you were me, and you had this information, who would you call?"

"I'm sorry, sir, I can't answer that. Goodbye."

The line went dead for the fifth time that night. Milton pressed the off button and searched in vain for a place to slam the cordless phone into something that wouldn't break it.

What I'd give for an old-fashioned phone with a cradle right now.

"Any luck?"

Milton shook his head. "No." He looked at his wife, Sandra, sitting opposite him at the kitchen table. "I guess we can only hope that this Echelon system works, and works quickly."

"What's Echelon?"

Milton leaned back. "Jim explained it to me once. Apparently, all phone calls, faxes, emails, pretty much every communication made into and out of the US, and around the world, is monitored. It's some sort of computer system that converts everything to a readable format, then searches the conversations for keywords like 'bomb' or 'anthrax,' and flags them for human review. It also searches for voices it knows, monitors specific phones—you know, it's basically Big Brother incarnate."

Sandra sipped her tea. "Sounds awful."

"Agreed, but I guess it's led to a lot of intelligence over the years that has saved a lot of lives."

"Yes, but at what cost?"

Milton shrugged. "Right now, if it saves Jim, I'm willing to live with the cost."

"Of course."

The phone rang. Milton nearly dropped it, not having found a place to put it down hard enough for his satisfaction.

"Hello?"

"Write this number down."

The voice was barely a whisper. But he recognized it.

He picked up the pen sitting on the table and grabbed his notepad. "Go ahead."

A number was slowly read to him, and he jotted each digit down.

"Thank you," he said, though it was to a dead line.

Sandra leaned over to see the number. "Who was that?"

251

"That was the base operator I was just talking to."

"Are you sure?"

"Pretty."

"Did they say who that number belongs to?"

"No, and there's only one way to find out."

He dialed the number.

It rang twice.

"Colonel Clancy's office. How may I help you?"

Milton quickly jotted down the name. "Hello, my name is Gregory Milton, I'm the dean of St. Paul's University in Maryland. I need to talk to Colonel Clancy about a very urgent matter, regarding a Delta Force member named BD or Big Dog, as well as Professor Acton, and the recent crash of the plane carrying the Pope. It's urgent that I speak to him."

"I'm sorry, sir, but it appears you were put through to this number by mistake. I'll transfer you to the main switch—"

"No, please, wait. Listen, my friend, my best friend, Professor James Acton, Jim. He was the one involved in London with the crystal skulls. He was involved last year with the Russians and the nuclear weapon. He's now a friend of one of your men, Big Dog. God, I wish I knew his real name, but I'm sorry, he forgot to mention it. He's alive. He's supposed to be dead, but he's alive. With the Pope. They survived the plane crash, and I'm his only hope at—" There was a click on the line. "Dammit!"

"What?"

"I think they hung—"

Another voice came on the line. "Dean Milton?" It was deep. Authoritative. The voice of someone who might be able to do something.

"Yes?"

"I'm going to hang up now. Please answer your door."

The call ended and before Milton could say anything, the doorbell rang.

Sandra rose from her chair. "I'll get it."

Milton shook his head. "No, it's for me, apparently."

Her eyes narrowed as she cocked her head, looking at him. "Now how could you possibly know that?"

He wheeled out of the kitchen, toward the front entrance. "I'll explain later." He opened the door, and a man whose wardrobe oozed government, stood there.

"Dean Milton?"

"Yes."

"This is for you." A phone was handed to him. It immediately rang. The man turned on his heel and walked down the path to the street where a plain black car idled, its tinted windows concealing its occupants.

Milton closed the door and answered the phone as he rolled back into the kitchen. "Hello?"

"Dean Milton?"

"Yes?"

"This is Colonel Clancy. We're now on a secure line."

"Oh, okay." Milton was still wrapping his head around what was going on. "How did you—"

"Your first phone call was monitored, and a secure line was dispatched to you right away, almost an hour ago."

Milton wasn't sure what to say. "Wow."

Are you kidding me? Did I just say 'wow' to a Delta Force Colonel?

Milton squeezed his eyes shut and took a quick breath. "If you monitored my call, then you know what's going on."

"Yes."

"Are you going to do something about it?"

"Yes."

"What?"

"That, I cannot say."

"I don't need details, I just need to know if you're going to save my friend."

"Rest assured, action is being taken. For now, I need you to sit tight and stop calling people."

Milton's ire was piqued. "If it was your friend——"

"I would have done exactly what you did. And now please leave it in our hands."

Milton slowly exhaled. "Okay, I understand."

"Thank you, Dean. Goodnight."

The line went dead and Milton put the phone down, his hands trembling. He lay his head on the table, cradled in his arms, and closed his eyes. His wife's hands were on his shoulders immediately, gently squeezing as his eyes burned.

Please, God, save Jim.

Somewhere over Turkish Airspace

I love this life.

Command Sergeant Major Burt "Big Dog" Dawson watched as wind whipped around the cargo hold, the ramp at the tail of their C-130H Hercules transport slowly closing as several of his men wrestled with the gear they had just skyhooked from the ground. They had received the call almost an hour ago. His men were exhausted from just finishing the mission in Iran, but when they heard who they were rescuing, each to a man had insisted they take part. Some were Catholic, so were doing it to save their pope. He was doing it because he respected Professor James Acton, as did his team.

And all were doing it because it was the right thing to do.

The ramp closed and he stepped forward to watch his men unload the gear. They had been extracted as planned from Iran without incident, and instead of flying south to Kuwait, they had flown north toward Al Sahra Airbase in Iraq, where the Hercules they now occupied had been dispatched. Their choppers hadn't even hit the tarmac when he and his men had hopped off and raced into the back of the Hercules. The moment the last boot had left the ground, Dawson had yelled for them to take off. The plane, already in position on the runway, rolled forward as the ramp closed, and was airborne less than a minute later.

He had formulated a plan based upon the intel he had been provided en route, and the necessary gear had just arrived. He stepped forward and took a knee, twirling his hand over his head. His team took knees in a circle, all ready for their final briefing. Dawson's eyes circled the group and rested on his friend, Red.

"Okay, ladies, here's the situation. Our three hostages are five klicks inside the Iranian border. Our mission is to eliminate any HTs, rescue the hostages, and escort them to the border, eliminating any local resistance if necessary."

"Why the wingsuits?" asked Niner.

"We can't let the Iranians know what we're doing. This plane will not enter their airspace. Team One will wing in from just over the Turkish border to their location, Team Two will parachute onto the Turkish side of the border and be prepared to hoof it in if we need help."

"That still puts us a good hike away with the type of terrain we're talking about," said Red.

Dawson nodded. "You'll be leading Team Two. Get your boots on the ground, in a position where you can cross without being detected, then sit tight for my signal. If it looks like we're going to need help, head in. Hopefully we'll have closed some of that distance ourselves."

Red handed the wingsuit he had been holding to Niner. "I guess I won't be needing this."

Niner took the wingsuit and hugged it. "If the superman suit came with these, they wouldn't need to put the label on it warning kids it won't make them fly." His voice was dreamy, wistful.

Chuckles filled the hold and Atlas smacked Niner on the back, sending him tumbling forward. Chuckles roared into laughter as Atlas helped him up. "Sorry, sometimes I don't know my own strength."

Niner made a show of dusting himself off. "You should come with your own warning label. You're built like Ahh-nold."

"Governator or Terminator?"

Niner knocked on Atlas' body armor. "Terminator," he said in his best Schwarzenegger impression.

Dawson smiled. The back and forth jabs might not be tolerated by some, especially when going into a mission, but they were returning from one, heading straight into another. He cut them a little slack, though there wasn't much time. "May I continue?"

"Sorry, Sergeant Major!" echoed Niner and Atlas.

"Niner, Jimmy, Stucco, Casey, Spock, you're with me. The rest are with Red. Team One will wing in to our targets' last known location, parachute in the rest of the way, take out any HTs, secure what we assume are three hostages, then escape on foot to the Turkish border five klicks away. If we meet resistance, we take them out. Any questions?"

"No, Sergeant Major!" yelled the chorus.

"Okay, suit up. ETA ten minutes."

3 Miles (5 Klicks) Outside the Green Zone
Iran

Gunfire erupted from the entrance of the hollow created by the three mighty stones they had discovered earlier. Acton had screwed up. He had assumed that Tino wouldn't leave the hostages alone, and he had been wrong. After spotting the Iranian convoy, he had made it back toward the camp and literally bumped into Tino coming around a rock, apparently having just relieved himself. The man had yelped and run, spraying bullets behind him, forcing Acton to dive for cover. By the time he recovered, Tino was secure in the cave, and a stray bullet had ruined the Beretta Acton had liberated from Federico, leaving him only with Navario's handgun.

And now Tino was in a panic.

The gunfire stopped while the man reloaded.

"Stop firing!" yelled Acton. "You'll give away our position to the Iranians!"

The cocking handle sliding back echoed. But more gunfire didn't follow.

"They're coming?"

Acton breathed a sigh of relief.

The enemy of my enemy is my friend?

"Yes, only a few miles out. Douse that fire, make sure there's no smoke."

"How do I do that?" It was clear from the man's voice he was more scared of the Iranians than he was of Acton.

"Use sand, not water."

There were pockets of sand all around them among the rocks, though it would mean Tino would have to come out of the cave. Acton debated shooting him. Then made up his mind. He positioned himself, weapon in hand, and took aim at the cave entrance. This was an opportunity he couldn't miss. A shadowy figure emerged slowly, hands raised.

"Don't shoot, it's me!"

Acton dropped to his haunches, turning around and pressing against the cold stone, its stored heat already radiated out into the night. He closed his eyes while pressing the equally cold barrel against his forehead.

Chaney!

His heart raced as he realized he had almost killed his partner in all this. He slid over and peered around the rock. Chaney was bare-chested, his shirt lying on the ground. He scooped handfuls of dirt and dropped them into the bright white dress shirt, then grabbed the four corners made from the sleeves and tails, and hauled the dirt inside. Within minutes, the small fire was noticeably dimmer, then dark.

It was nearly pitch black now, the only light from the stars and a low moon. Acton looked to the east and the headlights were clearly visible. He had no way of knowing if they were simply following a road that might take them right by, or if they were weaving in and out of the very rocks he now hid behind, on their way to where they had traced his satellite phone call.

No matter what, they were only minutes away.

His mind reeled as he debated what to do. He could convince his captor to let him rejoin the group—there was strength in numbers. But he doubted the man would agree to it, and there was little hope they could hold off an entire platoon or two of Iranian soldiers for very long. Besides, fighting back would only get them killed, and they would run out of ammo long before the Iranians. Not to mention it would give them an excuse to just kill everyone, which was what he had to assume their goal was, since they had clearly attacked the crash site.

No. His best bet, and everyone else's, was to stay out of sight. Monitor the situation, then if the Iranians captured his friends, tail them for when help arrived. He took another look at the headlights and cursed—they were making straight for them. He surveyed his surroundings, then at a crouch, ran as quickly as he could to an outcropping several hundred feet distant. He was sure they would search the area, especially if they knew how many people they were looking for. He took up position behind a rock and waited, the opening in the boulders housing his companions now small.

The dimly lit landscape was eerily still, occasionally interrupted by slices of yellow as headlights cut through the dark, the air filled with the roar of engines straining against the upward climb and the constant lurching of the suspensions as natural potholes swallowed tires. The first vehicle crested a nearby rise and stopped. Something was yelled in Farsi and men poured out of the vehicle, including those grinding to a halt behind the first. Within moments, the entire area was crawling with troops, at least a dozen, guns at the ready, moving closer and closer to the hiding place created eons ago.

His finger rubbed along the trigger guard.

Easy. There's nothing you can do now.

A soldier rounded the mass of stones and stepped inside the entrance. A burst of gunfire sent him flying through the air, his now lifeless body slamming unceremoniously on the ground. His comrades in arms raced toward the opening, spraying lead into the darkness. Acton prayed Chaney and the Pope were deep inside, shielded from the bullets, but he couldn't be sure. Gunfire continued to pour into the entrance, Acton's heart racing faster with each volley.

He was hiding so he could save them later. He had hoped to tail them until help could arrive.

If no one is left to save, then why are you hiding?

He sucked in a lungful of air then carefully took aim at the soldier closest to him, behind his comrades. He squeezed the trigger as he slowly exhaled. The man dropped, unnoticed with all the noise. Encouraged, he took aim at the next target, partly shielded from his friends by a large rock.

Exhale.

Squeeze.

Another dropped.

He forced to the back of his mind that these were human beings he was shooting. That didn't matter right now. They were the enemy, trying to kill the good guys. This was black and white, not gray. He squeezed off another shot, another dropped. This time one of his comrades noticed the gunfire behind him had stopped, and turned his head to look. Acton quickly took aim and squeezed. The man dropped, but he was in plain view of all the others.

Four down plus the one Tino had shot.

He counted eight more. And they had all stopped firing, now aiming their guns in his direction.

Sort of.

They had no idea where the shots had come from, only that four more of their platoon were down. If he fired again, they would have a bead on him, both from the sound and the muzzle flash.

The sound might echo. Empty the magazine, hopefully take a few out, then fall back, using the rocks as cover?

He checked to his right and saw a series of large boulders that would make perfect cover, the first less than five feet away. If he could only...

The platoon leader, using hand signals, indicated his men should fan out. He walked forward, flanked by two of his group. Acton picked his targets. First shot, left flank down. Second shot, the platoon leader, spinning to see what happened, took it through the neck while the third dove to the right, escaping the third shot meant for him, but now, prone and on his side, took the fourth in the stomach.

Gunfire erupted as Acton leaped from behind the rock and dove toward a larger boulder to his right. Ricochets surrounded him, bouncing off the very rocks he was using as cover, some of the altered trajectories coming close to hitting him. He rounded his new hiding place and made a beeline for another, farther behind and to the right. Crouching, he rushed behind the next boulder and pulled another mag from his pocket as he reexamined his situation. Their fire was concentrated where he was originally hiding. He had apparently successfully evaded them.

Now what to do about it.

He had taken out seven. There should only be five left. This was his last mag. Twelve rounds. There was no way he could take out five people with just twelve shots now that he had lost the element of surprise.

You did seven in eight. Why not?

Acton pulled the crisp night air in through his nose, filling his chest and stomach. He pushed the air out from between his lips, then dashed to the next rock.

Still unnoticed.

The gunfire had stopped, however. They were no longer convinced they were shooting at anything. Acton watched as the five stood, looking around, apparently uncertain what to do.

Cut off the head…

The headless snake of a platoon floundered for a few moments until one took the initiative and advanced, indicating to the others they should follow.

They did.

Organized again. Dangerous again.

He darted to the next boulder and his foot caught on a rock, tripping him. His finger, not on the trigger guard like it should be, but on the trigger itself, squeezed with the impact, a single round firing off into the night. Harmless to others in the vast wasteland he now occupied, though deadly to him, his position now given away. He scrambled the last few feet as bullets ripped up the ground where he had just been.

Now you're screwed.

Three miles in, Three miles up.
Iran

Dawson's heart pounded. Not from fear, but from excitement. He loved wingsuit flying. His arms were stretched out to his sides, his legs spread, the thin lightweight material increasing his surface area, giving him enough lift to control his direction of descent, and to slow him enough that his parachute wouldn't rip off when deployed. Niner and Spock were flanking him to the rear, with Stucco, Casey and Jimmy behind them, forming a flying wedge in the night sky. The terrain below whipped by at well over one hundred miles per hour, nearly a blur, and irrelevant. The Heads Up Display in his helmet told him all he needed to know. Altitude. Location. Distance and direction to target.

And they were close.

He eyeballed the ground, though could make out little, the night vision display mode showing nothing but rock and mostly barren terrain.

"BD, do you see that, straight ahead?"

Dawson raised his head slightly. Flashes. "Looks like gunfire." They rapidly closed on the position and an indicator pulsed in the bottom right of his display. "Deploy chutes, now." Each of his team indicated their deployment in his comm, but he waited.

"Shit, BD, deploy your chute!"

It was Niner.

"I need to get a little closer."

"You'll pancake, boss, and I ain't gotta spatula."

Dawson chuckled and watched his indicator. He yanked on his chord, the jolt as his chute opened above him tore him momentarily from reality. Now, floating gently to the ground, or at least slower, his descent still leg-breaking speed at the moment, he grabbed his toggles and scanned the action below him. "I've got five hostiles firing on a single target. Could be one of our hostages."

He adjusted his trajectory so he'd come in from behind those firing. He readied his M4.

"Coming in on your right."

"On your left."

Dawson's head pivoted in both directions. "How the hell did you two get down here so fast?"

"A whole lotta flarin' goin' on," said Niner in a rather poor imitation of an Elvis ditty.

"Okay, the rest of you provide cover from above once we hit the ground."

"Got ya covered, sixty seconds behind, BD," replied Jimmy.

An explosion rocked the scene below as a hand grenade exploded.

The firing stopped, and the person hiding behind the rock now stood, hands raised in the air, the weapon he was using held by one finger looped through the trigger guard. The attackers who Dawson now recognized as Iranian regulars, lowered their weapons slightly as one motioned for the man behind the rock to throw the weapon. It was tossed to the ground several feet to the man's right.

Not a good toss. I wonder if—

Dawson never had a chance to finish the thought.

Acton slowly stepped out from behind the rock sheltering him. There had been just too many bullets, and too many close calls, and once grenades entered the picture, it was over. Luckily for him, whoever tossed it was a pansy and it had fallen short, but it had done its job. He was finished. His hands raised, they yelled something in Farsi, and he tossed the gun a few feet away.

Just in case.

He rounded the rock slowly, his heart hammering. Would they take revenge for the death of their comrades? These weren't soldiers he could trust even knew what the Geneva Convention was. Then again, he wasn't a uniformed soldier, so it didn't apply to him. He was a civilian who had just killed seven of their friends. Seven friends who were trying to kill him, though he was certain that was semantics in their minds.

The one who had taken charge raised his weapon and fired. Acton had spotted the motion and was already diving for his gun when the muzzle belched its first round. He hit the ground, his hand grabbing the weapon. He rolled, straightening out his arm as he did so, and took a bead on the Iranian as the man lowered his weapon to regain his target.

Acton squeezed the trigger.

Gunfire filled the air and all five soldiers collapsed in heaps.

Acton turned his hand to examine his gun.

How the hell—

Something fluttered overhead. He rolled on his back and pointed his weapon, but didn't fire. He counted several chutes, all with what appeared to be winged demons under them, some type of material connecting their arms to their torsos and their legs together.

He lowered his weapon and they lowered theirs. He tossed his to the ground, only two rounds remaining leaving it useless, and rose to his feet, brushing off as the first man touched down less than ten yards away. The soldier smacked the center of his chest and shrugged out of his harness. He ran toward Acton, his helmeted head scanning the surroundings, his weapon following his line of sight. He came to a stop in front of Acton who silently prayed he hadn't been delivered from the hands of one enemy and into another. The man pulled off his helmet and Acton breathed a sigh of relief, his shoulders slumping and his head dropping slightly as he realized his ordeal was over. "Am I ever glad to see you."

Dawson grinned. "Just happened to be in the neighborhood. Thought we'd drop by."

Acton raised his head and smiled as he looked at the man who had once tried to kill him and the woman he loved, and who he now at least considered an acquaintance, and definitely someone he could trust. "You got my message."

"We got your message."

Acton let a long slow breath out and his eyes closed as he stared up and through them to Heaven, saying a silent thank you. He opened his eyes and extended his hand. Dawson's iron grip enveloped his.

"Good to see you again, Professor."

"Holy shit, Professor, did you do all this yourself?" Acton recognized the Asian member of the group from their last meeting as he jogged up.

He shook the man's hand. "Niner, wasn't it?"

"Ten-four, Doc." Niner looked about the area. "I count eight besides the group we took out. Is that right?"

Acton nodded.

"And you took them all out yourself?"

He nodded again. "All but one."

"Props, dawg!" laughed Niner as he extended a fist.

Acton shook his head with half a smile and a chuckle as he bumped fists with Niner. The third man walked up as three more chutes flared above. "Chutes secured." He smiled at Acton. "Hey, Professor. Judgin' by what I've just seen, I'm not sure you really needed us."

The tension of the moment gone, Acton loosened up again. "One more mag and I would have called off the rescue, but"—he patted his pockets—"out of ammo." He took a step toward Niner and leaned forward. "And I think I took out the guy who tried to shoot me. So that makes eight for me, four for *all*"—he swung his finger at the now six men—"of you."

Dawson laughed then the smile wiped off his face. "Secure the area, police the chutes. I don't want the Iranians knowing we were here." His men fanned out, and Dawson turned back to Acton. "Where are the others?"

"Oh shit!" In all the excitement, he had forgotten why he was fighting. He slipped around Dawson and rushed to the entrance of the shelter where only minutes before hundreds of rounds had emptied into it. He stopped at the entrance and stuck his head inside as Dawson stepped up behind him along with another of his team. "Is everyone okay?"

No reply.

"Chaney, Your Holiness, it's me, Jim. I've got the Delta Force team here with me. It's safe now!"

"The same bloody chaps that tried to kill us in London, and you say we're safe?"

Acton laughed in relief. "The very same."

Niner stepped forward but Acton placed a hand on his shoulder and raised a finger for him to wait.

"Is it safe to come in?"

"Yes. He's dead," echoed Chaney's voice.

Acton tapped Niner's shoulder signaling he was good to go. Niner entered, weapon raised, the night vision visor on his helmet lowered. Dawson stepped around Acton, following Niner in, his helmet once again perched on his head. He pointed at Acton then the ground. Acton gave a thumbs-up.

A few moments later Niner announced the all-clear. "Professor Acton, come on down!" yelled Niner in his best Bob Barker impression. Acton stepped inside, and a few feet in found the area lit by glow sticks, the green light illuminating the hollow nicely.

"Good to see you again, Professor." Acton turned toward the voice and saw Chaney and the Pontiff tucked behind a rock, the old man's hand on the forehead of the third member of the Keepers of the One Truth, drag marks indicating he had fallen dead several feet away.

Acton stepped over and knelt down. "You two okay?" Chaney nodded. The Pontiff didn't reply, his lips moving in silent prayer, his eyes closed. Acton motioned toward the body. "What's this?"

Chaney rolled his eyes slightly. "He insisted on giving him his last rites, so I had to risk my own neck to drag his corpse over here."

A voice boomed through the hollow. "BD! We've got company!"

Dawson pointed at the Pontiff. "Can he walk?"

Chaney shook his head. "No way, his feet are open wounds."

"But other than that, he can be transported?"

"Yes."

"Okay, get him outside, now." Dawson strode from the hollow as Acton and Chaney helped the old man to his feet, then, linking arms behind his back and hands under his thighs, created a human chair, shuffling him out of the stone shelter and into the night air, his feet never touching the ground. Several yards away, Dawson was talking to one of his men.

"At least half a dozen vehicles to the east, another maybe dozen to the south, all heading right for us."

"Distance?"

"Eastern group, eight klicks. Southern, three."

"Shit. Just for once I'd like things to go nice and smooth."

"Where's the fun in that?"

Dawson grunted then pointed at the nearby vehicles in which the first group had arrived. "Get two of those running, disable the third."

His man jogged toward the first vehicle as Dawson pulled a Velcro covering open on his sleeve, revealing a small touch screen computer sewn into his jumpsuit. He tapped the screen several times then spoke. "Zero-Two, Zero-One, come in, over." Acton couldn't hear the other side of the conversation, but it was short. "Zero-Two, Zero-One. Proceed with hookup, I say again, proceed with hookup, out." Dawson resealed the Velcro and turned toward Acton and his party. "How's he doing?"

"I will be okay, my son. God will get me through this, now that his angels of deliverance have arrived."

"Holy shit, BD, we're angels!" Niner slapped his hand over his mouth. "Shit. Sorry, your popeness, I didn't mean to, umm, you know, swear in front of you."

The old man made the sign of the cross at him. "Three Hail Mary's in the morning, and all is forgiven."

Niner mimicked the hand motion then jogged off toward the now roaring vehicles. The old man turned to Chaney and Acton. "Do you think he knows I was joking?" He laughed, but it soon turned into a chest-wrenching cough.

"Are you okay?" Dawson knelt down in front of him.

The man nodded as he slowly regained control of his cough. "Yes, just God's punishment for forty years of smoking."

"Priests smoke?" Chaney couldn't disguise the surprise in his voice.

"Yes. We even appreciate the beauty of women. We are, after all, men, not robots. The difference between you and us, is that we try to reserve our love for God and our fellow man, not one person or vice. We try to overcome our lust with prayer, not indulgence. Unfortunately, like all men, we fail from time to time. Me, I failed every day, several times a day, for forty years, until finally I wrestled my demon to the ground and won."

"How'd you quit?" asked Dawson.

"Lots of prayer, followed by two patches, not one. And a pack of Nicorette a day."

They all laughed until they saw the old man was about to join them and, worried he might start coughing again, stopped.

"Let's get you into one of those vehicles," said Acton. The three of them helped him up then carried him again to one of the jeeps. Chaney and Acton climbed in the back with him, flanking him, as Niner took the driver's seat, Dawson the passenger. One of Dawson's men jogged by and Dawson flagged him down.

"Give the Professor your sidearm and ammo. We just might need some more firepower in here."

He pulled the weapon out of its holster and handed it, butt first, to Acton, along with three mags. "You know how to use that?"

Acton gave him a look. "I just killed *eight* Iranians, plus two of the hostage-takers. I'll be fine."

The soldier shook his head with half a smile, then slapped Acton on the back as he left at a jog for the other vehicle. "You're okay, Doc," he called over his shoulder.

Dawson leaned into the back, handing Chaney his sidearm and three mags. "Now I know *you* know how to use this."

Chaney nodded. "I think our professor here might know better from what I've seen, but yes, I've been trained."

Dawson turned back to Niner. "Let's go."

Niner shoved the vehicle into gear and popped the clutch. The jeep jolted forward and raced toward a large boulder directly in front. He cranked the wheel to the right, easing off the gas as he slid it into second, his passengers grabbing onto anything they could to steady themselves. "Sorry, boss, just gettin' used to the old girl."

Dawson grunted and tore open the pouch concealing his tactical computer. A few taps and a map appeared. Dawson pointed slightly to the left. "That's where we want to head. Two-eight-zero degrees." He pinched the display with two fingers, slowly drawing them closer. The map zoomed out, revealing a flashing dot to the left.

"Red's on the move."

Fifteen Feet Inside the Green Zone
Turkey

Red's team had only landed minutes before, less than a mile from the border. A quick speed march and they were, according to the GPS on Red's wearable combat computer, only feet from the border, the only indication of its existence two dusty trails on either side where vehicles from both countries would patrol, likely at irregular intervals. Red scanned the horizon with his binoculars and spotted something to the south. He zoomed in.

"Looks like we've got a border installation a couple of klicks from here, Iranian with opposing Turk forces." He handed the binoculars to Atlas who took a bead on the outpost, then handed them back. "Looks like there's activity."

Red checked again and saw several vehicles leaving in a hurry, dust kicked up by the spinning tires reflecting the headlights and taillights of the mini convoy.

Red's comm demanded his attention and he replied to Dawson's call. "Zero-One, Zero-Two. Read you loud and clear. Be advised, we have activity here. Three technicals heading your way, over."

"Zero-Two, Zero-One. Proceed with hookup, I say again, proceed with hookup, out."

"Zero-One, Zero-Two. Roger that, out."

He checked his computer, zooming out, Dawson's position revealed. "Okay, they need our help, and we've got five klicks to go." He scanned the horizon again and spotted nothing beyond the outpost and the three vehicles now almost out of sight. "Let's go." He rose and at a crouch, crossed the border into Iranian territory for the second time today.

Two covert missions in one day on Iranian soil. That's got to be some kind of record.

They jogged at a crouch and in silence, picking their feet up so as not to kick up dust that might be noticed by a guard post doing its job, and were soon among the rock-strewn landscape. They wove their way through and around boulder after boulder, and Red quickly realized this would take longer than he had hoped if it didn't clear out soon. They crested a ridge and directly in front of them found a lone soldier, privates in hand, a healthy prostate allowing a strong stream of urine to flow onto the dry landscape. It cut off in spurts as the man's jaw dropped. Red drew his knife, still at a jog, and flipped the blade so the sharp end faced outward and parallel to his forearm. He drew his arm back at the elbow, then lunged forward, the blade arcing in the air, slicing cleanly across the man's throat.

Atlas grabbed the body by the shirt before it dropped, and lowered the gurgling but otherwise quiet man to the ground as the rest of the team raced by. Red continued forward, finding the hapless man's partner smoking a cigarette in front of the headlights of their still idling vehicle, making himself a perfect target, and Red, a mass of black on black with the man's pupils constricted in the bright light, an invisible force.

Idiot. Who trained you?

The man kicked a rock, turning toward Red. He flicked his lit cigarette toward the unseen killing machine. His eyes momentarily bulged as the black of night carried the glowing ember back toward him, then coalesced into Red's frame reflected in the ambient light. The man reached for his weapon sitting on the hood of the vehicle.

But it was too late.

Red's knife plunged into the soft belly of the man as his free hand covered the man's mouth, squeezing tight, cutting off any calls for help, and acting as a handhold for Red to lower him to the ground as he jerked his knife upward, impacting the ribcage. He pulled the blade out and controlled the man's collapse. Kneeling beside him, he cleaned his blade on the man's pants as the last of the life bled out of him. The body shook as Red's hand still clenched the man's face, the death rattle something he would never get used to.

Sorry, buddy. Wrong place, wrong time.

He removed his hand then closed the fallen soldier's wide-open eyes before dragging the body into the darkness and out of the light exposing him to anyone else who might be in the area. He dropped to his knee and scanned their surroundings, spotting no one but his own team. He shuffled to the side of the jeep, and using his body and the jeep as cover, ripped the Velcro seal open and looked at the map of the area. The trail they were on wound up through the hill they had to climb, then straightened out on the other side. If they didn't run into anyone, they could reach BD in minutes.

If.

2.5 Miles Outside the Green Zone
Iran

"We'd be faster on foot, BD!"

Niner double-handed the wheel around another boulder then geared down. Gunfire erupted behind them, but out of range. Dawson didn't bother looking, though Acton did. Headlights bobbed in the distance. At least half a dozen sets. And they were close, their drivers making better time.

"They must be on some sort of trail we don't know about. There's no way I can keep ahead of them."

"Just keep driving. His Holiness can't walk, so this is our only choice. Just keep going. We'll meet up with Red and make a stand if we have to."

"Leave me."

Everyone, including Niner, turned to stare at the Pope.

Dawson reached over without looking and pushed Niner's face back toward the front of the car. The vehicle jerked as he avoided a desk-sized rock.

"Your Holiness, with all due respect, stow that kind of talk. Everyone is coming out of this. Alive." Dawson turned back to his map, then pointed. "Half a klick, top of that ridge."

Niner nodded.

Something streaked over their heads and exploded against the top of one of the larger boulders, showering them with smaller debris. Both Acton and Chaney pushed the Pontiff down and covered him with their bodies. More explosions surrounded them as Niner continued to push toward the top of the hill they were now on. Dawson was typing something on his computer, apparently oblivious to the chaos around them. Another explosion and Niner jerked his wheel to the left.

"Christ, that one was close!" He checked his rearview mirror. "Sorry, Padre, I just hate RPGs!"

274

"You're forgiven!" yelled the old man, his voice muffled from being hunched over. Acton and Chaney exchanged a quick grin.

Another explosion behind them had Niner slide to a stop. "They took a hit."

Dawson leaped out and ran back to the second vehicle. Acton turned and watched as Dawson helped one of his men, apparently with a leg injury, toward the lone intact vehicle, the other one now resting atop a three-foot rock, the driver side quarter panel scorched from a hit that had taken out the tire and much of the engine compartment. Dawson put the injured man in the passenger seat, then stood on the running board as the other three climbed on the opposite side, the last one smacking the side. "Go! Go! Go!"

Niner floored it, almost knocking some of their hangers-on off, then rounded a large boulder, positioning himself with it at their back as bullets ricocheted around them. "They're almost on top of us."

"Just get to that ridge."

Acton saw Dawson turn to the three men now riding with them. "As soon as we reach the top, spread out, find cover. We make our stand there. Target their lights, tires, engine compartments. We want to be the only ones leaving this hilltop on wheels." He leaned down so Niner could hear him. "When we reach the top, park this thing behind the biggest damned rock you can find, turn out the lights, and protect it like it's your sister's cherry. It's still our ticket out of here."

Niner shoved the vehicle into third as he found a stretch of relatively clear ground. Gunning the motor, they sped forward. Another sharp turn to the left and Niner rounded a large boulder, skidding the jeep to a halt. "We're here!" he announced, killing the lights and turning off the engine.

"Spread out, pick your targets, conserve your ammo. Lights, tires, engines, and anybody who gets too damned close." Dawson leaned in. "Your Holiness, you sit tight. Professor, Detective, I'd suggest you take up positions on either side of this rock, and shoot at anything that moves that doesn't have its back to you."

With that, he disappeared. Acton turned to the Pontiff. "Will you be okay?"

"Don't worry about me, my sons. I will simply lie here, and pray for all those who have lost their lives today because of me."

Acton started to say something about it not being the old man's fault, but gunfire erupted from everywhere. He rolled out with Chaney and took up position as Dawson had suggested.

Ordered?

With everything that had happened today, he was certain he deserved honorary instatement.

I wonder how Laura's doing.

Acton spotted a figure sneaking up from their left flank. He took a bead and waited for him to move to the next rock.

He fired.

The man dropped, writhing on the ground. Acton turned his attention back down the hill. He could see Dawson and Niner about ten feet ahead of him, each positioned behind rocks about waist high. Both had their M4s out, resting atop their cover, belching controlled shots calmly, occasionally ducking and switching to the other side of their cover. Back and forth, several shots at a time. Never panicking. Acton wondered what was going through their minds. Were they calm? Were they disconnected? He thought back to earlier, when he killed all those men, and he hated to admit there was a disconnect. Not with Nazario whom he had killed with his bare hands. But those he had shot. Those faceless men. He felt nothing. They probably had wives, children. Families who loved them just as his loved him. His stomach churned.

He doubled over and vomited.

Enough thinking!

"You okay?"

Acton spat his mouth clean and glanced over at a concerned Chaney. "Just realizing what I've done today."

Chaney gave him a slight smile of understanding, then graciously returned his attention to the action below, leaving Acton alone with his thoughts.

Deal with this later. Now, you've got to focus.

He kicked some dirt over his emotional discharge and checked their flank again.

Clear.

His stomach growled.

Now you're hungry?

He pictured a Chicago deep dish. His stomach growled some more.

Not helping!

He watched Dawson and Niner as they fired, then turned his attention to the enemy below them, his eyebrows shooting up. There were almost no lights left, and he could distinctly see several vehicles listing to one side or the other, one or more of their tires deflated. He glanced to his left again and took aim. Three targets. He couldn't risk handling it by himself this time.

"Left flank!" he yelled, then squeezed the trigger rapidly, emptying his magazine. Two went down, the third dove for cover and returned fire. Acton fell back, hugging the rock, the angle too shallow to provide much cover. He looked over. The shots were ricocheting off the front of the jeep.

The front passenger side tire burst, the entire vehicle jolting as it collapsed several inches.

Shit!

"Jeep's out!" He glanced around the rock and saw the third man reloading. Acton took aim, and fired. Nothing. He ejected the mag, reloaded, and looked again. His target was safely hidden, his hand out as he indiscriminately sprayed the area with fire. Acton pressed against the rock again, his back chilled, the sweat of the moment clashing with the cold of the stone sending icy shivers through his body.

The firing stopped. He peeked out and saw a body tumble from behind the rock, then Dawson step into the open, giving Acton a thumbs-up.

Acton waved, pointed at the jeep, then gave a thumbs-down.

Dawson acknowledged the report and disappeared.

Now how the hell are we getting out of here?

"Chaney!"

The young detective glanced over at Acton.

"Are you clear over there?"

"Yes."

"Cover my side then."

Chaney took a final look around then slid over, taking up position where Acton had been covering. Acton pointed toward the left flank. "Watch there, four of them have tried to come up through there."

"What are you going to do?"

"See if I can change that damned tire. There's a spare under the rear bumper."

"Good thinking."

Acton ran to the back of the jeep and dropped to his stomach, rolling under the truck. He unscrewed the bolt holding the spare in place, then shoved it out. Underneath was a lug wrench. He unclipped it, then removed the jack. Sliding out, he tossed the jack and wrench beside the flat tire then rolled the spare over. Gunfire erupted over his head and he hit the ground.

Chaney squeezed off several rounds. "Got him!"

Acton shoved the jack under the frame and pumped rapidly. The gap filled, then the jeep lifted. He took the wrench and loosened the lug nuts, then jacked the car up far enough to pull the tire off. He removed the nuts, then the tire. Shoving it aside, it rolled down the hill, past

Chaney and out of sight. Acton lifted the spare, shoved it in position, replaced the nuts, then lowered the car until the tire touched the ground. Tightening the nuts, he tossed the wrench to the ground and gave the tire a good shake. It held. He removed the jack and the jeep dropped the rest of the way to the ground, once again on four good tires. He hoped no one told Laura—the last time they had a flat on a dig site, he had pled ignorance on how to change it, deferring to her greater automotive knowledge. The look she had given him made him certain she knew he was full of it, but when she had finished in half the time he could have, his manhood was thankful for the avoided embarrassment.

Beautiful and handy too.

He tossed the jack aside, knowing if they needed it again there were no more spares. He jumped behind the wheel and fired up the engine. It roared to life and he smiled, the few rounds that had hit the hood apparently not doing any damage.

Back in business!

Dawson watched a flat tire jerk its way down the hill, his eyes narrowing.

What the hell?

He took out another of the enemy as he evaluated their situation. Red should be here soon, doubling their number. Yet they still had no way out, and the second, larger group tailing them were at the bottom of the hill, their headlights in plain sight. Once they arrived, they might be outnumbered five to one. Surrendering was an option. It would create one hell of an international incident, but the survival of the Pope was paramount. He would die for certain if they were overwhelmed by the opposing force.

Though if we surrendered...

He activated his comm, selecting an open frequency their enemy could monitor.

"Control, Zero-One, come in over."

"Zero-One, Control. Go ahead over."

"Control, Zero-One, I need to speak to Control Actual, over."

There was a clicking sound as Colonel Clancy jacked in. "This is Actual, go ahead, over."

"Control, Zero-One, we're under heavy fire, about one klick from the Green Zone. About to face overwhelming opposition. Request extraction, over."

"Zero-One, Actual. Negative, extraction not possible at this time, over."

An engine roared to life behind him. Dawson smiled.

Fifty bucks says the Doc has something to do with that.

"Copy that, Control. We are surrendering. For the record, our entire team is intact at this time, only one non-fatal injury. Repeat, we are all intact, along with all three rescued hostages, over."

"Copy that, Zero-One. Entire team is intact. It's your call, will contact you in five mikes, over."

"Control, Zero-One. Copy that, five mikes, out."

Dawson switched to the team's channel. "Cease fire! I say again, cease fire! We're surrendering. Does everyone hear me five-by-five?"

A round of acknowledgments filled his headset, and the firing from their positions ceased, and with it, the Iranian fire dwindled, then stopped.

An eerie silence swept over the hilltop, interrupted only by the gentle idling of the jeep behind the rock. Dawson checked his tactical computer showing his position and Red's. He sent a text message advising Red of their situation.

A squawk echoed through the stones, then a voice over a megaphone sliced through the night. "American Imperialist Dogs, we have you surrounded. Surrender and you will not die. Resist, and you will burn in Hell for eternity."

Laying it on a little thick, aren't we? And where's the 'infidel' reference?

"You infidel American dogs have been captured on blessed Iranian soil, and are now our prisoners. Lay down your weapons, and you will survive. You have one minute to comply."

Dawson checked his display. It had been three minutes since his call to Control. The Colonel had said five minutes until next contact. He looked up as fresh headlights bounced into view. He counted perhaps eight vehicles, each probably carrying six to eight men. They were now facing an additional fifty to sixty of the enemy. If it weren't for the civilians, he'd count their chances pretty good, especially if Red were here. He glanced at his display. Down the hill, dozens of troops were now swarming among the rocks, rapidly closing the gap between him and his men. In the midst of these fresh troops strode a man whose insignia was the highest he had seen tonight. Colonel. The man took the megaphone and raised it to his lips.

"United States soldiers, I am Colonel Zarin. Surrender your arms, and you will be taken prisoner and treated with respect. After all, we know why you are here. This is a *rescue* mission. Are Professor Acton and your Catholic Pope with you?"

This man had a different tone. Less dogma, more chutzpah. But then again, if the good Colonel knew he had just used a Hebrew word to describe him, the man would try to slit his throat.

Try.

His wrist vibrated. He tapped the display and read the message. *ETA 60.*

This is it.

He rose from behind the rock, arms raised slightly. "Yes, they're with us."

The Colonel lowered the megaphone and climbed the final distance separating them, two of his men flanking him, the rest spread out across the hilltop. He stopped about ten feet from Dawson.

"I am Colonel Zarin of the Revolutionary Guard. Whom do I have the honor of addressing?"

"Command Sergeant Major Dog."

"Dog?"

"Well, it's spelled D-A-W-G." Dawson smiled. "I get teased all the time. It's really quite tragic."

This apparently satisfied the man. "Sergeant Major Dawg. Do you surrender?"

His wrist vibrated again. He glanced at the display. "Well, Colonel, I'd love to, but I'm not sure I can do that."

"Sergeant Major, you are on Iranian soil, surrounded by overwhelming numbers. You have little choice."

"I understand that, Colonel. But unlike others you may have dealt with"—he lowered his arms—"we're not hikers." He dove behind the rock he had been using for cover, narrowly missing the shots from the Colonel's guards. The scores of troops below opened fire, as did Dawson's men.

"Look!"

Dawson glanced at Niner, pointing to their left flank, down the hill. Dawson picked off two more guardsmen as they moved to flank his position, then looked where Niner was pointing. Heavy gunfire was concentrated on the rear flank of the now scattering troops as Red opened a second front. Dawson smiled and activated his comm. "Good of you to join us."

"Kind of busy saving your asses."

Dawson chuckled as he picked off another target. In the confusion of the second front opening, it was clear the Iranian colonel had lost all control of his men. Some of those nearer Dawson's position were firing on their own farther down the hill. In less than sixty seconds, half their opposing force had been eliminated.

A whooshing sound that Dawson recognized instantly caused him to spin around. And smile. Three Ghost Hawks, their almost whisper-quiet rotors slicing through the night air, rose above the hilltop from the other side, and cut an ominous silhouette against the moonlit sky. Dawson turned back to see their enemy fleeing, some diving in their vehicles and roaring away, others chasing them and leaping headlong in, and a few simply dropping their weapons and raising their hands.

"Zero-One, Ghost Leader, ready for retrieval on your command, over."

Dawson rose from behind the rock and gave a wave at the choppers, then activated his comm. "Ghost Leader, Zero-One. Find an LZ and we'll come to you, over."

"Zero-One, Ghost Leader. Roger that, LZ spotted two hundred meters west of your present location, over."

The three choppers banked and dropped below the hill, out of sight. "Bravo Team, Zero-One, rally point west side of hill, over."

Dawson, joined by Niner who covered their ascent to the top of the hill, rounded the large rock concealing their vehicle, and found the Pontiff lying across the back seat, with Acton and Chaney still covering either side of the rock. Dawson looked at both of them. "Excellent job. Both of you."

Acton nodded. "I suggest we use the jeep to take His Holiness to wherever those helicopters are going to pick us up."

"Agreed."

Acton walked over and holstered his weapon. He lowered his voice. "What the hell kind of chopper was that? It was like something out of Blue Thunder! I didn't hear it until it was right on top of us."

Dawson chuckled and leaned in. "It's the type of chopper that's so top secret, they're afraid to use the damned thing." Then he straightened and looked about.

"Wait a minute. What chopper? I didn't hear any chopper."

Niner laughed and sat in the driver's seat, Acton and Chaney climbing in the back with the now sitting pope, and Casey, his wounded leg not having kept him out of the battle, in the passenger seat. Dawson climbed on the running board as Niner gave it gas and popped the clutch, heaving them over the ridge and headlong down the slope, this side riddled with far fewer rocks.

Below, two of the choppers had landed, the third still in the air providing cover. Dawson scanned the scene and saw Red's group rounding the hill to his right. Behind them the remaining three men of his team descended backward, their weapons trained on the hilltop should any of their enemy rediscover their balls. Within minutes, the jeep skidded to a halt fifty feet from the nearest chopper. Chaney and Acton carried the elderly Pontiff to the helicopter as Dawson and Niner helped Casey. All aboard, the chopper lifted and rose quietly into the night sky, Red's team on the second nearly silent machine. They banked toward Turkish airspace, and within less than a minute, the pilot turned and gave the thumbs-up. "Green zone!"

Dawson returned the gesture then faced the rest. "We're safe." Fist bumps were exchanged by his men, Niner using his head to bump Casey's fist as he worked at redressing the leg wound. Acton and Chaney shook hands and the Pontiff made the sign of the cross, his eyes closed in silent prayer.

"Where are we going?" asked Acton.

"Diyarbakir Airbase. From there, I'm not sure where you'll be going. Rome, I guess."

"What about you?"

Dawson smiled. "We were never here."

Diyarbakir Airbase, Turkey

Reading elbowed Laura. "Look."

Laura peered out the window of the Gulf V and followed where he was pointing. Three helicopters, silhouetted against the night sky, cleared the roof of the hangar the bodies had been in earlier. They landed with a slight bounce and men poured out of two of them. Laura's heart leaped and tears filled her eyes as she recognized James. She raced from the seat and down the aisle, then stuck her head out the door. "James!"

He smiled at her and waved as he helped somebody off the chopper who Laura immediately recognized as the kidnapped pope. She grabbed the railing and descended the steps as fast as she dared, then dashed across the tarmac. James helped his charge onto a rushed-out gurney, then turned to look for her just as she slammed into him. He grunted from the impact as she wrapped her arms and legs around him, placing her head into his shoulder, the emotions of the past day pouring out uncontrollably. He hugged her back and said nothing, just squeezed her tight, breathing into her neck. She never wanted to let him go ever again. She thought she had lost him this time, and now understood what he had gone through when she had been kidnapped.

It was horrible.

She uncurled her legs from his waist and dropped to the ground, switching her arms from around his neck to around his torso, pressing her head in his chest. His hand gently stroked her head as she slowly regained control. Finally, she pushed away and gazed into his eyes.

"Thank God you're safe."

He smiled at her then jerked his head toward the gurney being pushed inside the hangar with the Pope, Giasson and the late-arriving Vatican entourage surrounding it. "I think He was on our side."

She smiled. "You and your jokes."

He hugged her hard, pushing her head back into his chest. "God, I missed you." He kissed the top of her head then let go slightly. She bent her head up and he stared at her for a moment, his eyes filled with the love they both shared, then he closed them, lowering his head. She closed her eyes and his lips touched hers, gently at first, as if rediscovering a passion thought lost, then with more fervor as they lost themselves in the moment, oblivious to the dozens of personnel, top-secret helicopters, and one Interpol Agent delighted to see his old partner safe. Her hands ran through his short hair, dry and caked in mud and sweat from his ordeal, and she didn't care. He gripped the back of her head with one hand, pushing her against his lips, his other hand on the small of her back, urging their bodies together. Her heart pounded in excitement and she tingled as the moment built.

Then he stopped.

A wave of disappointment rushed through her as he pressed his forehead against hers, his chest heaving with excitement, as if in time with hers. He stepped back, still holding both her hands in his and laughed. "I think we'll need to get a room."

She laughed. "Who needs a room? We've got an entire airplane." She jerked her thumb toward the Gulf V. Acton raised his eyebrows several times with a suggestive look. She leaned in and bit his earlobe, giving it a flick with her tongue. "There are quite a few people here who probably want to talk to you," she whispered. Then, her voice lower, throaty, she said, "but later, you're all mine."

"I'm going to hold you to that."

Laura noticed the group of soldiers who had been aboard the helicopter with James head into a nearby hangar. "Are those the same gentlemen we've met before?"

"Yup. Let's go say thanks."

Acton took Laura by the hand and walked over to the Delta Force team that had saved his neck. As they approached, he witnessed their exhaustion. Heads hung low, shoulders sagging, all sitting on whatever they could find, or on the floor of the hangar itself, dousing themselves in as much water as they could, several cases having been brought to them. Though tired, their wit, their camaraderie, was still intact. These men who wouldn't hesitate to die for their country, to die for each other, to die for us, these men knit together so tightly through constant training, socializing, and fighting, knew each other so well, had a bond so intense, that no civilian could understand it, no desk jockey could fathom it. They were, as has been said of others, brothers in arms, a family made from all parts of the fabric of the American mosaic, fused together in such a way as only combat could. Acton was proud to know his country had such men, and was proud to have fought beside them today.

"Does anybody know what the hell a Hail Mary is?"

Acton smiled at Niner's question.

I guess he didn't realize the old man was joking.

"Hail Mary, full of grace. You never went to church?"

"I'm Buddhist!" exclaimed Niner as he turned toward the voice. "Hey, BD, look who it is!"

Dawson glanced up and smiled, waving Acton and Laura over. He extended his hand to Laura who let go of Acton and grabbed Dawson in a hug, her head buried in his chest. "Thank you so much!" she cried. Dawson's arms, bent at the elbows and pointing out from his sides, awkwardly returned the hug.

"Just doing our job, ma'am."

She let go, and as she made her rounds, Acton stepped forward and began shaking hands in turn, and when done, they both sat on the hangar floor and chitchatted with the team.

"So, where are you off to now?" asked Laura.

"Hon, they can't tell you that."

"Yeah, or we'd have to kill you." Several of the team groaned at Niner's joke. He raised his hands palms up and shrugged. "What, too soon?" They all laughed at that, even Laura and Acton, as the events of London were recalled.

"What about you two?" asked Dawson. "Where are you off to?"

"Well, we *were* visiting my folks in Vermont before all this happened, so I think we'll head back there before my mother has a fit."

Dawson gestured toward the Gulf V. "Heading there in that?"

Acton blushed slightly. "Yes."

Niner whistled. "Sweeeeeeeet!" He leaned toward Laura. "Ma'am, if you ever get tired of this bozo"—he jerked his thumb at Acton—"you come look me up. I'm a very nice man, enjoy cleaning and cooking, and can hem a mean pair of pants." Laughter echoed through the hangar and Laura leaned forward, patting Niner on the cheek.

"As tempting as that offer is, I think I'll be toughing it out with him for a *long* time."

Niner dropped his head, feigning hurt, as several of his buddies slapped him on the back, pretending to console him.

"So, Doc, I get the impression you've been doing some training since we last met."

Acton nodded at Dawson. "Yeah, Laura hired a former SAS guy to teach us hand to hand, weaponry. A bit of everything."

"It shows."

Laura threw her arm over his shoulders. "My man did good?"

Niner leaned forward and pointed at Acton. "Good? Shit, ma'am, I'd let him watch my back any day!"

The rest of the team echoed the sentiment, causing Acton to blush.

"Jim!"

Acton glanced over his shoulder at Reading, who waved for them to join him. He stood and inhaled deeply. "Well, before I say something and ruin my newfound reputation, I'll say goodbye, and thanks once again." He shook Dawson's and Red's hands, then leaned in and slapped Niner on the shoulder, half a smile etched on his face. "And if you ever need my help again, you just call."

A round of guffaws erupted from the group of hardened warriors as Acton stepped back and took Laura by the hand. "Be safe," said Laura, waving as they turned and walked toward Reading. As they neared, a ridiculously deep voice rolled across the tarmac.

"That's one seriously fine woman."

"You can't say that when her boyfriend's within earshot!" exclaimed Niner.

Acton looked at Laura out of the corner of his eye, and saw her staring at him with a smile. "So, am I seriously fine?"

He reached down and squeezed her butt. "Damn fine." He let go and gave a secret thumbs-up behind her for the benefit of the Bravo Team, who responded with a roar of laughter.

As they neared the other hangar, the Pope, now in a wheelchair, was pushed out by Giasson, accompanied by Reading and Chaney. He rolled up to Acton, hands extended, a huge smile on his face. Acton took the proffered hands and the old man clasped them tightly, pulling him forward. For a moment, Acton thought he was expected to kiss the papal ring, but instead he was kissed on both cheeks. "Thank you, young man, for saving us all."

Acton bowed slightly.

Haven't been called 'young' in a while.

"You're welcome, Your Holiness. But I think the guys you really need to thank are over there." He jerked his thumb over his shoulder, toward the hangar they had just left.

"They're gone!" exclaimed Laura.

Acton stared at the empty hangar and smiled, shaking his head. "No. They were never here."

"That is most unfortunate." The Pontiff turned to Acton. "We must return to Rome now. Will you join us?"

Acton shook his head. "No." He checked his watch. "Today is my dad's birthday, and if we leave now, we might just make dinner."

The old man smiled. "I understand completely." He raised a finger. "But first, I must speak with both of you, alone." Giasson released his grip on the wheelchair and Acton stepped behind the Pontiff, pushing him toward a set of crates where he and Laura sat, facing the Pontiff in his chair.

His smile was gone.

"Evil was defeated today, but at what cost?" Acton was about to say something when the old man raised his finger. "Dozens have died due to a chain of events I initiated, and I must live with that. But *you*"—he pointed at Acton—"do not. The blood on my hands stains deep. Father Granger was a friend, who died in my service, attempting to retrieve something lost hundreds of years ago. In essence, we were trying to steal back what was stolen from us. And he paid the ultimate price. Detective Chaney, asked to participate in this folly, nearly died, and I, in my continuing denial of my age, chose to look for him when I did not find him in his chambers. I, too, almost paid the price, a price I would willingly have paid had I known the bloodshed that would result by my surviving.

"But I didn't. And living in the past is something that causes nothing but sorrow in the future. I will pray for all those who lost their lives, and I will pray for you, Professor Acton, in hopes you will find forgiveness within, for what you were forced to do. But"—he leaned forward in his chair, lowering his voice—"I pray for both of you, for I suspect, in saving me, you have been exposed to something no one should." He sat back in his chair. "You opened the chest?"

Acton nodded.

"As I suspected. It is written on your faces. You have seen evil, and it weighs heavily on your souls."

A tear rolled down Laura's cheek.

"Fear not, my child, for the Lord loves you. Put your faith in Him, and He will help you through this. Evil is real. We see it every day around us, hear about it every day on the news. There is no avoiding evil. However, we can fight it. By being better people, by refusing to give in to the temptation to do the Devil's bidding, we win the battle a little bit each day. You both were exposed to so much knowledge of evil, two thousand years' worth, in one sitting. I remember the night I was declared pope, and the secret was revealed to me. The horror I felt. My faith, a faith that had sustained me all my life, began to slip away. How could God, how could our Lord, even exist, with so much evil on this Earth.

"I sat all night, questioning my faith, but as the morning sun broke, I heard something tapping on my window. I recoiled in horror, my heart and mind filled with fear at what I had just read, but instead of some demon desperate to be invited inside to steal my soul, I found a lone dove, floundering with what appeared to be a broken wing, tapping on the glass. I opened the window and picked up this poor, wretched creature, and stroked its feathers. As I held it by its feet, it made no attempt to escape, though I was certain it must be terrified. That was when I found a plastic ring, some discarded piece of garbage, wrapped around the wing I thought broken. I gently removed it, and the poor creature was able to flap both wings again. I let it go, and if flew away, then returned moments later to rest on the railing of my balcony. It sat there for a minute, cooing, then flew away again, up, into the morning sky.

"I returned to my office, a smile on my face, and joy in my heart, that I had been able to help this poor creature and restore it to the life granted it by the glory of God. And it was then that I realized that I no longer doubted my faith, I no longer feared the evil that I had just discovered. God had sent me a messenger, that little bird, to remind me of the beauty of His creation, the innocence of His creatures, and the power He has granted us over His dominion. With His gift, no evil can triumph over Him."

He sat back in his chair. "Now, I believe you have a birthday party to get to, and I have a billion or so people to reassure that reports of my death were indeed greatly exaggerated."

He smiled and turned the chair around. Acton pushed him in silence back to the hangar, Laura trailing. Before they reached the doors, he indicated for them to stop. "Remember what I said. Believe in Him, and He will believe in you. Forget what you have seen and go home." He beckoned Acton closer so he could whisper. "And make an honest woman of her." The old man patted Acton on the hand and winked.

Acton chuckled, shaking his head, a smile spreading across his cheeks as he blushed a little. "That's an idea crazy enough to work."

Acton Residence
Stowe, Vermont

The doorbell rang.

Acton moved to get up but his mother waved him off.

"I'll get it." She rose from the dinner table, and a moment later the door opened and his mother gasped. It was a gasp of shock, not of happy surprise. He jumped from the table and rushed to the front door, his father, recognizing his wife's sound of distress, immediately behind him. They found her standing in the doorway, the door partially opened, their view blocked of who was on the other side.

Acton grabbed the door and yanked it open, stepping between his mother and whoever he might find. His heart hammered at who it might be. And what he found wasn't what he expected.

A lone woman, wearing a cloak resembling that of a monk, only black, stood on the doorstep. He glanced behind her and saw an SUV idling on the road in front of the house, several more pulling up. At the sight of Acton, the woman looked up, revealing a face far younger than he had been expecting. And far more beautiful.

"Professor Acton?"

He nodded.

"I am Sister Maria, may I come in?"

"What do you want?"

"Jim, is that any way to talk to a nun?" admonished his mother. "Of course you can come in, dear." She stepped back but Acton held his ground, blocking the door with both his arms.

"You're from the Order of the Blessed Virgin, aren't you?"

Laura gasped behind him, then footsteps pounded in retreat, up the stairs.

"Yes." The young woman held out her hands. Empty. "I assure you, I am unarmed, and am not here to hurt you in any way." Acton flashed back to the story Laura had told him of the battle on the streets of Rome. "Please, Professor Acton. I swear to God, to the Holy Virgin, I will not harm you."

Acton frowned but stepped aside.

The young woman crossed the threshold and Dorothy conducted her to the living room where she took a seat facing the large bank of windows extending across the back of the house. Acton and his parents sat in front of the windows as Laura rushed down the stairs, her satchel clutched to her chest. Acton jumped up as he realized what she had. They exchanged glances, her eyes begging the question, and he nodded, knowing exactly what that question was.

Do I give it to her?

The young woman looked at Acton, then at Laura who rounded the chair she was sitting in.

"I'm Laura, Sister Maria. And I think I know why you're here."

Maria smiled and pointed at the satchel still clutched to Laura's chest. "Is that it?" Acton could hear in her voice the excitement that her face refused to display.

Laura nodded.

The woman's hands slowly rose from the arms of the chair, toward the satchel. "May I?"

Laura started to open the satchel when Acton held his hand out to stop her.

"You tried to kill her last time. Why not this time?"

"It isn't necessary."

"What do you mean?"

"We vastly outnumber you, and you are stationary."

"Outnumber..." Acton's voice trailed off as he spun toward the windows. Laura gasped behind him and his parents jumped from the couch, rushing to the other side of the room, away from the windows. Extended from one end of the set of windows to the other, standing shoulder to shoulder, were a dozen robed figures, their heads bowed. Acton's father stepped into the kitchen then back out again.

"Looks like they're at every window."

"We surround your entire property."

"You said no harm would come to us!" said Laura.

"No, I said *I* would bring you no harm." She tilted her head at the window. "They might." She waved her hands in the air, as if wiping clean the sight of those surrounding the house. "Let us not get ahead of ourselves. I have no desire to take what is ours by force. None of us do. There has been enough death. Too much death." She pointed to the satchel. "Now, may I see it?"

Laura glanced at Acton, who nodded. She flipped open the satchel's cover then pulled the book from within. Maria gasped and Acton watched as tears rolled from both eyes, down her cheeks. A sound from behind him caused him to look. Several of the figures outside were pressed against the window. All were women. And all appeared as excited as Maria. He turned back to her, the book now held in her hands as gently as she could manage.

"Have you read it?" she asked Laura.

Laura shook her head. "There was never any time, then I forgot I had it."

Maria smiled, her hand slowly, gently, running over the cover. "Finally, after almost two thousand years, the Word of Mary is restored to its rightful owners."

"My understanding is that there are no other copies."

Maria looked up at Acton. "Correct. This is the only known copy to have survived."

"Then how do you know what's in it?"

"We don't. We know pieces that were remembered and passed down through the ages, but, no, we do not know what it contains."

Acton wasn't sure whether he should push the issue, but the archaeologist in him had to know what it contained. "The Keepers of the One Truth said you were wrong about what you thought it contained."

Maria regarded him. "What do you mean?"

"I mean, whatever you *think* that book has written in it, is not what *is* written in it."

The front door alarm chimed and footsteps echoed in the hallway. Acton placed himself in front of Laura as his father did the same for his wife. Two robed figures entered, both carrying large cases. Without a word, they both knelt on either side of the living room table, then cleared it of its contents.

"Let me do that," said his mother, but his father held her back with an arm and a look.

One of the women opened her case and pulled out another from inside that she opened and laid flat on the table. It had a black, velvet-like interior. Maria stepped forward and placed the book inside. The other woman pulled out a laptop computer, a portable printer, then a handheld scanner. The first spun the case toward her, then the second scanned the cover. Acton watched as a perfect image appeared on the laptop screen, then two copies spooled from the printer. The woman nodded, and the first carefully opened the cover then moved back so the first could scan both pages. They repeated this for several minutes, carefully turning the pages, scanning them, and printing them. Within ten minutes they were done, the book was closed, then sealed in the case.

Both women rose, bowed to Maria, the second handing one of the copies to her, then they left. The front door chimed as it closed, and Acton watched as the women surrounding the house filed past the window. Maria remained seated, however. She looked at Acton, then beckoned for them all to sit. They complied, and she turned back to Acton. "You said the Keepers of the One Truth said we were mistaken about what this contained."

"Yes," replied Acton.

"Well, they were wrong. Wrong about what they thought we believed. This book *is* a Gospel of sorts, the first, and only true, Gospel. It contains the word of Mary herself."

"You mean—" Laura stopped, tears filling her eyes.

Acton didn't get it. "What? What does it mean?"

"The words written here"—she shook the sheaf of papers—"were originally written by a mother...and a son. They are not about the teachings of Jesus, or the telling of his exploits. They are letters from her to him, and from him to her, over a lifetime. They are a record of correspondence between the greatest man to have ever lived, and the mother who gave birth to him. They are written proof that he existed, that she existed, and that the New Testament is true."

"Then why hide it?" asked Laura.

Maria frowned. "Because men of the Church decided that the masses should think of Jesus as the son of God, and not the son of Mary. That they should think of him as a god walking among men, as opposed to a man. A man with emotions, with not only knowledge to give, but love. This book reveals the man, as he revealed himself to his own mother, while he traveled the land spreading the word of God. He is flawed, he has doubts, he falls in love, he cries, rants, and questions. It is all in here. And the Church didn't want any image of Jesus that wasn't perfect to be shared with the masses, so they banned the book, and destroyed all copies but this one."

"And what will you do with it, now that you've got it?"

Maria rose. "We will share it with the world. Not at first, of course, we have to have the book authenticated so when we are questioned, we can defend our beliefs, but in time, all will be shared." She held out the copy for Laura. "But *you* will be the first."

Laura took the pages and looked up at Maria. "Why me?"

"Because you are the reason we have it now. You rescued it from its hiding place, and kept it rather than give it back to those who would conceal the truth."

"But I simply forgot I had it!"

Maria smiled. "Did you? Or did your conscience tell you that these words were not evil, that these words were meant to be read by the world, and that these words should never again be hidden away in the vaults of the Vatican?"

Laura said nothing, simply staring at the bundle of pages she now gripped.

"I'll be going now. Thank you all for your assistance."

Maria walked toward the door, Acton and his father following. She flashed them a quick smile with a turn of her head, then skipped with excitement to the SUV waiting for her.

As soon as the vehicle was out of sight, Acton closed the door and bolted it. His father placed a hand on his shoulder.

"These past couple of years have been eventful."

Acton chuckled. "That's one way of putting it." He looked at his father. "Sorry for getting you guys involved."

"Well, at least this time there were no guns."

"Oh, I don't know about that. Something tells me if we hadn't given up the book, there would have been a whole lot of guns showing up."

His father frowned. "You're probably right." He patted Acton on his back. "Let's see how our women are doing."

They walked into the living room and found Laura translating the text, in a low tone, to his mother. Both were crying.

"What's wrong?" asked Acton.

They looked up, both shaking their heads.

"It's so beautiful," said his mother.

Laura agreed, wiping her nose with a tissue, then holding her hand out. Acton took it and sat beside her.

"What is it?"

She stared at him with a smile. "I no longer fear evil."

Acton put his arm over her shoulders and squeezed the back of her neck. "In just a few pages?"

She smiled, running her hand over the page. "This will change the world."

"Why, what does it say?"

"Let me read it to you, to you all."

Acton leaned back and closed his eyes as the love of his life began to read.

And before the first page was done, his eyes burned with the tears he was keeping at bay as his heart filled with hope.

This will *change the world.*

THE END

ACKNOWLEDGMENTS

The concept for Broken Dove was born from a discussion with my father during a family visit. We were spit-balling ideas for another Acton adventure, and as one outrageous idea after another were batted back and forth, an idea leaped to mind, and I stopped.

"I've got all I need," I said. "A murder at the Vatican."

The result of that one idea is this book. The concept of the female pope wasn't even considered, as I wasn't aware of this part of hidden history until researching something else for the book. And once I stumbled upon that, more of the concept took shape. I hope you enjoyed the effort, regardless of whether you buy the concept of a female pope.

As usual, people need to be thanked. My parents, my wife and daughter, Brent Richards, Christian Leroux, Mario Giasson (who I couldn't figure out how to kill) and his family.

To those who have not already done so, please visit my website at www.jrobertkennedy.com then sign up for the Insider's Club to be notified of new book releases. Your email address will never be shared or sold.

Thank you once again for reading.